The FEAST OF THE TRICKSTER

ᴛʜᴇ FEAST
❖ OF ᴛʜᴇ ❖
TRICKSTER

BETH HILGARTNER

Houghton Mifflin Company
Boston   1991

Library of Congress Cataloging-in-Publication Data

Hilgartner, Beth.
The feast of the trickster / Beth Hilgartner.
p. cm.
Sequel to: Colors in the dreamweaver's loom.
Summary: Five companions from another world visit earth on
a mission to return a woman, earlier woven into their world, back
to their true home.
ISBN 0-395-55008-4
[1. Fantasy.]   I. Title.
PZ7.H5474Fe 1991   91-9705
[Fic]—dc20   CIP
                          AC

Printed in the United States of America

VB 10 9 8 7 6 5 4 3 2 1

For Ernest,
who asked for a book about real kids,
and
for Josh, Naomi, and David

THE FEAST OF THE TRICKSTER

PROLOGUE

June in Vermont is either heavenly or dismal. This afternoon, a determined rain thudded on the corrugated roof of the horse barn, and the comfortable smells of hay, horses, and leather were mixed with raw dampness. Angel scrubbed her dirt-caked bridle, pushed a coil of blond hair off her forehead, and sighed. Mark looked up from the saddle he was cleaning.

"It's so *boring*," Angel said. "I mean, the first day of summer vacation and we're *cleaning tack*."

"So go for a trail ride in the rain," Brice suggested. "No one's stopping you."

Angel rolled her eyes. "It's not the *rain*; it's that nothing ever happens here."

Brice set aside the boot he'd just polished and reached for its mate. "What do you *want* to have happen, Angel?"

"Something exciting—" she began. "Something different; something out of the ordinary; something *amazing*—do you know what I mean?"

"Like mad dogs?" Brice offered. "Or an earthquake?"

"Or a nuclear plant accident?"

"Oh, *Mark!*" Angel said with great disgust.

"Well," he said, "how about an alien invasion?"

"Exactly!" Angel cried. "Aliens would do nicely! Maybe they'd carry you off!"

"For it to be really exciting, they'd have to carry *you* off," Brice put in. "I can see the headlines now: 'Girl, fifteen, abducted by UFO.'"

She tossed her grubby sponge at him. The arrival of their boss, Kelly Sebastian, cut short their discussion.

"You guys planning to ride today?" Kelly asked. "I've got a pair of beginners coming for a three-thirty lesson, so if you want to ride inside, you'd better get moving."

As she left, Brice leaned toward the others. "Maybe the aliens would carry off *Kelly*!" he whispered.

Mischief lit Angel's hazel eyes. "Even aliens wouldn't *dare*," she replied. "Besides, it had better be more like close encounters, if the excitement is going to last us all summer."

Mark shook his head. "You're weird, Angel; but I don't know what we'd do without you. I'm going to get Churchy ready. Aren't you guys going to ride?"

1

The Weaver sat at the Loom, a frown lodged between his brows as he studied the pattern. Things were desperately wrong. The fabric of Fate was not as closely woven as it should be. There was a spreading weakness he could not put right. And the pattern! The orderly world he knew was spinning into chaos; the pattern showed it, shot through as it was with the vivid purple of the Trickster's color—a thread he could not control. The Feast of the Trickster was fast approaching, heralding the season when her power was greatest and the influence of the Loom weakest. Long ago, the other gods had felt it necessary to curb the Trickster's wildness, so they had, over the Weaver's protests, used the Loom to bind her power. It was not the Loom's way to destroy power. As the Weaver had foreseen, the Loom would only limit the Trickster's ability to use her power; during the time the Trickster was able to wield her power, there was a great deal of it at hand. The result was that most of the time, the Trickster was unable to upset things through her perversity. Only during the few years preceding and following her Feast (which fell every twenty-one years) was she troublesome; but because of the Loom's binding, she had access to enough of her own stored power to be extremely troublesome indeed.

The Weaver thinned his lips. There was another problem

with the gods' solution: it made the Trickster angry. With each passing of her Feast, she had striven more determinedly at the Loom's binding. She wanted to be free; the Weaver could feel her anger and her strength even now, like a salmon too strong for the angler's line. With each cycle, she had gained in subtlety; she flexed her power to find new weak places in the Loom's bonds. The Weaver feared this Trickster's Feast, as he had never feared it before; when the Trickster came into her full power, she might rip free, unraveling the whole of reality.

The Trickster played her game with masterly skill. She was angry enough not to care that her freedom would bring the end of the Loom, and with it the Weaver, and would shake the foundations of their world. The Trickster fed and fostered whatever chaos she could work into the pattern, to prevent the Loom from strengthening itself. But the Weaver knew his work; he had found the point from which the weakening had begun. He could see that everything began to change the instant the Stranger, 'Tsan, had been torn from the Loom by the Trickster's malice and flung across the void to another world.

'Tsan. He shook his head. She was such an enigma. He had strung her color in the Loom at the request of his sister, the Forester. Three and a half years ago, the people of the forest, the Orathi, had been threatened by the conniving of the City and the violence of the desert people, the Khedathi. The Forester felt that they needed a Wanderer, a leader from beyond the forest's borders. The Weaver had agreed; but when he strung a Wanderer's color on the Loom, for some unguessable reason, 'Tsan had been pulled from her own world into his. Although it hadn't been easy for her, the Weaver knew, 'Tsan proved stronger than she had thought herself; somehow, she had knit together a band of misfits to ask a boon of the gods. But the Trickster had chosen that moment to test her own weakening bonds. She had set the companions a further quest,

4

one fraught with greater difficulties; and then, when they sur-
mounted even these odds, she had loosed her malice on them,
"rewarding" them with bitter, unwelcome gifts; 'Tsan was
ripped from the Loom and cast across the void to the land
whence she had come. Even the hard-won boon—to save the
Orathi—was twisted as only the Trickster could devise. Now
the City itself was endangered by the threat of its own Tame
Khedathi turning feral; the fragile truce between the
shapeshifters and the desert Khedathi was at the point of shat-
tering. The whole world was poised on the brink of violence
and war.

"And the Trickster's thread runs through it all," the Weaver
whispered. With an explosive sigh, he began to weave. Vivid
colors shimmered as he wound them into the pattern: gods' colors—deep blue, clear gold. When he finished, he spoke two
names—gods' names: "Dreamer, Namegiver." His siblings
appeared in a swirl of moving air. At his gesture, they
approached to study the Loom.

The Namegiver's voice was grim. "Chaos, Destruction,
Doom. Weaver, I do not like your pattern."

"My pattern? It is hardly that."

"How has she grown so strong?" the Dreamer demanded.

"Her power grows as her Feast approaches," the Weaver
responded. "It is the price of the Loom's binding upon her."

"I know that," the Dreamer snapped. "But in the past, the
Loom has constrained her. She has caused trouble at her Feast,
but never anything like this. The Loom is failing, Elgonar."

"Do you think I cannot feel it? I am bound to the Loom
more firmly than even the Trickster. I fear it is only a matter of
time before she will tear free, and the whole will unravel."

The Dreamer laid a gentle hand on the Weaver's shoulder.
"But El, why?"

"She has weakened the fabric of Fate," he said heavily.

5

"How, I'm not certain, though I suspect it has something to do with the way she cast out the Wanderer."

"Well, weave her back," the Dreamer said.

"No!" the Namegiver cried.

A sour smile twisted the Weaver's lips. "I've tried. But the Trickster thought of that. I strung 'Tsan's color, but when it touched the Loom, it turned to the Trickster's purple. It is not an experience I am anxious to repeat."

"But your Wanderer is the answer, I think," said the Namegiver. "What if she were brought here another way?"

The Weaver considered her question. At last he answered, his words deliberate. "Since the Trickster has anticipated me, I cannot use the power of the Loom to summon 'Tsan from her far world; but were she here, within the Loom's sphere, then, yes, I could weave her into the pattern—and her presence would strengthen it. But how to get her here? I don't think I can withstand the Trickster at her Feast."

"You needn't stand alone, you proud idiot," the Dreamer said hotly. "I am with you. This is too great a matter for heroics."

"Irenden took my very words," the Namegiver said. "We will aid you however we may."

"I thank you," the Weaver said. "We will need one another's strengths if we are to prevail. But without the Loom, I do not see how we three can bring 'Tsan across the void."

"We need other allies," the Namegiver said. With one finger she traced a thread in the Loom's pattern. "Minstrel." Her finger moved to another strand. "Swordswoman." A third: "Shapeshifter." There was a hesitation as she sought the fourth. "Prophet. And to bind them together," she concluded, "the Heart-mender."

"'Tsan's companions," the Dreamer breathed. "What can they do?"

6

The Weaver's face brightened. "We shall set them another Quest. Yes! If anyone is equal to the task, surely they are." He reached for the shuttle. "Leave me now. I must weave them together. When all is in readiness, I will call." He sent the shuttle flying through the warp with more energy than he had felt in many, many weeks.

In the City, the Street of the Artisans was not as busy as one might expect on a fine spring afternoon. There was little laughter or bright patter from either sellers or buyers. A pall of anxiety hung over the market; no one was strong enough to lift it.

Remarr the Minstrel sat on a worn blanket beside the silversmith's booth. His fingers pulled music from his harp, but even he seemed to have succumbed to the tension in the air. His melodies called up images of early winter, of the fading of things, of loss, death, and sorrow. There was no eager crowd gathered to hear the magic of his harp, and the battered tin cup on the pavement before him was empty. For the last two days, his cup had been empty when the market closed at dusk, and he had gone to bed with no supper whatever. The Vemathi merchants were sick with apprehension; the Tame Khedathi had turned surly, no longer spending the odd coin on the trinkets the Street of the Artisans offered. Lean times had come; everyone's belt needed tightening.

The sound of a coin falling into his cup snagged Remarr's attention—but his music faltered into silence. This coin was heavy, yellow, and the size of his circled thumb and index finger. He looked up, seeking the hand from which the coin had fallen. Efiran Moirre watched him. Efiran Moirre: head of the powerful House of Moirre; father of Remarr's friend and companion of years past, Vihena Moirre Khesst. He remembered, with an odd twinge of loss, that the tin cup he used for begging was marked with the badge of House Moirre—the last remnant

7

of the provisioning Efiran had given 'Tsan and the Orathi twins for their journey to Windsmeet.

For a long moment, Remarr and Efiran studied each other. Remarr saw an aging Vemathen, still handsome, though his dark hair had faded to gray and his eyes were shadowed. Efiran saw a young man; judging from his white-blond hair, golden skin, and dark eyes, a Khedathen, whose hands were callused from the harp and not the sword. He lacked the feline grace of the Tame Khedathi Efiran knew. The minstrel's face was drawn, his skin too tight to the bone, his eyes too large and dark in their sockets. Efiran shook his head.

"You are too thin, Remarr."

He shrugged. "Indeed. No doubt hunger blunts her claws on the thick walls of your fine house."

"No doubt," Efiran agreed. They regarded each other warily. Then Efiran sighed. "I came," he said, "to give you news, and a warning. You know of the tension between Edevvi and Belerann?"

Remarr nodded. Belerann spoke for the Tame Khedathi; Edevvi, one of his lieutenants, was known to be dissatisfied with his leadership. The talk hadn't worried Remarr; Edevvi was no friend of his and would make his life unpleasant were she in power, but Belerann was too shrewd to rise to her bait. Remarr had always believed that even if Edevvi forced a challenge, Belerann had nothing to fear from her blade. Now, though, Efiran's manner struck an ominous chord.

"Edevvi challenged Belerann this afternoon—and won."

"Merciless gods, *how?* She isn't half the fighter he is."

Efiran clenched one fist. "She had the Trickster's own luck. He cut her early on; and—soul of honor that he was—he offered to spare her if she put up her sword. Despite her wound, she fought like one possessed. He slipped in her blood. It was over in an instant." He shook his head. "That's the news," he

8

went on, heavily. "Now the warning: there are two things that young hothead wants badly enough to have risked death on Belerann's sword. One is the City; she'll have to wait for that, I wager. But the other is the head of one blond harper. Don't stay in the City for her sycophants to find you."

Remarr studied Efiran's face, as though he could peel away his skin and see the motives in his mind. "Why are you telling me this?"

A curious expression, almost a smile, flitted across Efiran's face. "It will annoy Hobann."

Remarr's eyes narrowed at the name of his one-time employer. "Hobann is dead." The merchant had fallen in one of the Lord of the City's purges, two years ago.

"Forgive me," Efiran said. "My jests are all of a dark hue these days. That was why I took 'Tsan and the Orathi twins into my House: to annoy Hobann. 'Tsan guessed what was in my mind—gods know how—and asked me who Hobann was. I've never forgotten it. But I haven't answered your question. If my daughter Vihena is accepted as Khesst, then surely you are almost Moirre? Perhaps I came to warn the son I never had."

"Are you naming me Moirre?" Remarr demanded in disbelief.

Efiran hunched an elegant shoulder. "No. But if you came courting my daughter Anfeh, who knows where that might lead?"

"Anfeh is just a little girl," the minstrel protested. *And an impossible brat as well,* he added inwardly.

"And you are hardly in a position to come courting. I speak of what may be, not what is, Remarr Khesst."

The minstrel's face went still as a carving. "Not Khesst," he said, his flat tone covering the pain he felt at hearing his birth-name. "Khesst isn't as open-minded as you, Moirre. If they welcomed Vihena and tolerated me for her sake, they would yet

9

slice me to ribbons if they heard me style myself Khesst. *They cast me out.* I am neither Khesst nor Moirre. I thank you for your news and your warning, but I do not want your daughter, nor your gold, nor your pity." He snatched up the tin cup, and made as though to toss the coin back at Efiran Moirre, but the look on the older man's face stopped him.

"Buy a horse—a fast horse. Consider it a loan, you stiff-necked harper. Pay me back if we both survive the brewing storm. And I don't pity you, Remarr; not at all." Then he strode off, moving with surprising energy for an old man. Remarr watched him go, the coin in the westering light still bright on his own palm.

Remarr hugged himself as he began to shiver. "The Weaver's at his Loom," he whispered to himself, "and it's my thread he draws into his pattern. But gods—*oh, merciless gods!*—with whose destiny is he tangling mine, this time?"

He stowed his harp in its case, gathered his possessions, and walked away. He found himself whistling. Things were stirring; there were changes in the air. He could feel it.

The Weaver laid the shuttle aside. It had taken delicate work, but the first of them was in motion. Now for the swords-woman—and swiftly!—for the minstrel might have need of her. He studied the pattern for several moments; with a decisive nod he reached for her color, and set to his task.

10

2

The Star Sower had done her work with a prodigal hand, Vihena thought as she sat in the cold starlight of the desert night. She had volunteered for the night watch because it was one of the few duties within Clan Khesst that permitted solitude. Not that the Clan wouldn't understand if she said she needed to be by herself—but to have to suffer their curious glances was more than she could bear.

Why were things so complicated? Before she came to the desert, she had pined for the freedom of the sands, for a world where she could pursue her Weapons Discipline, hone her skill and speed in the hiss and clash of swordplay. She had longed to wear anonymous desert robes when she slunk around the City dressed as a boy: the notorious hoyden of House Moirre, of whom rumors whispered that even her vast dowry could not buy her a husband. It was true that life with Clan Khesst had freed her from the City's contempt, but the desert was not the paradise of which she had dreamed. And now, with Tedevarr courting her, life was awkward at best.

Tedevarr was a good man, kind to his hound and his horses; he liked children; he was almost her match at the sword. But she didn't *love* him. When Vihena had told this to her foster mother, Emirri had laughed.

"Love? I didn't think you had any soft City-notions left in

11

you, foster daughter," Emirri had said. "When you have his child at your breast, you will understand. Marry him, Vihena, and bear many strong sons. You have my blessing."

Vihena had responded with what was in her heart. "I don't want your blessing, foster mother. I don't want to marry him."

Emirri had gestured in disgust. "What is wrong with you? He would make you a fine husband. He is good to look at, strong and kind, rich—not the richest in the Clan, but no pauper. He has no vices—he doesn't even gamble!—and he is *fond* of you. Vihena, what do you want in a man?"

"I don't know—but not Tedevarr."

"The Trickster's hand is in this," Emirri said.

That had angered Vihena. "*It is not!* It's my own perversity—not hers!" In a gentler voice she added, "Emirri. Foster mother, can't you let me be young and confused?"

The older woman had taken Vihena's face in her hands. "Be young and confused if you must, Vihena, but don't be a fool. Don't refuse him until you've really, *really* thought." Then she had turned away. Vihena was still no closer to an answer. *Am I mad,* she thought, *not to want him?*

Not mad. Contrary—indeed yes—but not mad.

The answering thought catapulted Vihena into memories. Ychass, the shapeshifter—one of 'Tsan's impossible companions—had communicated thus, with the voice of her thoughts. Vihena and the shapeshifter had not begun the journey as friends, but 'Tsan's gift had knit them closer than kin. It had been harder than Vihena had anticipated to stay with her adopted clan when she realized it meant leaving at least two of her companions behind. The Khedathi were enemies of the shapeshifters, whom they viewed with deep contempt, and Remarr would not remain among the desert clan that had cast him out.

'Tsan. Vihena smiled sadly at the memory. What a time that

had been; the world hung in the balance, and the six of them—
'Tsan, Vihena, Ychass, Remarr, and the Orathi twins Iobeh and
Karivet—had tipped the scales. It had been the first time anyone had made her feel important, unique in a *good* way. It had
been heady indeed to have friends who relied on her. Oh, she
belonged in the Clan, despite the gray eyes and dark hair that
set her apart from them in looks; but as one of 'Tsan's companions, her every action had been heavy with destiny.

Vihena sighed. Once, she had thought that loyalty and love
were straightforward; that good and evil were clearly delin-
eated; that victory was always cause for celebration. How simple the world of childhood had been, before she encountered
ambiguity—and confusion. She smiled sardonically as she
noticed her thoughts' circle: from Tedevarr through 'Tsan and
back to Tedevarr. But what *was* she going to do about him?
Even if she told him she wouldn't marry him, he wouldn't
believe her: none of them would. Emirri clearly thought her foster daughter would come to her senses in time. Without a reason Tedevarr would understand and accept, the whole Clan
would simply assume she was being young and foolish and that
she would marry him in the end. The awful thing was Vihena
knew they were right. Eventually she *would* give in; her resolve
would crumble; she would marry the man, bear his children,
and end up either wondering what the fuss had been about, or
discontented for reasons she would never be able to name. *So
how do I get out of this?* she asked herself.

Flee.

That was more than memory. The desert was still; only the
stars trembled. *Ychass?* she thought. *YCHASS!*

Softly. I'm nearby, the shapeshifter's thought-voice answered.
*You know the standing stone a mile to the west of here? I'll meet
you there in two hours. Bring extra water—but no horse. There
are* some *advantages to shapeshifting, even in the dry lands.*

13

Leave tonight? Without saying goodbye?

I gave you two hours; that ought to be time to say your farewells—if you think they'll let you go.

Ychass, wait. Why are you here? I'd have thought the desert was the last place you'd choose to visit—especially now. The Khedathi and the shapeshifters had begun raiding across one another's borders for the first time in living memory. The dry lands were not the place for the lone Outcast Ychass.

No. The familiar dry humor tinged the shapeshifter's thought-voice. *I'm not visiting: I'm on an errand. I've been living in the forest. Do you remember Ohmiden?*

The Dreamweaver's helper? Of course. She had met the old man only once, but he had made quite an impression on her; and the Dreamweaver had maintained that she could never have woven that Fate which aided them in their quests without his vision and support. *He sent you?*

He had a dream—about us, and 'Tsan, and the Trickster.

If 'Tsan was in this—though the gods alone knew how!—so was Vihena. She had been tangled in the gods' weaving once before; her Clan would understand and wish her well. She trotted down into the camp, with a sense of purpose and a curious feeling of peace.

The Weaver sighed in relief. The old man's dream had been a gift indeed. Now that three of the Five were moving, he could breathe more easily. He rose. The Loom could mind itself for the moment. Something made him look back at the pattern. A splinter of purple had begun working itself into his carefully crafted pattern. His fists knotted. "No. Not now!" But the Loom did not respond to his voice, and the Trickster paid him no heed.

14

3

Being raised in the desert had one clear advantage, Remarr thought as he shifted his weight in the saddle: he had an eye for a good horse. The mare he had selected was fast, with tolerably comfortable gaits; the *rider,* on the other hand, was lacking a few crucial muscles. He would be stiffer than cold pitch by morning. He knew better than to try to hole up somewhere in the farmlands bordering the forest. The sort of harmless vagabond who would sleep in someone's hayloft was unlikely to be mounted; the farmer would assume the horse was stolen.

An unwelcome sound caught his attention: horses approaching at a rapid pace. A patrol from the City? He looked for a hiding place, but the fields provided no cover. He cursed. Were they already looking for him? If not, he would certainly arouse interest by galloping off at their approach.

He decided to run for it, anyway. As he cantered up the rise that shielded the City from the forest, he heard shouts and the quickening thunder of pursuit. Standing in his stirrups, he urged his mare on. She charged forward. The sounds of pursuit faded. The looming forest promised safety. Remarr made for the Gate Oaks, two huge trees that marked the beginning of the Forest Road. The old roadway would serve a lone rider even if it were too neglected for heavier traffic.

He eased his horse to a trot as they passed into the shadow of the Gate Oaks. The moon chose this moment to shake herself free of the clouds. As they moved into the last stretch of meadow before the forest began, the moon lit the dew-silvered grass like a stage. At the edge of the trees Remarr saw movement. An enormous cat, half the size of his mare, slunk toward them. The mare halted, her eyes rolling white. The cat growled, a low rumble that made Remarr's shoulders tense; then it sprang.

The horse reared, thrashing at the cat; then, with a scream of terror, she spun away, galloping back the way she had come. Remarr's muscles failed him; he was shaken loose. Winded in the damp grass, he waited for the cat to make an end of him, and hoped that it would be reasonably quick about it.

Nothing happened. Then he heard a sound. Not a growl: a laugh. The cat was gone. A woman stood in the moonlight, wrapped in a voluminous cloak.

He looked up at her; she was very tall. "You find this amusing?"

"Indeed. You realize that you'd have gotten away if your horse hadn't shied. I find such—quirks of fate very amusing indeed, Minstrel Remarr."

"You know my name."

"Of course. Your situation wouldn't be so diverting if I didn't. And you know mine—though I don't think you've ever seen my face." She pushed back her hood and shook wild hair out of her eyes. The moonlight muted her coloring, but Remarr knew her.

"Trickster," he said quietly. It wasn't a question. Then the sound of hoofbeats recalled him to his plight. He leaped up, heading for the trees. Before he had taken even three strides, he found his feet frozen to the ground.

"I regret, Remarr, that I can't let you run. You might yet elude them; they are stupid. And I mustn't disappoint Edevvi."

"I should think you might find Edevvi's disappointment entertaining," he said.

16

"Perhaps. But not useful." The Trickster put her hand under his chin and forced him to meet her eyes. "Such a nice head. Perhaps you can persuade Edevvi to let you keep it."

Remarr regarded her for several heartbeats. Then, with great deliberation, he spat in the Trickster's face.

Her eyebrows rose; Remarr saw a glimmer of respect. "A new experience. Even the Weaver hasn't dared to *spit* at me. What a world of wonders." She touched his forehead. "Sleep," she commanded; he crumpled. She bent and wiped her face on his tunic. As the first of Edevvi's riders crested the rise, she vanished.

The Weaver watched in helpless fury as the Trickster muddled his subtle pattern with her vivid purple. He wondered whether she had learned—somehow—that he, the Dreamer, and the Namegiver were allied to thwart her, or whether her interference this night was no more than random troublemaking. On that hope, he made no effort to counter her directly. He waited for her influence in the Loom to subside before he tried to salvage his careful plans.

It took great effort. The shapeshifter and the swordswoman were even now thundering toward Orathi territory. The City was not a sensible destination for either of them, but they were the only hope the minstrel had. Unless—a thread of inspiration wound into his thoughts—he had allies. Decisively, he cast the Dreamer's color into the pattern.

"Irenden," he said as the Dreamer's vibrant blue grew on the Loom. "I need your help."

"What is it, Elgonar?" Moonlight clung to the Dreamer, for this was the time of his greatest power.

The Weaver showed him Remarr's plight. "I thought you might influence his captors."

The Dreamer frowned. "I can try, El, but it is difficult to

17

guess how a mind not open to me will respond to my touch."

The Weaver sighed. *"I can weave hesitation for them, and haste for the shapeshifter and the swordswoman; perhaps they will be able to free the minstrel before irrevocable harm is done to him."* He gnawed his lower lip. *"I don't like it. There is fire in the new Voice's hatred, and the Trickster is in it already; but perhaps it is the best we can do."*

"Wait! See!" The Dreamer pointed. *"Here, and here: those two I can influence, and they in turn may be able to curb the new Voice. You weave the dream, El, and I'll cast it; and then we shall see what they draw into their minds' nets!"*

Pifadeh Moirre woke. Tears clung to her lashes; she scrubbed them away, but the dream would not be so easily torn loose. She had thought herself beyond such nonsense. Her husband treasured her calm; Efiran admired the serenity with which she faced every calamity. But this dream would not leave her. She went to her window. In the garden, the fountains glittered with moonlight. Then, as scudding clouds snuffed the moon, the diamonds faded into shadow. She struggled to hold back tears. The sparkling life she loved was passing into darkness, into war. A tear scalded the back of her thin hand. A flood followed it. Pifadeh found herself weeping as she had not wept since she was a girl.

"Pifadeh!" Efiran's gentle hands turned her to face him. "The world must be ending if my Pifadeh weeps."

"Don't make light of me," she pleaded. "Efiran, I dreamed a bitter dream indeed."

"These bitter times leave us prey to bitter dreams and mad urges," he said. "Do you know what I did this afternoon? I went to the Street of the Artisans and gave a coin and a warning to a minstrel there."

His words struck her like the waves of destiny. "Remarr."

18

His name was half a sob. "It was he of whom I dreamed." The words spilled rapidly from her lips, as though there were not time to give the message in her usual unhurried manner. "The horse he bought wasn't fast enough. They have taken him, and they will use him—our soul son!—as *bait* to lure Vihena. When Edevvi has them both, she will kill them. Their cries will shake the world loose from its foundation, and their blood will blot out the stars, and the world will end in terror and darkness."

Efiran drew Pifadeh away from the window. He jerked the bell pull. A moment later, Pifadeh's sleepy maid looked in.

"Wake Monegal," he said. "I want the household moved to Moirresharre by morning. He knows where the boats are and what to do. Then fetch Anfeh and her maid and help my lady wife make herself ready. Do you understand?"

The maid nodded, wide-eyed, then fled to the servants' quarters to wake the butler. As soon as she was gone, Efiran went to the secret panel that hid House Moirre's valuables.

"What are you going to do, Efiran?" Pifadeh asked.

Without slowing in his removal of jewel boxes and coffers, he replied, "I will try to ransom him."

"And meanwhile I must wait for you, or word of your fate?"

He closed the plundered coffers and faced her. "I will work better for knowing that you and Anfeh are safe at Moirresharre."

She nodded. The traces of her tears and weakness were gone. "Then I will wait," she told him tenderly. "Waiting is women's work; and I have been well trained."

He tucked the two heavy purses he had filled into his shirt and went to her. As he kissed her brow, she murmured, "May the Dreamer and the Weaver guard you, my husband."

He held her close. "And the Namegiver," he whispered. "Don't forget the Namegiver."

19

4

Efiran Moirre hesitated outside the door to Edevvi's quarters. He could hear arguing voices, muffled by the iron-bound doors. He touched the reassuring weight of the purses in his shirt, then smiled wryly at himself. He knew he shouldn't rely upon gold for peace of mind, but it was gold and a soft life that had tamed the City Khedathi in the past. He pounded on the door. The arguing ceased.

The door was opened by one of Edevvi's lieutenants, a Khedatheh Efiran knew only by sight. She stared at him in surprise.

"I would like to speak with the new Voice," he said. "I realize it is late, but the matter is of some urgency."

"I shall return with an answer in a moment." When she reappeared, she ushered the Head of House Moirre inside.

Edevvi sat at a long trestle table before the hearth. Her wounded arm rested in a sling. A tankard of mulled cider sat by her elbow; with her good hand, she toyed with the silver medallion on a chain round her neck. She eyed Efiran with the look of one interrupted untimely. There were four other Khedathi in the room: two in the shadows beside the hearth, the woman who had brought him, and the fourth seated beside Edevvi. Bodyguards, Efiran judged. He wondered why she feared a lone old man.

20

"What urgent matter could drive you from your comfortable bed at this hour, Moirre?"

"My errand concerns a minstrel."

"Then you want the Musicians' Guild, Moirre."

"A *blond* minstrel. You have him, Edevvi, and I want him."

A muscle jumped in the warrior's jaw; her gaze sharpened on Efiran's face. Before Edevvi could speak, the Khedatheh who had let him in demanded, "Why do you want him, Moirre?"

"Rakhela, stay out of it," Edevvi growled.

"It's *important*, Edevvi," she persisted. "Moirre, *why do you want him?*"

"My wife dreamed of him: not only where he is, but of terrible consequences should he come to harm."

The hiss of caught breath was loud in the room. Rakhela cried, "So! Didn't I tell you? Edevvi, we've been dream-warned."

"I told you to stay out of it!" Edevvi snapped. "You can't have him, Moirre. He's mine; and I intend to make him suffer."

One of the men by the fire stirred uneasily. "You should give him up, Edevvi. He's god-touched."

"*Dream-warned? God-touched?*" Her contempt scalded them. "Am I surrounded by fools?"

Efiran removed a purse and upended it. The coins chimed and gleamed—more gold than most Khedathi mercenaries saw in a lifetime. "I do not come as a beggar," he said. "House Moirre does not ask for charity. I want the minstrel; name a price."

"Oh gods," the Khedatheh at the table whispered. "That would buy my mother's farm twice over."

"Shut up," Edevvi snarled. "I'm not selling, Moirre."

"Don't be a fool, 'Dev," Rakhela pleaded. "You've a king's ransom on the table. What are you playing at?" She turned to the man who had called Remarr god-touched. "Merivatt, fetch him."

"Yes, do," Edevvi agreed. "Maybe I can show Moirre there are things that—even with all his money—he can't do."

Merivatt returned with the minstrel. He was bound, already showing signs of rough treatment. Surprise flickered in his eyes when he saw Efiran.

"So, Singer," Edevvi taunted. "Moirre here wants to buy you. What do you think you're worth?"

"It depends upon what sort of condition I'm in by the time you're ready to sell," he replied.

She struck him across the face. "He's insolent," she commented to Efiran. "Are you sure you want him?"

"Name your price, Voice; I have said as much already."

"And *I* have said I'm not selling."

Merivatt said, "He's god-touched. You are playing with fire, Edevvi. Take the man's money but let the Singer go."

"*God*-touched. Superstitious nonsense! The gods have no interest in this sniveling weakling."

"But they do," Remarr said softly. "The Trickster threw me to you, Edevvi, like a bone to a dog; if she wants you to have me, no doubt others would thwart her. You think me cowardly; but I *am* desert born—and not such a tyro as to be parted from my mount when we were already clean away."

"So it takes the hand of a god to part you from your horse?" she mocked.

"Indeed not. I am merely telling you that it *was* a god's action that parted me from *this* horse, *this* night."

"You are lying."

"I wouldn't lie to the Trickster herself—much less *you*. I have my honor, even if I can't wield a sword to prove it."

"You make a *mockery* of honor!" Her lips curled as she

22

strove to bridle her rage. "The gods are mere stories for wayward children, yet you would tell me that you have seen the Trickster. What sort of fool do you take me for?"

"With every word you speak I take you for a greater one. The gods are no children's tale and you do ill to mock them."

"*Mock* them?" Her laughter rang wildly. "I have barely begun to mock them." She drew her knife. "Merivatt called you god-touched." She placed the point of her dagger beside his eye; with a swift, downward stroke, she scored a bloody line from temple to jaw. "I shall play the Namegiver and name you Dagger-Touched." She slit the lacings of his shirt one by one, then lodged the dagger's point in the hollow of his throat. Remarr swallowed convulsively. She laughed. "I name you Coward, and Liar." The blade bit. Behind her, the door crashed open; a gust of wind extinguished the lamps. Shadows leaped away from the sullen glow of the hearth.

A cloaked figure strode into the room. "Light," a woman's voice said. The lamps rekindled. The Namegiver faced Edevvi, the lamplight striking fiery glints in her unbound hair. "The peril in giving names comes when they are not apt. One cannot name a brave man Coward, nor an honest one Liar in my name—even in jest." She drew Remarr gently out of Edevvi's reach. Her finger traced the wound on his face. "Dagger-Touched, yes," she said sadly. "And God-Touched." Her gaze swept to Efiran and Rakhela, "And indeed Dream-Warned." Then, her eyes imprisoned Edevvi's. "You killed a good man to make a different name for yourself. But the Voice must speak with wisdom, with justice, with compassion. You have not learned those lessons; until you do, I name you Silence." She turned to the others. "You must choose another Voice to speak for your people, for Silence is mute."

Edevvi's mouth worked, her face grew red, then pale; but she

23

made no sound. She snatched up her tankard and hammered it on the table; and though she sloshed cider on herself and on Efiran's gold, the pounding gesture was noiseless.

"Silence," Efiran breathed. "Keep the gold. It has served me well." He went out, to make his way to his island stronghold before the storm, brewed by the night's events, broke.

As Remarr watched Efiran go, he felt the Namegiver's eyes on him; he returned her gaze warily.

"Will you come with me, Minstrel, that I may shorten your journey?" At his nod, she reached a hand toward him. His bonds fell away. "Take my hand." When his cold hand closed on her warm, strong one, god and Minstrel vanished into a swirl of wind and mist.

The sun was swathed in an early fog when Iobeh rose to tend her goats. After she finished the milking, she turned them out to graze in the high meadow above the stone house she and her twin, Karivet, had built.

The goats were strays or castoffs from the village herds. Iobeh had found the first over a year ago, injured and starving. She had soothed the creature, fed her, and tended her hurts. When the goat was well, Iobeh had taken her into the village to find her owner—but no one would claim her. The other goats had come in similar fashion. Many other animals came to Iobeh as well: an orphan deer; an otter with a broken leg; even a mountain cat, once, with an abscessed wound; and others. But the goats stayed, while the wildlings returned to the forest.

Iobeh took the pan of milk back to the house. Karivet was still sleeping—his anxious dreams worried her peace like distant thunder. Perhaps if she made enticing breakfast smells he would waken.

By the time Iobeh had warmed the leftover *kemess*, Karivet had risen. He looked very much like her: small and delicate, with curly dark hair and wide brown eyes. But this morning, he was haggard; he appeared older than his fourteen years.

What is it? Iobeh signed, using the hand-language she and her twin shared.

He shrugged. "There are portents in the wind. The Weaver's at the Loom, but I cannot guess what pattern he is weaving." He gave her an apologetic look. "You could Ask me."

Do you want me to? she signed.

"I think it may be important that we know."

She hid her reluctance. She hated to use the voice that had been the gift of the Trickster. Iobeh had been born mute, a difficulty she had overcome with her hand-language—and in other ways. She "heard" the feelings of others, and could project her own when she chose. This ability gave her skill with animals, but it also made her unwilling to speak. The voice the Trickster's malice had given her was an ugly croak; because of her empathic gifts, she knew it was painful to others. Steeling herself, she took Karivet's hand and met his eyes. "What troubles your dreams?" she croaked.

Karivet answered in the flat voice in which he prophesied. "One comes; two follow; three guide."

"Who comes?"

"The Minstrel Remarr."

Iobeh's eyes widened. *Remarr!* But her hand still gripped Karivet's and her eyes held his. She Asked again. "Who follows?"

"The Swordswoman Vihena and the Shapeshifter Ychass."

"Who guides?" she Asked; her croaking voice quavered.

"Weaver, Dreamer, and Namegiver."

Her free hand clenched. "To what end?"

"To reclaim 'Tsan, and halt Fate's unraveling."

Iobeh dropped his hand. *Karivet!* she signed. *What can this mean? I don't know whether to be horrified or delighted.*

25

"Nor do I. Do you suppose they want us to look for her?"

Why else would they send 'Tsan's companions here?

"Why else, indeed. Well, Iobeh, what do you think? Should we look for her?"

Iobeh felt tears near the surface. She gripped her twin's hand, caught his eyes, and Asked, "Is 'Tsan happy where she is?"

"She is beset by loneliness and stalked by madness."

Then of course we must go after her, Iobeh signed. *We owe her too much to let her suffer.*

Further discussion was cut short by a knock. Karivet smiled at Iobeh. "Come in, Remarr," he called.

Remarr looked in, smiling wryly. "I should know better than to try to surprise a prophet."

Before he had finished speaking, the twins had flung themselves into his arms. There was a great deal of hugging and back-pounding; Iobeh's were not the only damp eyes.

"Have you eaten?" Karivet asked. "There is *kemess*."

Your face! What happened to your face? Iobeh signed.

Bitterness twisted his lips. "Namegiver said I was god-touched; they need to trim their claws. But let me tell you the whole." When he had finished, he said, "I don't suppose you can explain what this is all about?"

"I think we will be sent to rescue 'Tsan," Karivet replied.

"Rescue 'Tsan?" He laughed. "I can't imagine her as a damsel in distress."

She may be different in her own world, Iobeh signed. *When she first came to us, she was very unsure of herself.*

"She would not believe she was in any way special," Karivet recalled, his eyes growing distant. "I remember her saying that she was a very ordinary person, and if the gods had chosen her, they had made a bad mistake."

Remarr was silent. He, too, could remember that time. "I do

26

not think I shall like a world that can change 'Tsan so much that she *needs* rescuing."

But you will *help?*

He tousled Iobeh's hair. "Yes. I owe her that—besides," he added sourly, "I'm rather deeply in the Namegiver's debt. Do we know when Vihena and Ychass will arrive?"

Karivet shook his head. "You could Ask me."

"Do you mind?" Remarr pressed, remembering how reluctant Karivet was to use his prophetic gift; there had been too many times when the question had been the wrong one, or the truth too brutal. Karivet gave his hand to the minstrel. Remarr met his eyes. "When will Vihena and Ychass arrive?"

"They will come with the dusk."

He released Karivet's hand. "Good. I could sleep for a week, but all day will do for a start."

Let me tend your hurts first, Iobeh signed; she had already heated a bowl of water and herbs. When Remarr finally fell asleep in their loft, his wounds and bruises hardly ached at all.

The Weaver and the Dreamer both breathed sighs of relief. That had been hard work; Edevvi did not respond predictably to the guidance of the Loom. It had been pure luck that had made her choose to mock the Namegiver—who had been waiting for an excuse to intervene.

The Dreamer smiled. "This gives me new respect for you, El. I never thought choosing the Loom's pattern could be so hard."

The Weaver sighed. "Only when you care about the outcome. If the threads are merely colors, you can lose a shade of blue and not miss it; but none of 'Tsan's companions are mere threads to me. The Mother would say that I've lost my objectivity."

27

"I would say," the Namegiver said as she stepped from the shadows, "that you have engaged your heart."

"But is that good or bad?" the Weaver asked.

"Both," she replied, "and neither."

The Dreamer chuckled and laid a hand on the Weaver's shoulder. "That's our sister's way of saying you'll have to wait and see. I must go. If you have need of me, call."

"I will, Irenden," the Weaver promised. When the Dreamer was gone, he turned to the Namegiver. "Thank you. I think Edevvi would have killed the minstrel if not for you."

She shrugged. "Perhaps. In any case, it pleased me to bind silence onto that rash hothead. Belerann was a good man."

"Engaging your heart isn't new to you, is it?"

"No." The Namegiver's smile was enigmatic. "El, I've been thinking: should we not let your Wanderer know what's afoot? The three of us ought to be able to reach across the void—at least with a dream."

"Yes. You're right—but not now. I'm spent. If we drew—resistance—I'm not fit to face it. But later—I'll summon you."

With a gesture, the Namegiver wrapped herself in wind and mist. Her voice remained, after she had gone. "Rest, El. You're a wraith."

Elgonar smiled as he rose and stretched. Leave it to Yschadeh to have the last word.

5

Ychass and Vihena arrived at dusk, but not alone. They brought the old man, Ohmiden, and the Dreamweaver, Eiko-heh. There was quite a reunion in Karivet and Iobeh's cottage, with much laughter and embracing.

While they ate, they shared their news. Ohmiden related the dream that had sent Ychass into the desert to bring Vihena out. Remarr's tale caused a stir; it was alarming that the Trickster and the Namegiver had both touched his life in a single night.

"It worries me that the gods are moving in this so clearly," Remarr said. "I do not trust the Trickster and though I do not think the Weaver or the Namegiver wish us ill, they *are* gods, and their touch is not over-gentle."

"No," Karivet agreed. "But there is 'Tsan to think of. She is beset by loneliness and stalked by madness. Whatever the gods' motivation, the thought of 'Tsan unhappy is enough to drive me to seek her."

"We all feel that way," Ychass said. "And the gods know it—or have guessed as much. The questions are: what will this quest require of us; what aid—or hindrance—will the gods give us; and what will become of us all at the end of it?"

"Those are questions we cannot answer," Vihena said. "I am a woman of action; I want to know what we should *do*. Do we wait here or do we journey to Windsmeet to ask the gods?"

"I think," Eikoheh said, "that I should string my loom for a Fate and cast the Weaver's color in the pattern. Then he can tell us what is afoot."

"But you must not weave a Fate for us, Eikoheh," Karivet protested. "It is dangerous for you, and tiring—"

"And I am old," she interrupted him. "Karivet, I *am* old; I don't hear as well as I did, nor move so nimbly. But my heart loves as strongly as yours, and my courage is undiminished. I cannot go with you, for I am bound to the Forest and my loom. But I can weave for you. You are all willing to die for 'Tsan—I can see it in your faces. So am I. Further, I am not willing to live if you fail because I withheld my aid."

"You always were an outspoken harpy," Ohmiden told her fondly.

"And you, my sweet Ohmiden, have the winning ways of a skunk; but I'll give you this: you *can* cook."

Iobeh beamed. *It is wonderful to be together again.*

Yes. Ychass's thought-voice spoke in each of their minds. *But we won't truly be gathered until 'Tsan is with us, too.*

It was easy, the three gods found, to touch 'Tsan's mind. Even across the void, her strong presence shone like a torch. The Dreamer left a dream in her mind: a powerful dream of her friends, of rescue, of the need the gods had for her. The Weaver hoped it would wake her but she slept on. And the gods could not see the tears that wet her pillow.

Alexandra Scarsdale woke to the beastly shrilling of her alarm clock. She rolled out of bed. Usually, she woke long before the clock rang. Now if she wanted breakfast, she would have to hurry.

As she dressed, she tried to occupy her mind with daily matters: her exams, her two research papers; if she spent the day in

30

the library, perhaps she could avoid worrying about that dream. But the images surfaced—beyond her power to suppress. The dream worried her; the several months after her father's death, three and a half years ago, were a gap in her memory. She knew she had been with some cult—but she could remember no details of that experience. Instead, the hole in her memory was filled with impossible things: shapeshifters, walking gods, friends dearer than life itself; crazy delusions. Why couldn't she remember something—*anything!*—from her time with the cult? Why did the people of the world she had invented in her grief seem so much more real than the students and professors? And why, *why, WHY* did she have to *dream* about them?

She raked the comb through her red hair. She had cut her impossible hair short, so that it clung severely to her skull. The style emphasized the strong bones of her face and the sharpness of her jawline. She would never be pretty, but she could be striking. Now, she just looked thin, shorn, and desperate.

She was the last one through the breakfast line; they were out of eggs. She made do with oatmeal, then selected an empty table beneath one of the huge windows. Dunster House had one of the nicest dining halls at Harvard, but she didn't bother to admire it. Instead, she propped a book open in front of her for a screen against the outside world. It worked this morning, as it had for the past three years; no one tried to join her. Even a dedicated extrovert was daunted by the shell she used to hide the troubled young woman inside.

It was nearly dusk before Eikoheh was ready to string the Weaver's color on her loom. The five companions crowded around as the old woman picked up the shuttle wound with the Weaver's shimmering gray thread. Ohmiden hovered in the background.

31

The gasp of wonder from the watchers drew the old man's attention. Where the Weaver's silvery gray left the shuttle and entered the pattern, he could see how it became three strands: a deep, iridescent blue and a thread of clear gold wound themselves into the pattern with the Weaver's color.

"More company than planned," Eikoheh remarked. "The Weaver is bringing the Dreamer and the Namegiver with him."

A knock sounded. Eikoheh went to the door while the companions hovered. The Weaver came in first, looking much as he had when they had first seen him, three years ago, in his bower in the far mountains. He was followed closely by the Namegiver and the Dreamer. Except for their red hair, the three did not look much alike. The Dreamer's eyes were a blue so dark it was nearly black, and his skin was more golden than the Weaver's. The Namegiver was taller than her brothers, and thinner; her eyes were very pale gray, like water over stones: shapeshifter's eyes.

"Greetings," the old woman bade the gods. "I can't say we expected all of you, but you are welcome nonetheless. Will you eat with us—or don't you eat mortal food?"

The Weaver answered for them. "We are grateful for your summons, and more than pleased to accept your hospitality."

Eikoheh ushered them to piles of skins and cushions before the hearth. "Sit, and eat. We have much to discuss."

Over the meal, the gods explained the situation and outlined the task they had in mind for the Five: go to 'Tsan's world and bring her back.

"You make it sound simple," Remarr commented, "but surely it will be harder than that?"

"We know nothing of the world from which 'Tsan came," the Dreamer answered. "There will doubtless be perils. You are intrepid and resourceful; you have overcome impossible odds before. We are laying all our hopes upon your shoulders, but I

32

know of no others to whom I would rather entrust the very fate of our world."

"I find such confidence frightening," Ychass said. "It was 'Tsan who knit us together; I don't know how we will manage without her."

"You may not have to manage without her," the Namegiver said. "We have touched 'Tsan's mind across the void and left a dream there. Once you arrive in her world, Ychass, you may be able to reach her mind. In any case, we will continue to send messages: dreams, and perhaps even more. So before you have been long in her world, she will know of your presence."

"It is only fair to warn you," the Weaver said, "that the Trickster may be able to act directly against you. The bonds that hold her in check are strained; I don't know how far they will stretch. She may follow you across the void—or failing that, exert some influence to hinder you."

"Which is why they need my help," Eikoheh said. "I will weave allies for you, in the world whither you are bound."

The Weaver looked anxious. "A Fate that spans the void?"

Eikoheh drew herself up. "Yes."

"I admire your courage," the Weaver told her.

"I shall help her," Ohmiden put in. "I have already dreamed of 'Tsan. If my dreams can span the void, I think the Dreamweaver's Fate will have no trouble."

"You are resolved to go," the Dreamer said to the five companions. "And you are resolved to aid them as you can," he added to Ohmiden and Eikoheh. "Faithful friends, indeed."

"We are resolved to go," Karivet acknowledged. "When—and how—will you send us; and how will we return?"

The Weaver answered. "Together, the three of us can send you across the void without touching the Loom's power. Once you are there, we will follow your progress as best we can—through the Dreamweaver's Fate, and by direct means; we are

33

able to scry beyond the void. When you are ready to return, link hands and call upon us. Use my true name: Elgonar. I will hear you, and the three of us will draw you back. We will send you"—he spread his hands—"when the Dreamweaver tells you all is in readiness."

"The Fate is strung," the old woman said. "And as for mundane needs—" she gestured to the door, to a cluster of bulging knapsacks for the travelers—"Ohmiden has seen to it."

The Namegiver held up one hand. "Wait. One thing more. We must give them the language, so that they need not waste time learning to speak to 'Tsan's people."

The Weaver and the Dreamer agreed. While the gods took counsel together, Iobeh, Karivet, and Eikoheh exchanged glances; it had fallen to them to teach 'Tsan the Senathii, the speech of the peoples, when she had first come. It had not been easy.

The Weaver spoke again. "If we pool our power, we will be able to give you the language and we can send you across the void whenever you choose. Perhaps in the morning?"

Let's do it now, Iobeh signed. *I won't get any sleep for worrying, if we wait.*

The others agreed. They said their farewells to Eikoheh and Ohmiden, then clasped hands in the center of the room. The old woman began flinging the shuttle through the warp. The gods linked hands and called their power. For several moments nothing happened, then air hissed past them and they were swept into swirling darkness.

Once the Five were gone, the gods took their leave. Eikoheh sat late at her weaving; while Ohmiden cleaned up, he heard her mutter, several times: "Allies. I must weave them allies."

6

Angel let out a yodel and urged Gabe into a mad gallop up the slope Brice had christened "Black Stallion Hill." The two boys followed Angel's lead; they reined in laughing on the crest of the hill. Angel saw the sun glinting on the Orange Reservoir; out of habit, her eyes sought the forlorn bulk of the Blocktower, a derelict square structure, rather like a Saxon fort, built by some summer people. If you didn't know where to look for it, it tended to blend into the landscape. Suddenly, Angel tensed.

"Look!" she pointed. "Smoke—by the Blocktower. I wonder what's going on."

"Probably someone having a picnic," Mark offered.

"At nine in the morning?" Angel scoffed.

"Maybe someone is camping there," Brice suggested.

"Let's check it out." Angel and Gabe set off without waiting for a response. Mark and Brice shared long-suffering looks before they followed.

The steep path up to the Blocktower was badly eroded by the frequent passage of dirt bikes. Angel tried to set a sedate pace, so as not to startle anyone who might be around, but Gabe took the bit and thundered up the path. At the top, Angel reasserted control. Smoke rose from behind the tower. As she and her friends slowly approached, a figure swathed in outlandish white robes sprang from the grass. Churchy shied

35

violently, nearly unseating Mark. Angel gasped as she realized the figure barring their way held a sword. Brice gave a low whistle, then said in an under-voice that almost hid his tremor of apprehension, "Angel, your aliens have landed."

"We're friends," Angel told the unwavering sword. "We're peaceful. We're harmless!" Her voice crackled with panic.

When Mark had Churchy under control, he took the reins in one hand and extended his open palm toward the robed figure. "We're unarmed," he said with a calmness Angel envied.

The figure sheathed the sword. "Come with me." It was a woman's voice. "Perhaps you can aid us."

"Take us to your leader," Brice whispered; he and Angel had to stifle nervous giggles. They followed. The woman and her companions had cut back some of the turf and laid a campfire. Meat was roasting on a spit, and steam escaped from a lidded kettle set in the coals. There were four others, all similarly robed. As Angel and the boys stared, one of the others rose, swept his hood back from a halo of white-blond hair, and bowed.

"I trust we have not invaded your territory," he began. "We are strangers here; we do not mean to offend."

Angel waited for Mark to answer; she'd been impressed with his calm in the face of the swordswoman. But when he said nothing, she drew a deep breath to steady her voice. "We don't own the Blocktower, and I don't suppose Old Man Chandler will notice unless you start a brush fire. We saw the smoke and came to check it out."

"You're not sentries for this—Old Man Chandler?"

Angel made a face, partly puzzled, partly exasperated. "*Sentries?* We're just kids. We keep our horses over at Horizon Stable and we ride around here." She took the offensive. "Where are you from, anyway? And how did you get here?" she added, as she noticed there was no trace of any vehicle.

36

"We are from a distant land," one of the others said: another woman; she, too, pushed back her hood, revealing a sharp-featured face and shrewd, silvery-gray eyes. "We are on a quest and hope that you can aid us."

Brice laughed. "I get it. You guys are into that Dungeons and Dragons stuff. Look, we don't want to interrupt; we'll just head out and let you get back to your game."

"Wait," the young man said firmly, and Brice hesitated in spite of himself. "We are not playing a game. We *do* need your help. At least hear us out before you refuse."

The three kids exchanged looks; Mark whispered, "This is really weird, but it can't hurt to listen, surely."

Angel turned back to the young man. "So explain."

"As my companion said, we come from a distant place; three of our gods sent us across the void to this world. Our quest is of the utmost importance. In the land whence we come, the very fabric of reality is weakening. We must find a woman of your world, a friend of ours, who was drawn to our world to fulfill her destiny. When her quest was accomplished, the Trickster cast her out, tearing her thread from the Loom of Fate. Alas, her thread was tightly woven into the Loom, and the Trickster's deed did grave damage. We seek our friend in hopes that she may heal the Loom and save our world." The young man smiled wryly. "That is the noble side of our quest. But there is a human side, as well. 'Tsan is our friend, and she is not happy here. After all she has done for us, she deserves better. We seek her for the gods' sake, for our sake, and for hers. Will you aid us?"

There was silence when he finished. The thin woman laughed harshly. "It's no good, Remarr; they don't believe you." She pinned Mark with her eyes and asked, "What is 'Waterbury'?"

Mark flushed and stammered, "W–Waterbury?"

The woman nodded patiently. "You were wondering whether we had escaped from Waterbury. I can assure you we haven't. We don't even know what—or where—Waterbury is."

Angel felt the imp of mischief prod her. "There's a state mental hospital in Waterbury," she said. "I bet that's what Mark was thinking of."

"'State mental hospital,'" the woman repeated; then her eyes widened. "You think we're mad."

"You're not exactly normal," Angel replied brightly. "Do you want a turn to—you know—tighten up your friend's story?"

The woman frowned. "What would convince you that we are, indeed, from another world?" Angel said nothing, thinking that maybe this had gone too far. These folks might be dangerous. Waterbury: Mark wasn't far off base. She started fishing for a tactful exit line; the woman interrupted. "*Watch.*"

The woman's form blurred suddenly; as they gaped, her shape changed, reassembled: a woman no longer. A wolf confronted them, the woman's gray eyes strangely intelligent in its face. Angel bit her tongue to keep from screaming. The wolf regarded them. *Convinced?* Her sarcastic voice spoke directly in their minds.

"Can you all do that?" Angel squeaked. "And can you do any shape you want or just wolves?"

The wolf melted into a red-tailed hawk with human eyes. *Only I. My companions have other gifts.* Then she resumed her human shape. "I am called Ychass; this"—she touched the blond man's shoulder—"is Remarr." Indicating the woman with the sword, she said, "Vihena. And Iobeh, and Karivet." The last two were younger; as Ychass introduced them, they pushed their hoods back, revealing curly dark hair and faces with a great deal of resemblance to one another. Only the swordswoman still wore her hood; all they could see of her face was a pair of cold eyes.

38

There was a long silence. Angel found herself suspended between terror and jubilation. (*Aliens! They really ARE aliens!*) Then she realized she hadn't retained a single name. Before she could confess, though, the one who had changed shape repeated the introductions. This time, Angel found she could actually *look* at the five of them without her mind flinching.

"Iobeh and I are twins," Karivet said, explaining their resemblance. "And my sister does not speak. If you can help us find our friend, we will be ever in your debt."

"Do you have any idea where she's staying—the town or city?" Mark asked. He sounded officious; Angel realized he was as overwhelmed as she, but was coping in his own way.

"Town?" Karivet echoed. "No, we haven't."

"This may not be as simple as you hope," Mark warned. "There are nearly five hundred thousand people in Vermont alone; and I don't suppose you're even certain she is in Vermont."

"What is Vermont? Is it a town?"

Brice answered; his voice sounded as though part of his mind were elsewhere. Angel knew the feeling. "No, a state; a region. We're in Vermont, now, in the town of—Orange, I guess; or Plainfield. Those are little towns. If your friend is in one of them, it ought to be easy to find her. What's her name?"

"'Tsan," Karivet responded.

"'Tsan?'" Angel echoed doubtfully. "Is that *it?* I mean, she's not from around here with a weird name like that. Here, people have at least two names: I'm Angel Newcomb. And this is Brice Crowley, and Mark Harrington."

"'Tsan was what we called her," Remarr clarified, as he dredged his harper's memory for her whole name. "Alexandra Scarsdale," he said when it surfaced.

"It could be worse," Brice pointed out cheerfully. "At least we're not looking for a Jane Smith."

"*We?*" Mark broke in. "Have we decided to help?"

"Of *course* we'll help!" Angel retorted. "They're my alien invasion."

"Angel," Mark began, in his most annoying 'let's-be-reasonable' tone; but Brice cut him off.

"They're just looking for a friend, Mark. It's not like we're being asked to slay a dragon. Where's your sense of adventure, anyway?"

Mark regarded his friends seriously before his wry smile surfaced. "The last time you asked me that, Brice, I ended up staying after school every day for a month."

Brice grinned. "Yeah, but it was worth it."

The Five watched their exchange, puzzled. "Will you help, or not?" Ychass asked at last.

"We'll help," Angel replied. Suddenly, she registered a sound that had been growing in the distance: dirt bikes. "Uh-oh, we may have company. Look, you guys: hide in the Blocktower. In those billowing white things, you look like a bunch of super-bleached Hare Krishnas." She turned to her friends. "We've *got* to get them some real clothes."

"First priority," Mark agreed. "I can scrounge some of my older brother's stuff."

Angel nodded. "In the meantime, you guys stay here. We'll deal with the dirt bikes and come back later with clothes. While we're gone, don't talk to anyone else. We'll be back as soon as we can." With an ordinary task at hand, Angel wasted no time. The strangers had barely absorbed their plan before the three kids turned their horses toward the sound of the bikes. Soon, they were herding a pair of dirt bikes ahead of them. They were halfway home before the bikers escaped them.

"Hide?" Vihena snorted. "I wouldn't *hide* from the Trickster herself. Who do those three think they are?"

40

Perhaps they are the allies Eikoheh promised to weave for us, Iobeh suggested.

"Let's hope not," Vihena retorted. "You heard them: their first priority was *clothing.*" She turned to the twins. "I doubt *clothing* was the first thing you thought of doing for 'Tsan."

"No," Karivet agreed. "Teaching her the language was."

There was a silence, which Remarr broke. "Ychass, what do you think? Could those three be the allies Eikoheh promised?"

The shapeshifter shrugged. "We are strangers; they may be useful. Then again, they were very frightened of us. They look full grown, but their thoughts are young. One of them—the one called Brice—wondered what his mother would say if she knew."

"Wonderful," Vihena snapped. "I'm certainly not planning to hide from anyone! If others come along, we should approach them, in hopes that they are our allies, instead of these *children.*"

"I won't dispute that, Vihena," Ychass said. "Surely it can do no harm to ask questions."

7

More dreams! Alexandra thought with disgust. *Can't they leave me alone?* That thought made her flinch: *they* weren't doing anything to her; this was her own impossible subconscious. Was she getting paranoid on top of everything else?

She rose. Though she had slept, she did not feel rested. What was she going to *do?* The past three years had not been easy, but she had thought she was through the worst of it. Now, her dreams were again tormenting her with glimpses of her delusional world. And she *missed* it — that was the crowning irony.

"I'm going over the edge," she said aloud. "And part of me *wants* to."

She used her morning routine to stifle her uncomfortable thoughts. After she mopped her dripping face, she caught sight of her wan reflection in the bathroom mirror. She grimaced; her reflection suddenly wavered. Instead of her own familiar image, she faced the Weaver. *'Tsan,* he spoke in her mind.

Alexandra screamed. She snatched her hairbrush and hurled it at the mirror. The glass shattered, taking with it the terrifying reflection. "No, *NO!*" she shouted. "Get out of my head! Leave me alone! *Leave me alone! LEAVE ME ALONE!!*"

Concerned voices and a knock on the emergency fire door doused Alexandra's hysteria. "Are you okay in there?"

She struggled for control. She didn't even *know* these next-

42

door neighbors. She didn't want them prying into her madness. After several deep breaths, she spoke. "Sorry! I'm okay. *Really.* I didn't mean to alarm you." Her voice sounded shrill in her own ears; but she prayed the neighbors would buy it. If they came through the fire door, the resulting alarm would rouse the whole dorm. The thought appalled her.

"You sure?" the voice was doubtful. "It sounded like you were being murdered."

"I'm sure, I'm okay. Thanks. I'm so sorry to have alarmed you!" Her voice sounded better this time; fortunately, her neighbor couldn't see the shuddering that wracked her body. He made some acknowledging noises, then left her alone. Alexandra returned to the bedroom, collapsed on the bed, and buried her face in her hands. The shudders turned to sobs; acutely aware of her neighbors, she muffled her face in her pillow and cried as though the world were ending.

The grinding rumble Angel had called "dirt bikes" returned to trouble the morning. Vihena listened intently. If the sound were as distant as it seemed, it was quite loud. She wondered what sort of animal would make so much noise. At least it wasn't hunting; such a racket would drive prey into hiding.

"I would guess that it is approaching," Remarr said. "Are you certain we shouldn't take our visitors' advice?"

"And hide?" Vihena's eyes flashed. "I am not so craven."

"No one doubts your *bravery,*" the minstrel retorted. "But is it *wise* to confront the unknown so rashly?"

"This whole venture was rash: a leap into the unknown, Singer. Surely it is late to counsel caution?"

Remarr eyed her coldly. "I have a name—a given one, if not a clan name. Use it."

"Indeed, Remarr. And what honorific should I use? Lord Remarr? Master Remarr? Remarr of the Golden-Throat?"

Stop it! Iobeh interposed herself between them. *You sound like cats battling over territory. The noise is close. Leave your argument until we have at least figured out what it is.*

It was impossible to guess Vihena's expression behind her veil, but Remarr looked sheepish. "My apologies, Iobeh," he murmured; but further discussion was cut off by the appearance of two peculiar beasts. Vihena pushed herself in front of Iobeh and Remarr, raising her sword.

The beasts halted; their roars changed to a purr. Instead of feet, they had wheels that enabled them to travel very quickly. A single eye glowed between two thin antlers; and oddest of all, perched on the back of each purring creature was a strange, human-like figure with a round, hairless, oversized head that was utterly without features. The Five gaped. The largest of the humanoids dismounted, raised both hands to his head and removed—his helmet! Recognition, like the sighting of a familiar landmark on a desert horizon, washed over the Five. These two were people—mounted rather strangely, but about the same age as the three who had arrived earlier on horseback.

"What do you think you're doing?" the unhelmeted boy said belligerently. "This is private property!"

Ychass, who had been lounging nonchalantly against the gray bulk of the Blocktower, sauntered toward him. "So it is," she agreed. "And we well might ask you what business *you* have on Chandler land."

The second rider spoke, his voice muffled by his helmet. "If they've got permission—"

The first boy's gesture cut him off. "Old Man Chandler isn't going to give a bunch of freaked-out cultists permission to do their crazy rites on his property." He glared at Ychass. "So what are you doing here?"

Remarr answered. "We come from a different world; we are on a quest set us by the gods. Perhaps you would aid us?"

The boy clenched his fists and took a step toward the minstrel. "Hey! Don't go trying to make a fool out of me, or you'll get more than you planned on!"

"Come no closer," Vihena said, raising her sword.

"You think I'm afraid of some chick with a toy sword? Get real!" Lowering his head, he rushed Remarr. Quicker than thought, Vihena's blade hissed toward him, deftly slicing his leather belt.

"No closer," she said in a voice that froze blood. "This is no toy, and I am no frail lady."

"Come *on*, Travis!" the younger boy bleated. "Let's get out of here!" He retreated down the hill.

Travis hesitated, but in the face of Vihena's blade, his courage failed. He crammed his helmet on as he ran back to his mount. With a vicious kick he set it snarling down the hill after his companion.

Ychass frowned. "They were more frightened than the first three—*and* more hostile. This is a strange world. I wonder what a 'state trooper' is? One of them considered summoning one."

Vihena shrugged. "No doubt a 'state trooper' can be as easily routed as these two; and if it is not hostile, may the Weaver grant that it will be of more use to us!"

When Angel, Mark, and Brice reached the yard of Horizon Stable, the horses were nearly cool. The kids were so distracted by their excitement and urgency that not even Angel noted the promptness with which Kelly Sebastian greeted their return.

"Good; you're back," she began briskly. "I forgot to tell you there's a buyer coming to look at Charity. Angel, turn Gabe out with the other geldings, then get Charity ready; I want you to ride her before the buyer does. Mark, switch the horses in the paddock; Brigid's coming for a lesson and Rex needs to get out.

When you've finished mucking, Brice, the jump standards need another coat of paint. I'm going home to grab some lunch. Call me if the buyer shows up before I'm back." Without waiting for comment, Kelly climbed into her battered pickup and drove out of the yard.

Angel clapped her hands to the sides of her face in a theatrical gesture of dismay. "Oh *no! Now* what do we do?"

Mark blinked. "What Kelly says."

"But—" Angel protested.

"But nothing," Brice asserted. "Our weird friends will just have to wait; even for your aliens, Angel, I'm not crossing Kelly Sebastian."

"Where's your sense of adventure?" Angel muttered.

"I'm adventurous," Brice retorted, "not *suicidal.*"

With a rebellious glower, Angel started on her tasks. Usually, she liked riding Charity, an Anglo-Arab with nice gaits and enough of a stubborn streak to be a challenge. At another time, Angel would have been flattered to be chosen to display her to a buyer; today, she ground her teeth with frustration. But by the time she had the little mare saddled, Angel's attitude had improved. Brice and Mark were right. They were Kelly's working students for the summer; and if the summer was to be bearable, they had to do what she said. Kelly was a good teacher; she ran a well-managed barn; but she had no use for working students who wouldn't pull their weight. The aliens at the Blocktower would just have to be patient.

Kelly's truck pulled into the yard minutes before the buyers arrived. Kelly introduced Charity, giving her history, then led the mare into the arena. Angel, sensing her cue, fastened her hard hat and mounted. She put Charity through her paces; after a while, Angel got off to let the buyers ride. Angel watched for a minute or two before she took herself off.

Mark was in the aisleway, giving Churchy some juice from a

juice box. Angel hid a smile at the sight of a large horse-mouth wrapped around a straw, and instead adopted a schoolmarm's expression. "You'll spoil that horse," she prophesied direly.

"It's Tropical Fruits," Mark reproached her. "His *favorite.*" As if in emphasis, Churchy banged his stall door. "It's *gone,* you greedy brat."

In mock disgust, Angel flounced off, only to discover that Mark and Brice had mucked her stalls, too. "This *isn't* the start of a trend," Brice warned when she thanked them. "It's just for today, so we can get out of here sooner."

"What I want to know," Mark put in, "is what we're going to do with them after we get them real clothes. Like where are they going to stay? They can't camp at the Blocktower forever."

"Stay?" Brice asked. "They're looking for their friend—"

"A needle in a haystack!" Angel broke in. "Mark's right: they'll need to stay *somewhere* while we comb the library's phone book collection for this Alexandra Scarsdale person."

"Right," Mark agreed. "So where will they stay, and how are we going to explain who they are?"

"Fresh air kids?" Brice suggested.

"AFS students!" Angel countered. "That will explain any cultural misunderstandings."

"But there are five of them," Mark protested. "No one has five AFS students at once."

"Picky, picky," Angel scoffed. "How about foreign relatives? Have you got any European cousins, Brice?"

"Wait a second!" Mark cut in. "This is a story to tell our *parents;* the explanation *can't* have anything to do with any of us! I can just imagine my mother telling Brice's: 'It's so wonderful you could have those nice cousins to visit,' and her saying, 'What nice cousins? Aren't they *your* cousins?' No way."

"So think of something," Angel retorted. "But let's figure out how to get them normal clothes first. I can get stuff for the two

47

kids—Mom has a whole closet full of things waiting for a rummage sale—but I'm not going to be able to help with the other three. They're all taller than I am."

"Don't look at me," Brice said. "I don't have any way to get home before tonight."

Mark nodded. "I think I can come up with stuff for the other three."

"This is so *exciting,*" Angel said, "I don't think I can stand it." She damped her enthusiasm when she saw Kelly approaching. "These guys forgot their lunches," she told her. "I said I'd make sandwiches if they came over to my house."

Kelly turned to Mark. "Take the truck. I'm going to work my horses before my afternoon lessons. When you get back, set up a moderate course in the upper arena; Brigid's having a jumping lesson. Then start chores."

At Angel's house, the breakfast dishes were piled haphazardly in the kitchen sink. She left the others to forage while she reconnoitered. No one was home. She rooted in the rummage sale closet, bundled up a generous assortment of clothes, and returned to the kitchen. The boys had made her two enormous ham and cheese sandwiches, which she wolfed down in the truck on the way to Mark's house. As always, Angel was struck by the contrast between her untidy home and Mark's, which looked like an illustration from a new-age *Better Homes and Gardens*. Again, no one was home. It took Mark longer to select stuff he didn't think would be missed, but he remembered necessities like belts, socks, and handkerchiefs. By the time they left, Mark's faded laundry bag bulged like a sausage casing.

"I hate being the worrier, Angel," Mark began, "but have you thought about how we'll get this junk up to the Blocktower? Kelly would think it odd if we took our horses out again today."

48

"Let's stop off now," Brice suggested.

"You need four-wheel drive to get to the Blocktower," Angel explained. "We'd have to park in the Chandlers' yard and walk about a mile. Kelly would be wondering where we'd gone long before we were back."

"Besides, we'd have to get past Mr. Chandler," Mark added. "Hey! Maybe *one* of us *could* go. We have blanket permission to ride Princess while Harriet is away. One of us could take her up there while the others did chores."

Angel stifled a groan. Princess. The idea of the mare on the trail by herself did not appeal. "I'll do chores since you guys did my stalls," she offered. It was easily the lesser evil.

Brice volunteered to deliver the clothes. When they got back to the stable, he tacked up while Angel and Mark set up jumps for Brigid Chandler's lesson. They were placing the last jump when Brigid drove in. She paused to assess their handiwork.

"Kelly threatened me with this," she said with a laugh. Brigid was a tall young woman in her late twenties, with an infectious smile and unruly reddish-brown hair. Her horse, Rex, was a big bay gelding with more muscle than sense and a fast gallop. "But it looks like you haven't been too unkind. This will make Rex's day—he's sick of dressage; and it will be good for me, too, if I survive. Has he been out?"

"He's out now." Angel pointed. "He looks pretty mellow."

"He always does when he's not under saddle," Brigid retorted as she headed for the barn.

Angel gripped Mark's elbow, barely managing to keep her voice down. "I've got it!" she crowed. "This is *perfect!* They're *Chandler's* European cousins."

As Mark considered, calculation was replaced by a conspiratorial smile. "You're right; it *is* perfect. And I bet Brigid will play along."

49

Angel's imp reappeared in her smile. "Yeah. She will. But we'd better come up with a good way to get her into this; she'll never believe us if we start with a plain explanation."

Mark began evolving strategems. As they headed to the barn to start chores, they passed Brice on his way out with Princess. From the gleam in his eye when Angel said, "Chandler," he had had precisely the same thought.

8

Eikoheh fought; the shuttle seemed to have an independent will. Though she had brought the threads of the Allies close to those of the Five, they had not meshed into her intended pattern. Now, she felt a disturbance—threads she did not weave, with a faint hint of purple in their colors: the Trickster's influence. Behind her, Ohmiden cleared his throat.

"What?" she demanded curtly.

"There's stew. Will you eat it while you work, or would you prefer to rest awhile?"

She laid the shuttle aside. "I know what you intend, old man: you're trying to tell me I'm perilously tired. And you're right. But the loom never stops. There are forces loose, Ohmiden, forces I cannot control. Who knows what may happen to the Five while I eat and rest?"

"What will become of you if you don't eat or rest?"

She stood. "They are resourceful—and the stew smells good. Consider your task accomplished."

"For the moment, old woman; only for the moment."

The roaring of the dirt bikes retreated; peace and birdsong returned to the woodlands. Inside the Blocktower, Iobeh and Remarr tried to climb to the second floor of the building. There was a trap door in the wooden flooring above their heads, and

51

a route upward for someone agile, utilizing the window casings and a large iron spike that must have once anchored a ladder. It took several tries, but at last, Iobeh—with a rope looped over her shoulder—got the trap door open and scrambled within. She reappeared several moments after securely fastening her knotted rope to a ringbolt embedded in the wall. She dropped the other end to Remarr, who joined her.

The room was not large, but it was bright and airy. The openings in each wall gave a view of the countryside.

"It wouldn't be much shelter in a driving rain," Remarr commented, "but it will probably be more comfortable than sleeping on the dirt floor below."

Iobeh nodded, then signed, *And if we need to hide, just pull up the rope, close the trap, and sit quietly.*

"Yes. But don't mention 'hide' to Vihena."

Iobeh gestured chidingly. *We must work together.*

He spread his hands. "Was *I* the one being impossible?"

You both were. It takes two for argument, Remarr.

Indeed! The shapeshifter's thought-voice sounded in their minds. *But do I hear more dirt-bike noise in the distance?*

After a hurried conclave, they decided Iobeh and Ychass would remain hidden upstairs; not only did this allow them to conceal their rope ladder, but it kept Ychass in reserve. She could fly down in bird-shape for a surprise attack. Karivet would remain out of sight in the ground floor room, ready to be of help without being an obvious target if the newcomers were not of a mind to parley. This left Remarr and Vihena to have the first contact with any visitors, Vihena for her prowess with the sword, and Remarr for his diplomatic speech.

By the time everyone was deployed, the noise was much closer. This growl, deeper than the dirt bikes', sounded confident—and larger. Remarr felt certain that this creature would be more of a threat than their earlier visitors. He kept his con-

52

victions to himself; there was no sense in inviting Vihena's scorn.

A moment later, Remarr's hunch was proven. This thing had four wheel-feet instead of two. It lumbered powerfully up the hill. Roughly rectangular in shape, its neckless head was about a third as tall as the rest of its body. It had two shiny eyes, separated by a grate of silvery teeth. Its hard shell was shiny in places, but mostly a dull green in color. It halted and fell silent. When it opened an unsuspected wing, a tall man climbed out of its guts. He wore livery of a dark greenish color, with some insignia on the sleeves. He pushed the wing of his beast, which it pulled to its side with a thump, then he leaned back and studied Vihena and Remarr.

"Well, I'll be damned," he said at last. "And I thought Travis was telling wild stories. I don't suppose you folks would like to tell me what you're doing on Mr. Chandler's land?"

"We mean no harm," Remarr began.

"That's not the point," he interrupted. "You're breaking the law—and you don't have any business threatening kids with a sword, for God's sake."

"Truly, we did not realize that we were breaking rules—"

"*Didn't know?*" the fellow demanded. "Why, Old Man Chandler's got Posted signs up, thick as mosquitoes, around every *inch* of his boundaries. What do you mean you didn't *know* you were trespassing? How'd you get here, anyway?"

"We were sent by the gods from a distant world. We mean no harm. Indeed, we are much in need of your help."

"*I'll* say you need help," he muttered, then turned his attention to Vihena. "Now look here. There's no need for that sword. Why don't you just put it down, nice and slowly, and then I'll take you and your friend off to get some help."

Vihena shook her head. "Why should we trust you? What kind of help can you give us?"

"Take it easy. Look: I'll take you down to Waterbury; there are lots of nice folks there who'll get you straightened out in no time. It's nothing to be afraid of."

"Waterbury," Vihena repeated. Her sword point snapped up as she recalled its significance. "You think we're mad! But we are not—and we will not go to this Waterbury."

"Look, I don't want to get rough with you," he said.

"Just try!" Vihena challenged.

He removed an object from a leather case at his waist. "I'm not exactly helpless." He pointed it in her direction. "Put that sword down—*NOW!*" Authority crackled in his voice.

"Never," Vihena vowed. Before she could lunge, there was a blast of sound, the object in the man's hand spat fire, and she collapsed to the ground, a red stain blooming at her shoulder.

"Vihena!" Remarr knelt beside her. The man flung her sword over the edge of the hill. Then he went to Remarr's side.

"I'm sorry," he said. For the first time, Remarr saw how white he was. "But she was going to go for me. Help me get her into the jeep and we'll take her up to the hospital."

Ychass! Remarr thought frantically.

Go with him, the shapeshifter responded. *He is genuinely concerned for her. I will follow in bird-shape; Iobeh and Karivet will remain hidden here.*

In a daze, Remarr helped the man move Vihena into the thing he called "jeep." When she was stowed comfortably, the man showed Remarr where to sit, and they bounced and jolted away.

After a time, the track turned to an actual road; the jeep traveled faster than any cart. Under pretense of checking on Vihena, the minstrel kept looking out the window in the back, hoping for a glimpse of Ychass.

I am with you, her thought-voice assured him.

54

Vihena moaned and opened her eyes. "Remarr!" Remarr put a reassuring hand on her unhurt shoulder.

"All is well. Do not fret yourself."

"*Well?*" she demanded, struggling to prop herself up on her good arm. Remarr pushed her gently down, signing to her in their hand-language.

Lie still; you'll start bleeding again. The man has promised to help us. Ychass is following. The twins wait.

With effort, she brought up her good hand to reply. *Are we prisoners?*

I don't think so.

"Is your friend awake?" the man asked.

"Yes," Remarr told him.

"Well, we'll be at the hospital soon."

Do you know what he's talking about? Vihena signed.

No. But Ychass said he is genuinely concerned about you.

Vihena dropped her hand wearily. Remarr noted that the woodlands and meadows had been replaced by scattered dwellings; the road was wider and smoother, and the fenced fields they passed were dotted with black-and-white cows. The jeep halted, then proceeded onto a new kind of road—black rock, with a vivid double yellow line running down the center of it. The jeep picked up speed on this smoother surface.

Ychass, are you with us? Remarr thought.

Yes. Watch for landmarks. If you gain much more speed, I may lose sight of you and need your guidance.

Remarr noted for Ychass that they bore right at a large, dilapidated red barn, then passed into an area of many dwellings, very close together. At a crossroad with a floating, flashing red flare above it, they again halted before turning right. They continued downhill, into an area where the build-ings were even closer together, much bigger, and made of a strange, muddy red stone that was cut into small, rectangular shapes. There were no patches of green between the buildings, and the streets were dirty. There were also many other magic carts, in a dizzying array of colors and shapes, crowding the street and slowing their progress.

I've caught sight of you again, the shapeshifter said.

Despite her assurance, Remarr watched landmarks. After a time, they turned onto a much wider road, where all the other magic carts went the same way they were going. The jeep flung itself up the hill. Suddenly, they came to a huge crossroads, with more of the floating flares. They turned right, then pulled into a drive leading to a massive fort, made of the strange red stones and huge plates of glass, that sprawled around them. The jeep stopped by a doorway with a long ramp leading to it, and the man jumped out.

"I'll get a stretcher," he told Remarr. "You wait here."

"What do you suppose a 'stretcher' is?" Vihena asked. "I don't think I could bear to stretch, now."

The man returned, then, with others in white livery and towing a rolling bed. They put Vihena on the rolling bed and wheeled her inside. In panic, Remarr climbed over the seat and flung himself out the back way. The man in green livery stared.

"Wait!" Remarr said. "Where are they taking her?"

"Inside to get treatment. Now, why don't you just come along with me? I've got some questions to ask you."

"I must go with her," Remarr protested. The man's hand closed around his arm—none too gently.

"Not so fast. I said I had some questions. You can see your friend after you've answered them."

Remarr struggled, but the man held him. After a moment, the minstrel allowed himself to be guided into a small room, where he was set in a chair. The man closed the door behind them.

56

The man took a small book out of a pocket and flipped it open. "Name?"

"Remarr."

"And your first name, Mr. Remarr?"

"I don't understand. I am Remarr the Minstrel. What other name do you want?"

He looked up from his writing, staring at the young man. Then he shrugged. "Let's leave it for now. Your address?"

"My *what?*" There was something wrong with the language the gods had given them: there were too many words that were mere sound. Remarr's hands grew clammy.

"Where do you live?"

"We were camping by the old fort."

"I know that," he said patiently. "Where do you live when you aren't camping by the Blocktower?"

Remarr gazed at the big man's face while his mind cried out, *Ychass, help me!* "In the loft," he answered slowly, "over the silversmith's stable."

"What town?"

YCHASS!!

Patience, she scolded. *Vihena's having troubles, too.*

What should I say?

Say you don't understand.

"I don't understand."

"You know: town. Like a city. Like Barre. Like Plainfield."

"I don't understand."

"Like *Waterbury!*" the man said, his temper fraying.

Remarr frowned. "I thought that Waterbury was a madhouse."

"It's a *town,* with a madhouse—I mean, a mental illness treatment facility—in it. You *must* have escaped from there," he added in a mutter.

"No. I swear it."

"Great. Well, let's try another tack. Why did your friend attack me?"

"She thought you were hostile," Remarr offered.

"*Hostile?* Oh, good Lord. I'm a *trooper,* not some crazy vigilante. I don't shoot except in self-defense!"

"What is a 'trooper'?"

The trooper stared. "What *planet* are you from?"

"Planet?"

He raked his fingers through his hair. "God," he muttered.

"Which one?" Remarr asked.

Before the trooper could pose further questions, the door swung open.

"Raymond?" Another man in white livery poked his head in the door. "You know anything about that woman you brought in?"

"Nothing about her background. She rushed me—with a *sword,* no less. I had to shoot her."

"Will she recover?" Remarr put in anxiously.

"She's stable. The bullet's been removed and the bleeding has stopped. Blood loss wasn't too severe, and the bullet didn't hit anything vital."

"Bullet?" Remarr repeated.

The white-coated fellow smiled, stuck his thumb up as he pointed his index finger at Remarr. "From the gun. K'pow."

Remarr's eyes shifted to the strange implement in the case at the trooper's waist. "May I see my friend?" he asked at last.

"Sure. She's heavily sedated, but I'll take you up to see her. Want to come along, Ray?"

Together, they went out into a hallway lit with a strange white light that did not flicker or cast shadows. The white-liveried man led them through a maze of corridors. He pushed a door open, and waved Remarr inside.

Vihena lay on a bed. Her veil was gone and her lashes were dark against her pale cheeks. Beside the bed, a metal tree supported a pouch like a wineskin, with a long tentacle attached to the swordswoman's arm. He pointed. "What is.that?"

"An IV," was the cryptic reply. "We're replacing some of the fluid she lost."

Remarr went to the bedside. "Vihena, can you hear me?"

Her eyelids fluttered, but she made no other sign.

"*Vihena?*"

The white-liveried man laid a restraining hand on Remarr's shoulder. "She's sleeping. She's pretty doped up; we gave her pain meds and a tranquilizer. Don't try to wake her."

"When will she wake? I need to talk with her."

He shrugged. "It may be several hours."

"Who *are* you?" Remarr asked him, while he cried out silently to the shapeshifter. *Ychass?*

"Sorry!" the fellow laughed, pointing to a badge on his livery. "I'm Dr. Kemper. Peter Kemper."

"Are you a trooper, too?"

"No. I'm a doctor. Come on."

Go with him. He means well. And don't ask questions. They both think you are very peculiar. I'm going back to Iobeh and Karivet. They tell me that one of the children from this morning has returned; we will all take counsel together. Be of good courage, and if you need me, call; I will be listening.

Remarr went with the doctor and the trooper, leaving Vihena to her dreams.

9

As Brice approached the Blocktower, his heart sank. He saw no signs of life; even the turfs had been replaced in the firepit. What a letdown if it turned out to be a mass hallucination. Then, Princess shied violently; Brice brought her around in a tight circle to make her face the tower. One of the twins—Karivet, he thought—emerged, his white robe flapping in the breeze.

"Greetings," Karivet began. "It's Brice, no?"

Brice smiled and nodded. "And you're Karivet? I brought the clothes we promised; I was the only one who could get away. So far, the plan is for you to camp here tonight—" he broke off at the look on Karivet's face. "Is something the matter?"

"Yes. You and your friends were not the only people who came up the hill today."

"Oh-oh. Didn't you hide? Angel told you to."

The flicker of a smile touched Karivet's face. "Vihena doesn't hide. There were two—'dirt bikes?'—and after she had driven them off, a—'state trooper.' Vihena couldn't frighten him away, and when she made to attack him, he pointed an object at her that barked and spat fire, and she fell down—hurt."

Brice gripped the front of his saddle. "He *shot* her," he whispered. "Is she—Karivet, is she *dead?*"

"No. The trooper took her away. Remarr went with him,

60

and Ychass followed in bird-shape. They took her to a big castle on a hill, full of people in white livery. And they are making her better. Ychass says she is sleeping."

"Ychass says—" he repeated, feeling stupid. "But how?"

"She speaks with her mind. She doesn't have to be terribly close. She is returning, now. Iobeh called her when she saw you coming. Come within. Can you tether your horse?"

Brice slung the stuffed laundry bag down to Karivet, then dismounted. "Princess won't go anywhere as long as she can eat. Maybe we could all sit out here?" Almost before they were settled with their backs against the tower, there was a thunder of wings and a hawk landed on the grass. It became the shapeshifter, who joined them.

"Vihena is—'stable'," she told them. "But she is sleeping. Remarr remained there with her; the trooper wanted to question him, but the one called 'doctor' suggested he wait and question them both when Vihena wakes."

"Can you talk to Remarr right now?" Brice asked.

"Yes."

"Tell him *not* to answer any questions, and *especially* not to try to say that he's from another world."

"I have told him to say he doesn't understand," Ychass said. "What will happen if he tries to explain?"

"They'll think he's crazy and ship him off to Waterbury or something." Brice's mouth went dry as the weight of responsibility settled on him. "Listen: we have to get them out of there! How seriously is Vihena hurt?"

Ychass concentrated. "Remarr tells me the doctor said she had not lost too much blood, and that the bullet didn't damage anything vital."

"Well, that's a relief. We've *got* to spring them." A hundred science fiction movie plots spun in his brain. *What would Angel do?* he thought. *A daring abduction by car*—Mark *can drive*—

that's it! "I've got it," he said aloud. "Ychass, we'll need you, but you others had better stay here. Mark, Angel, and I will work out details. We'll meet you, Ychass, at the hospital with Mark's car. When we arrive, you signal to Remarr, and he brings Vihena to the car. *Vroom!*—off we go into the sunset: no questions, no more police officers. Just a mystery for the hospital computer. Oh yeah," he added. "Can you hear *my* thoughts, Ychass?" *I'm thinking about the toe of my left boot.*

I can tell—the shapeshifter's thought-voice rang in his mind—*though it seems an ordinary boot to me.*

"All right!" he said. "Then you can relay messages. When I get back, I'll think at you to confirm the plan. Okay?" At their nods, he jumped up. "Good. I've got to go. Put on the clothing so you won't arouse curiosity if other people come." He swung into the saddle and started for home at a brisk trot.

Ychass sighed. "If even half the things Brice was thinking are true, Vihena and Remarr are in great danger. But he is difficult to read. He looks like a young man, but his thoughts are child-like. He was worried that he would be late returning and that his mother would be waiting. These people are odd."

Perhaps they think we are the odd ones, Iobeh signed.

Ychass nodded. "There is absolutely no doubt that they do, Iobeh; none whatever."

Vihena's sleep was restless. Her body resisted the strange com-pounds that coursed through her veins while her mind was troubled by dreams. The Weaver came to her as she slept, his face worried. "There is a force," he told her, "which bars me from 'Tsan's mind. It must be of the Trickster's making, though I cannot find her mark upon it. I came to warn you that your quest may be more difficult than we had thought."

Vihena had questions, but her dreaming mind drowned her in a sea of images: magic carts that lured people within to be devoured; carnivorous metal trees, which used spiked tentacles to suck people into dessicated shells; strange devices that exploded into pain. She fought the nightmares, thrashing against the bedclothes; fought the metal tree, ripping its clinging tube from her arm; fought the white-clad women who came to soothe her; fought; fought; *fought!*

The doctor and the trooper escorted Remarr to a waiting area. Remarr thought the trooper Raymond would go back to questioning him, but instead, the trooper ordered him to stay at the hospital, and went away. The doctor went away as well, promising to have Remarr called when Vihena awoke. So Remarr waited, as the afternoon waned slowly toward dusk. Others in the waiting area stole looks at him, but no one spoke. When Remarr found himself wishing for the tenth time that he had brought his harp, he resolved to cast the day's experiences into a ballad. He had composed a melody and nearly three stanzas when Ychass relayed Brice's plan to him; by the time one of the nurses told him Vihena was awake, he had composed eight stanzas.

They had tied Vihena to the bed; when Remarr entered, she was shouting abuse at two cowering nurses.

"Remarr!" she snapped. "They have *bound* me! Release me!"

"We had to restrain her," one of the nurses whispered. "She kept tearing her IV out."

"Surely, now that she is awake, she will listen to your advice," he said, loudly enough for Vihena to hear. He moved to the bed side. "You know they are only trying to help, Vihena. Say that you will behave, and I will ask them to untie you."

"*Behave?*" she began, but subsided when he took her hand and squeezed a warning. "Of course I will behave," she added meekly. "I was having nightmares, but now I am in my right mind."

"There," Remarr said to the nurses as he untied the restraints. "You see? It is as I said."

"Well, then; we'll leave you to your visit," one nurse said, then rather spoiled the effect by almost scuttling away.

As soon as they were gone, Remarr explained the plan to Vihena and asked whether she thought she could walk unaided.

"Who knows? They have given me so many strange potions that I cannot even *feel* my shoulder, much less tell how badly it is damaged. I will try. If I can't, carry me. I will not spend a night in this unchancy place."

Remarr, Vihena, Ychass spoke in their minds. *Our three allies are approaching. Pay attention. There is a small door at the end of the hall where they have put Vihena. It will take you directly outside. Mark will stop his magic cart just outside, and I will be perched on top of it so there can be no mistaking it. When I give you the signal,* and not before, *come outside and get in as quickly as you can. We must not waste time; someone may try to stop us.*

Wait, Vihena thought to the shapeshifter. *They took my sword. I must retrieve it.*

Don't be a fool. A sword is not as important as escaping, the shapeshifter responded.

Remarr, who could only guess at Vihena's thoughts by Ychass's reply, hastened to reassure the swordswoman. "The trooper did not take your sword. He flung it away after you fell—no doubt he was afraid *I* would take it up."

"If you are lying to me—" she began, but Remarr's fist struck the metal bedframe, jolting her silent.

"I am *tired* of being treated like a beast without honor because I do not carry a blade!" he whispered passionately. "I do not fit the role in which my form would cast me. Of all people, Vihena, you should understand *that!*"

She was shamed by the scalding bitterness in his voice. "Forgive me. I spoke without thinking."

"You speak without thinking far too often! Just because you can wield a sword doesn't mean you need not use your judgment."

Taut silence stretched between them until Ychass's summons. Vihena pulled the IV out of her arm. When she stood unsteadily, they made a terrible discovery: the clothing the castle provided was very skimpy; it did not even reach to her knees, and there was barely enough material to wrap around her. Remarr ripped off his veil and tied it around her waist; even so, she felt indecently clad as they slipped into the hallway.

Other patients ambled along the hall. Striving not to look furtive, they made for the doorway about which Ychass had told them. They found themselves in a small alcove with another doorway and a flight of ascending stairs. A flat metal bar, inscribed with strange symbols in red, held the door closed. Remarr gave it a mighty push. As the door swung open, the air was rent with a shrill ringing.

Over here! Ychass urged. *Hurry!*

Remarr heard running feet behind them. He swept Vihena into his arms and made a dash for the magic cart. Angel hauled them inside and Remarr slammed the door as the magic cart roared forward. They charged down the drive and out into the road, leaving a bevy of nurses gaping after them.

"A good thing we pasted cardboard over your license plate," Angel commented, to the bafflement of Remarr and Vihena. "As soon as we're out of sight, pull over and I'll take it off."

"Just say: 'I think of everything,' and be done with it," Brice suggested.

The magic cart stopped, Angel hopped out, returning a moment later brandishing two rectangular boards. "Disguise removed! The Rescuemobile returns to civilian usage. Don't worry about your clothes," she added to Vihena. "You were far too conspicuous in those robes; we brought some normal stuff up to the Blocktower."

"I hate to be a spoilsport," Mark put in, "but how can we *get* Vihena up to the Blocktower? This thing's no Land Rover, but I wouldn't think Vihena's up to walking over a mile—especially without shoes."

I will carry her, Ychass thought at them. *I can take horse-shape to do it. We owe you three a debt of gratitude; you have proved good friends and resourceful indeed.*

"Oh, hey! All in the line of duty." Angel laughed, grateful for the darkness that hid her blush. "But listen, about tomorrow: we're going to have to do some serious talking. We'll ride over for a real powwow. We've *got* to get you away from the Blocktower before the troopers go back to look for you. Do you think you could hide, this time, if anyone else came up there?"

"I think we could," Remarr said. "We are unfamiliar with the hazards, here, and must rely upon trusted advice."

"Very well," Vihena agreed grudgingly.

When Mark halted the magic cart, they waited until Ychass caught up to them and then all climbed out. The three kids' breath caught as Ychass became a beautiful, pale gray mare. Remarr boosted Vihena onto her broad back.

"You know how to get there, don't you?" Mark asked.

I know the way, Ychass assured them.

After goodbyes and thanks, the two parties set off for home. The quiet of the nighttime woods surrounded the shapeshifter, the swordswoman, and the minstrel as they made their careful way back to the Blocktower.

Eikoheh groaned, more than half with relief. Events had escaped her guidance, and it had been taxing indeed to realign

66

the course of her Fate. Spanning the void with her pattern was hard work. Events moved quickly, and she could assert control only sporadically and with great effort.

"It's as though I were swimming in honey," she said to herself, "while everyone else moves through open air."

She got up. Ohmiden was asleep in a nest of cushions by the hearth. She laid another log on the fire, then climbed the ladder to her waiting bed. She slept deeply, too deeply to hear the distressed noises Ohmiden made once he began to dream.

The Blocktower was quiet. All the occupants, save Ychass, were asleep, looking odd and vulnerable in their unfamiliar clothing. As Ychass's anxious gaze lit on Vihena, she smiled wryly. It hadn't been easy to convince the swordswoman to don the strange apparel.

Though Ychass was weary, she was not ready for sleep. All day, off and on, she had been casting for 'Tsan's mind. And all day, she had felt mired in minds: more people than she had dreamed could exist, all busily thinking of mundane things. She believed she had touched 'Tsan, once or twice, but then had lost the unique shape of her mind in the whelm of others' thoughts. She hoped that the night would aid her, as sleep stilled thoughts, leaving 'Tsan's mind exposed by the ebb like a shell on the sand. When Ychass sent her mind questing yet again, she found her, almost immediately. *'Tsan! It is Ychass. We are here, searching for you.*

The shapeshifter was unprepared for 'Tsan's answering wave of terror. Awash in a torrent of fragmented thoughts, Ychass clung to her own identity, to avoid being swept into madness. *I am Ychass!* she insisted, driving her message into 'Tsan's brain. *I am no enemy, but your friend: Ychass! You named me, 'Tsan; you cannot repudiate me!*

I do not—cannot—I don't know you—you aren't—here—

you can't be—can't—mustn't—madness—I'm over the edge!
Hearing voices—no! There's no Ychass—you never were—
no—I made you up—a dream—a nightmare—no, no, no, no,
NO, NO, NOOOO!

Ychass had to break contact. She cradled her pounding head
in her hands. Suddenly, she felt the touch of Iobeh's hands,
heard her silent question.

"Go back to sleep," Ychass told her. "I'm all right."

Iobeh touched the shapeshifter's face, capturing a tear on her
finger. *You're weeping,* she thought.

"Yes, I am. Go back to sleep." There was nothing rough in
her tone, just sadness and deep weariness. Iobeh studied her
face for a moment longer, then with a small sigh, went back to
her bedroll. The shapeshifter stayed awake, and for a long time,
the moonlight silvered her tears.

10

Alexandra had given up sleeping. Her dreams had become too vivid. After her hallucination in the bathroom, she had covered every mirror; she closed her blinds, to avoid reflections in night-darkened windows. There had been no more visions, but all day, a voice whispered in her mind, though she had tried to shut it out. The voice tugged at her memory like that nagging feeling when one has forgotten something really crucial.

The night was bad. Her body pleaded for sleep, but she could not relax. As soon as she let down her guard, the voice began: clearer now, claiming to be Ychass, one of the people from her delusion. She fought the voice in her mind, fought her own panic, fought sleep. And when dawn came, she dressed and went to breakfast, determined to pretend that nothing was wrong.

Despite her intentions, however, she couldn't help looking over her shoulder periodically; and she inspected her dishes in the dining hall.

Though even Angel managed to goad her parents into getting her to the stable earlier than usual the next morning, the three kids were not able to make an early start. Kelly was in one of her efficient moods. Before they'd even said good morning, she had given them a long list of chores. Though they set to with a will and a sense of urgency, it was nearly noon before they were ready to start tacking up their horses. While they were all diligently currying, Brigid Chandler walked in.

"Hi, guys," she greeted them. "What are you up to?"

"Trail ride," Mark responded. "Want to come along?"

Brigid considered then nodded. "Why not? The worst that can happen is that Rex and I will start a stampede." As she went off to get her horse, Angel gave an emphatic thumbs-up.

"But what are we going to *tell* her?" Brice whispered.

"Why don't we let *them* explain—and then tell Brigid we plan to say they're her cousins." Brice wrinkled his nose. "If you have a better idea," Angel snapped, "I'd love to hear it."

Further debate was cut off as Brigid returned with her horse. "Don't forget halters and picket lines," Mark reminded, slightly officious.

Brigid fell in with their plans, and soon, they were off. Not daring to hurry, they threaded their way through the maze of tracks and old roads with carefully feigned nonchalance. When their meandering progress led them past the Blocktower, Angel suggested they make their picnic on the hill. As they dismounted, the shapeshifter emerged from the tower and joined them. Brigid eyed her with surprise.

"We brought a friend who may be able to help," Angel explained to Ychass. "Brigid, this is Ychass. She and her friends need our help—but I'll let them explain while we eat."

There was food enough for an army. The Five investigated the unfamiliar food, then helped themselves. Angel couldn't believe the transformation the clothing wrought on her aliens. They looked normal—except Vihena, whose sword rested on her blue-jeaned knees. Not only was the weapon incongruous, but Vihena, unveiled, was beautiful. Her pallor and the shadows under her eyes only made her beauty more striking. She looked remarkably well for someone with a bullet hole in her. While Angel gawked, Mark made introductions. Brigid

70

repeated each of their names as she looked around the circle; her eyebrows rose. Then she said, with enviable calm, "So what's this all about?"

Remarr answered. "We were sent to this place from a different world, to perform a quest set by the gods: to seek a companion who is lost in this place. The fate of our world depends upon our finding her. We need your help; we are strangers and we understand neither your customs nor your people."

Brigid laughed. "What kind of a put-on is this?"

Ychass spoke then. "We speak the truth. We *are* from a different world. If you need proof, I can give it to you."

Brigid laughed again, though with a note of unease. "Try me," she suggested.

Ychass's form blurred and shifted. In her place stood a beautiful gray mare that watched them with pale, intelligent eyes. Brigid clenched one hand. "Holy God," she whispered. Then, the horse disappeared; Ychass sat back down on the blanket.

Silence stretched. Iobeh fidgeted, but the others remained motionless. "You said you needed help," Brigid managed to gasp at last. "What sort of help?"

Remarr explained their quest in more detail, and told the tale of yesterday's misadventures. Brigid frowned. "If you can't be any more specific about your friend's whereabouts, I'm not sure what use we'll be. There are a lot of people in this country and—" She broke off suddenly. "Wait a minute. *Scarsdale.* I wonder if your Alexandra is any relation to the author—you know, Alister Scarsdale: *Meeker Street* and so on. He had a daughter; there was some scandal about her when he died. You could check it out."

"*You* could check it out," Angel insisted. "*You're* the one who works in a library."

"I'm not sure I want to get involved," Brigid began, but Angel and Brice overrode her.

71

"You *have* to! We need you!" Angel asserted.

"*C'mon,* Brigid; it'll be exciting. And they need us—after last night, they can hardly go to the state police for help."

Mark met Brigid's eyes. "Desperately seeking Alexandra Scarsdale. Mostly, we need to camouflage Angel's aliens until we can complete a phone book search or a Personals ad campaign."

"How did *you* ever get talked into this?" Brigid asked him.

He smiled ruefully. "I'm not sure—just like you did."

"But I haven't said—" She made a last ditch effort.

"*C'mon,* Brigid," Mark wheedled. "It'll be fun."

"I have the sense of impending disaster," she remarked, shaking her head as though amazed at herself, "but all right."

"*Yay!*" Angel crowed. "We really *do* need you. Camouflage: we figured you had some European cousins—or something."

Brigid considered. "As in, here for a visit? Oh, Lord. Anything's possible—but *not* cousins. They don't look enough alike to be all from the same family, and if we have more than one branch of European cousins visiting at once, it'll look odd— even for Chandlers. Besides, my parents keep up on our family tree; they'd be suspicious of a horde of unknown relatives. But we can probably get away with European *friends. My* European friends—I have lots of them, and my parents haven't met them all."

"Good point," Mark affirmed. "So friends it is. The next hurdle is where they will stay. They *can't* stay here: it's pure luck that the troopers haven't been back already. Can they camp in your apartment, Brigid?"

"It's a one bedroom apartment with a dinky living room," Brigid reminded him.

"We can lend you sleeping bags. Besides, I can probably get Mom to say a few of them can stay with us—as a special treat after it's clear how much we like each other, and all that. But to

72

make *that* work, she'll have to see them all a few times at the barn first; then I can spend a week talking about how neat they are to prepare her for the big request. I'm pretty sure I can talk her into it." He made a quick assessment of the Five. "Maybe Iobeh and Karivet."

"I have the perfect solution," Brigid admitted. "My parents are away and I'm keeping an eye on the farm for them. There's plenty of room. You could use the truck . . ." She broke off. "I don't suppose any of you drive?"

"You mean a magic cart?" Remarr asked. "Does it not require special powers to guide them?"

"Just practice," said Brice, "and you have to be old enough to get a license."

Angel cut in on the discussion. "Look, you guys. We're pushing our luck. Someone could come looking for you any minute. We should take you down to Chandlers' right now. Brigid can check in on you later, and we'll figure out what to do next."

Brigid sighed. "Okay. Let's do it before I lose my nerve."

Iobeh and Ychass cleaned up the remains of lunch while Remarr and Karivet broke camp. Vihena chafed at her inactivity, while the others tended their horses. In short order, they were ready to leave. "I'll take someone up with me," Angel offered.

Iobeh clambered on behind Angel. Karivet rode with Brigid, and Ychass turned into the gray mare again to carry Remarr and Vihena. The group set out at a sedate pace through the woods.

The Chandlers' place was a brick farmhouse with a big screened porch. It was on the end of a town road, with the nearest neighbor half a mile away. The troupe waited in the yard until Brigid had located the spare key and unlocked the door.

"Come on in," she called. "I'll show you around."

Vihena was particularly impressed with running water, and Brigid had to explain the operation of the stove and the function of the refrigerator more than once. Finally, she left them to settle into their new surroundings.

"I told them I'd be back later this afternoon to feed the ponies," she told Angel, Brice, and Mark, "and that I'd see how they were getting along. Tomorrow morning, I can bring them all up to the barn with me so we can discuss what to do next. I'm taking the day off to get Rex ready for Vershire, so I'm coming out to the stable anyway. God, I hope they don't burn the place down. Mother would strangle me."

Vihena watched from the window as the four riders left the yard. She turned back to the others with a wry smile. "They make unlikely rescuers, even after last night. Now, let's explore this place more thoroughly, before my strength gives out."

They began in the kitchen, opening cupboards and drawers, puzzling out purposes for the strange utensils they found. From there they moved to the living room. Iobeh fingered the plush upholstery on the sofa, while Remarr investigated an oddly shaped piece of wooden furniture that resembled a cross between a table and a box that was trying to be triangular. It had a row of black and white teeth on one side of it, which Remarr touched gingerly. He jumped at the faint chiming noise, then struck the note again, with more force. A moment later, he was sitting on the bench, experimenting with scales and chords. Iobeh shared a rueful look with her twin.

We've lost Remarr, she signed. *Shall we leave him to it?*

They went through the dining room and the hall and up to the master bedroom. While Karivet examined the woodworking in the furniture and Iobeh and Ychass discovered closets, Vihena fiddled with a peculiar box with a dark crystal face on one side. There were a number of small knobs and buttons. Greatly daring, Vihena twisted one. She leaped back in alarm as

74

light bloomed in the depths of the crystal face, accompanied by a shred of music and a voice. When the image steadied, she stared at small people. Though unnerved, Vihena forced herself to approach the box and again twist the knob. There was a sharp click and the images vanished. There were several other bedrooms, a bathroom, and a room full of paper clutter dominated by a heavy oak desk. It reminded Vihena of her father's office. She restrained an impulse to rummage through drawers by imagining her father's reaction to a trespasser in his private domain.

When they had finished exploring, each of them spent some time unpacking their things in the rooms Brigid had described as guest rooms. When Remarr tore himself away from the instrument, he listened with interest to Vihena's description of her encounter with the magic box. Remarr was all for conducting experiments of his own, but before he could get started, they were interrupted by the purring roar of a magic cart. Suddenly, its noise was stilled, one of its wing-like doors extruded from its sleek, black side—and Brigid Chandler climbed out. Iobeh and Karivet exchanged relieved looks. It was not the trooper returning.

Brigid greeted them and set a large brown paper sack on the kitchen counter. "I brought some food," she said. "I don't know about you, but I'm starved." She unloaded the sack: meats, vegetables, fruit, all encased in a strange, clear skin. Ychass fingered the covering on the steaks doubtfully.

"You eat meat, don't you?" Brigid asked anxiously, noting the shapeshifter's distaste.

Ychass nodded, then pinched a piece of the clear skin between two fingers. "But what is this skin? I've never seen its like."

Brigid's expression cleared. "Oh, that's plastic," she explained, then, with the air of a field commander, deployed

75

her troops and prepared supper. As soon as the meal was ready, they gathered at the table.

"Tell me," Brigid began. "Why—exactly—are you looking for this Alexandra Scarsdale? And why do you think she'll agree to go back with you?"

Somewhat to Brigid's surprise, it was Karivet who answered her. "'Tsan came to us from a far place at a time when my people had great need for a leader. She was drawn into our world by the power of the Weaver to champion our cause. She took my sister and me to meet with Vihena's people, and when it became clear that even that would not be enough, she led us on a quest to ask the gods to intercede on our behalf. We faced many difficulties and dangers together. 'Tsan grew into her destiny; I believe it was the first time she ever found people with whom she felt she belonged. When our quest was ended, 'Tsan was reft from the Loom against her will. We all believe that she would have stayed had it not been for the Trickster's cruelty.

"But there is more at stake. When the Trickster flung her back to this world, 'Tsan's thread was torn from the Loom of Fate, weakening the very fabric of reality. The gods believe that we must bring 'Tsan back to strengthen the Loom and to prevent the end, the unraveling, of our whole world.

"We do not pretend to know 'Tsan's mind, but I have the gift of prophecy, and have learned that she is tormented by fear and stalked by madness. She has done too much for my people and our world for her to be left desolate; and I think that she would not wish to see our world fall into darkness."

Brigid tried in vain to imagine the sort of responsibility that went along with being chosen by some gods to save a world. And she tried to imagine having to choose between her world, with all its uncertainties and problems, and some primitive culture. Brigid's imagination boggled. It didn't sound as though this 'Tsan faced an easy choice—or an easy life, whatever she

76

decided. Brigid couldn't envy her being the chosen savior; *she* would feel the weight of the gods' trust as a tremendous imposition. Her own culture taught that humans were masters of their destiny and not servants of it. Brigid noticed Ychass studying her intently, and with a mental shrug, she went back to her meal.

"What will happen tomorrow?" Remarr asked. "How will we begin our search?"

"Well, we'll check phone books first. Brice—"

"Wait," Vihena said. "What is a 'phone book'?"

"Sorry! It's a book that lists lots and lots of people's names and tells you where they live and how to reach them by telephone." At their blank looks, Brigid tried to clarify. "The telephone is my people's way of communicating over a long distance. Anyway, Brice is going to bring as many phone books as he can find to the stable and during the day, tomorrow, you can take turns looking for Alexandra in them." They were uncomprehending. She fetched a phone book and handed it to Vihena. "This is the book for this area: Montpelier, Plainfield— all the towns around here. The names are listed alphabetically, by surname, so look for Scarsdale." As Vihena flipped the book open and stared at it blankly, alarm dawned in Brigid's eyes. "Can't you read?"

Vihena pushed the book back into Brigid's hands. "We have no use for books in the desert."

Brigid looked around the table. "Oh, Lord," she muttered, reading their expressions. "Wait'll I tell *that* to Angel."

Brigid left them after dinner, reminding them that tomorrow morning, she would take them to the stable. "Vihena," she said, "please leave your sword behind. You've seen what kind of trouble it can get you into. People don't use swords here." Recognizing rebellion in the beautiful young woman's face, Brigid softened her request. "Perhaps you could leave it in the

77

truck while we're at the stable, so it would be close to hand but won't cause questions." She didn't wait for Vihena's response, but headed for the door. "See you tomorrow."

After she had gone, Vihena sighed irritably. "I'm surprised she didn't tell you to leave your harp behind," she said to Remarr. "Interfering woman."

Remarr shrugged. "Perhaps a harp is easier to explain." He turned to the shapeshifter. "What did you think of her, Ychass?"

Ychass considered. "There are shadows in her mind."

"Do you mean duplicity?" Remarr asked.

"No, not betrayal; but fears, worries I don't understand. I sensed the like in 'Tsan, on occasion." She debated sharing the gist of her contact with 'Tsan with the others but decided against it; it would alarm them, and it might simply be a snare of the Trickster. "I think," she went on, "that Brigid will make a good ally. She hides her fears well. And I cannot blame her for being afraid; we threaten beliefs she has held since childhood. But she is curious and even eager to help us—if only to see what will happen."

Is that all we are to them? Iobeh signed. *An amusing diversion? Don't they understand the importance of our quest?*

Ychass smiled sadly at her young friend. "I don't think we seem very real to them."

"We are figures out of legend in a land where legends have stayed safely dead for many long years," Remarr added.

They each fell prey to their own thoughts and doubts. Remarr looked sharply at Vihena. "You look weary. Go to bed; there's no sense in tiring yourself."

"Don't mother me." Vihena's voice lacked the usual spark of indignation. "I'm going."

"So am I," said Karivet. "Do any of you remember how to extinguish these lamps?"

11

Ychass woke at dawn. From the window she saw, through a shrouding mist, webs of silver threads and dew that decorated the grass. The air was sweet, rich with birdsong. Ychass went outside. She yielded to a sudden urge to run; she took her horse shape, and set off at a reckless pace through the orchard. As she neared the hilltop, she heard hoofbeats, and the horse part of her neighed greeting. There were three ponies in a pasture, trotting along the fence. Ychass watched them for a moment before she angled back through the orchard toward the road. She sailed over the stone wall bordering the road and pounded off at a canter. Suddenly, she became aware of another noise: a familiar roaring growl. As she halted in the middle of the road, a magic cart bounded around a curve, then shrieked to a stop in a scatter of grit. Brigid Chandler leaped out, her face white.

"Easy there, big guy," she soothed, approaching the horse. "What are you doing so far from home?"

I rose early and went out to explore, Ychass replied in her mind. *Did I do wrong?*

Brigid looked sharply at Ychass, then her expression eased. "Oh, it's you. I thought we had a loose horse. You shouldn't run around like this. You might have been hit by a car."

Ychass shifted back, sensing that her thought-voice made Brigid nervous.

"Hop in," Brigid suggested. "I'll give you a ride." The vehicle was full of odd, somewhat unpleasant smells that made Ychass's nose wrinkle.

"You make a beautiful horse," Brigid remarked. "Are you always a gray, or could you be any color?"

"I suppose so; I can make myself take the coloring of other people, though I cannot change my eyes. But gray suits me."

"Why can't you change your eyes?"

"My eyes are who I am. I can change myself so much—beast, fish, bird—but something besides my mind must remain constant."

"And you talk with your mind when you're in a beast shape?"

Ychass nodded. *And other times as well.*

Brigid started. "Someday I may get used to that—in about six million years. But here we are," she added as she coasted to a stop. "I came along early to see whether I couldn't help you all get breakfast."

"Without burning down the house," Ychass added, voicing Brigid's thought aloud.

Brigid blinked. *Goes both ways, does it?* she thought clearly.

Ychass smiled with approval. *You're no fool.*

They found the others in the kitchen, trying to produce breakfast by trial and error. Ychass watched as Brigid moved in and took over. In no time, she conjured up a skillet, found some butter, and began cooking scrambled eggs and cheese. In short order, they were gathered around the large dining room table, stuffing themselves. Brigid stirred a spoonful of sugar into her coffee, took a long swig, and steeled herself for explanations.

"After we've eaten, we'll leave for the stable," she began. "I had a long talk with Angel last night, and the plan is that you will pose as a bunch of my foreign friends." She looked at them dubiously. "We had a bit of a time deciding where you are from, since you're all so different looking."

80

"Get to the point," Vihena suggested.

"The problem is languages," Brigid replied. "In our world, different peoples speak different languages; some people speak more than one. We tried to pick a country whose language very few people here speak. You can say you are from Greece—and if anyone asks you to say something in Greek, just speak in your own language. You are from Athens and I met you when I was visiting my cousin who works at the American Embassy. Can you remember that? I'll try to get it all out for you when I introduce you to people, but you'd better know the story." She collected somber nods, then went on. "Okay. The next problem was names. In this world, most people have at least two names. Your names don't sound very Greek, but they'll have to do— it's too much to expect you to remember a lot of new names; but you need last names, too. Vihena, you, Iobeh, and Karivet could pass as brother and sisters so we thought we'd call you Marakis; that's Vihena Marakis, Iobeh Marakis, and Karivet Marakis. Is that clear? Remarr Papadopoulos and Ychass Zaousis. Your last names won't be used much, I hope, but you need to remember them. Another thing—maybe the most important thing: there's a lot you don't know about our culture. If anyone starts asking hard questions, just look confused and say, 'I don't understand,' or 'I beg your pardon,' and *stick with that*. They'll assume you don't understand the language. Okay?"

Karivet delivered his best puzzled expression and said, "I beg your pardon?"

Laughter eased the tension. "Today," Brigid continued, "when we're at the stable, just be friendly and try to get to know Angel, Brice, and Mark better. They are hoping to invite some of you to stay with them before my parents come home. And if you can help out with chores, we'll all take turns checking the phone books Brice brings."

81

"Is this elaborate subterfuge necessary?" Vihena asked.

Brigid sighed. "Yes. It's going to take some time to find your friend—unless we luck out with the phone books. If they don't give us any leads, I'll do some research in the library. As for subterfuge, this is an organized world. We need to explain your presence. I know it's frustrating, but it's the best we can do." She looked around at them. "Let's hit the road."

Riding in the truck was a thrilling experience. Ychass rode in the cab with Brigid, intrigued by the gauges and dials on the dash, puzzled by the glove compartment ("It's so *small* when you have all this room!"), and delighted by the fan. In the truckbed, the other four felt they had never traveled so fast in their entire lives. The air whipped around them, and even the jostling bounces seemed smooth compared to the jolt of an unsprung oxcart. The countryside that sped past so swiftly was fascinating. They passed houses, in bright, unusual colors, with cars and other vehicles in their yards. They roared by a huge red barn with two tall blue towers; they swept past a person riding on a two-wheeled metal framework that looked like a skinny, silent dirt bike. And finally, they drew into the yard of a large barn. They all clambered out, leaving Vihena's sword and Remarr's harp in the truckbed.

"This is it," Brigid said. "My home away from home: Horizon Stable. Come on; I'll show you around."

Alexandra still hadn't slept. As she went through her daily routine, her actions often lost their focus. Alexandra only barely managed to remember which summer-session classes to attend. Her German class was the easiest to keep straight, since it met every day.

This morning, when she arrived, Herr Bergemann had already begun. As she murmured an apology, his gaze sharpened on her. He watched her collapse into her chair without unslinging her bookbag, then he turned back to the other students.

"I want you each to write a letter to your Tante Amalia. Make the letters as outrageous as you dare, and as your vocabulary permits. I've got to step out for a few minutes, but when I come back, you will read them to one another. All right?"

"Jawohl," the class wit responded.

While everyone got started, Herr Bergemann took Alexandra by the elbow. "Come on. Come with me."

Bemused, she rose at his insistence. They went outside into the Yard. "What?" Alexandra finally managed.

"You look *awful*," he said without slowing his brisk pace. "Aren't you sleeping at all?"

"I'm all right," she bristled. "Who says I'm not?"

"It's written all over you! You look worse every day. I don't know what's going on in your life, Alexandra, and I don't need to know; but it's clear you need help. I know someone who can help you, and I'm taking you to him."

"You're taking me to Health Services," Alexandra said.

He nodded. "Dr. Marchbanks got me through a tough time, my first year as a grad student. I think you should talk to him."

It was too much. She burst into tears. Herr Bergemann put his arm around her. "It's all right, Alex. Dr. Marchbanks will be able to help."

"But I'm not sick," she gasped, "I'm crazy."

He herded her on. "Dr. Marchbanks is a psychiatrist."

It was a relief to abandon her pretenses. Alexandra went obediently where her teacher led.

Elgonar felt his color move in the Dreamweaver's pattern. He wrapped his power around him as he was drawn to her cottage. She waited in the doorway, her face grave.

"Something terrible is happening," she said. "I feel it in the pattern. And I cannot wake Ohmiden from his dream."

83

The Weaver looked past her. Ohmiden lay in a nest of cushions by the hearth. Sweat beaded the old man's face; he moaned like a woman in travail. Elgonar went to the loom, wove a strand of the Dreamer's blue into the pattern, and said, "Irenden."

The Dreamer appeared in a swirl of mist and ran to the old man's side. He laid a hand on Ohmiden's wrinkled brow, his own expression echoing the old man's pain. "Awake," he commanded. "Awake!"

Ohmiden jolted awake. His eyes brimmed with tears as his breath caught in gasping sobs. "'Tsan's in terrible danger," he whispered. "Terrible! She has met the man who can cripple her spirit—who will destroy her in the name of healing her."

"Look!" Eikoheh cried, pointing in horror to the loom. With no hand touching it, the shuttle hissed through the warp, laying down a thread of vivid purple. Scarcely had Eikoheh spoken when the door of her cottage slammed open. The Trickster strode in.

"Trickster," she said, mimicking the tone the Weaver had used to name the Dreamer. "And here I am. What a touching scene. Did you seriously believe your meddling would escape my notice, Weaver?"

"Meddling?" the Weaver retorted. "The Loom is my province."

"Not so! During my Feast, anything that interests me is my province—and I find your attempts to interfere with me more and more objectionable. So, I take action." At her gesture, a thread of pure gold wove itself into the pattern. "Namegiver."

The Namegiver appeared, leaning against the door frame with her arms crossed. "Arrogant," she said. "Prideful. Rash."

"I quite agree," the Trickster replied. "But which of you is which? You must be Rash, for naming my chosen Voice Silence."

As the Trickster spoke, the Weaver could feel her gathering power, preparing to act against them. Though he longed to send Eikoheh and Ohmiden to safety, he dared not, for the Trickster watched him. Her lips shaped a poisonous smile.

"It would be amusing," she purred, "to cast you across the void. I would enjoy watching you struggle with a mortal's limitations, stripped of language, in the world where your Wanderer grapples with madness." Her hands moved; the straining power of the Loom gripped the Weaver. He struggled for breath.

Then, the Trickster staggered backward, as she was struck by a flung stoneware pitcher. The gathering power ripped free of her control. The Dreamer and the Namegiver shielded the two mortals while the Weaver dove for the loom. He snatched Eikoheh's shuttle, throwing all his power into the weft. He wove furiously, binding the power the Trickster had loosed and strengthening the Dreamweaver's pattern. But before he could finish, the Trickster clutched his throat. As the world began to dissolve into dizzying sparks, the Weaver took desperate action. With almost the last of his strength, he wove the Trickster across the void. At the instant the Weaver collapsed to the floor, the Trickster, with a shriek of rage, vanished.

12

"Good morning, Brigid," Kelly Sebastian greeted her, grain scoop in hand. Her eyes widened. "What's this? An entourage."

"Hi, Kelly. These are some Greek friends of mine. I met them when I was staying in Athens." She began pointing. "Ychass Zaousis, Remarr Papadopoulos, Vihena, Iobeh, and Karivet Marakis. This is Kelly Sebastian."

"Do you ride," Kelly asked, "or are you spectators?"

"We ride," Vihena answered.

"After a fashion," Ychass added, hearing sudden worries from Brigid about styles of riding.

"Well, we don't rent horses for trailriding, but if you'd like to take lessons while you're visiting, let me know." With that, Kelly started off.

Brigid shooed her charges into the tack room. "Now," she said. "There's some time to kill before Brice gets here with the phone books. You guys want to learn to clean an English bridle?"

When Brice and Mark arrived, they were greeted by the sight of the Five diligently cleaning every bridle in sight. Brice raised eyebrows, nudged Mark, and feigned outrage. "Brigid Chandler, are you trying to make us look lazy?" He examined the bridle in Iobeh's hands. "That's *Twitch's* bridle! That hasn't been cleaned since last year's beginner camp week."

"No Angel?" Mark asked. "I swear she'd be late to her own funeral."

As though her name had summoned her, Angel appeared in a breathless hurry, her arms full of horsey things. "Wow!" she said when she took in the industry; then her look grew calculating. "I don't suppose you lot would see that Gabe's bridle gets done?" Without waiting for a reply, she dumped her load on top of her tack trunk and went off to start turning horses out.

Brice gestured to the phone books he'd piled on his trunk. "I've got all the Vermont books. Who wants to start?"

Brigid picked up a book and flipped it open, explaining that the Five couldn't read. While Brice was still reeling from that information, Kelly poked her head in. "Give Angel a hand with the turnout, Brice," she ordered briskly, and Brice, well trained, hustled.

Mark rose. "I'd better start the mucking. Kelly gets grumpy if she has to remind us."

"Why don't you all help him," Brigid suggested, "while I go through the phone books?"

Mark put the Five to work, and in a remarkably short time, they were done. When they returned to the tack room, Brigid was on the last phone book. After scrawling something on a piece of paper, she laid the book aside. "Pretty slim pickings." She sighed. "There's a Victor Scarsdale in Cavendish and a Margaret Scarsdale in Island Pond. Does your Alexandra have relatives?"

Karivet answered. "She told me her father was dead. I do not know whether she had other kin. She never spoke of relatives or close friends."

"I wonder if it's worth calling," Brigid murmured. "I suppose it can't hurt. I'll try these numbers tonight—when folks are apt to be home from work—and let you know what I find out. Her father is dead?" At Karivet's nod, she looked thoughtful.

87

"Maybe she *is* Alister Scarsdale's daughter. As soon as I get a chance, I'll research him in the library, and we'll see what there is to see."

"When?" Vihena pressed.

"I might have time tonight," Brigid replied. "If not, it won't be until the day after tomorrow. Tomorrow, we're all going to the horse show at Vershire. Speaking of which, who wants to help me give Rex his bath?"

The chores associated with readying four horses for the Horse Trial at the Vershire School took most of the day. Iobeh proved invaluable during the task of bathing Tigger, who had never reconciled herself to water; when Iobeh used her empathic gift, the little mare stood as though a bath were her idea of bliss. After the horses were clean, their manes were braided, their whiskers clipped, and their hooves polished. Then, the four riders packed their gear in their tack boxes and loaded everything into Kelly's truck. The four-horse trailer was swept out, haynets filled, jerry-cans of water and extra bales of hay lugged up. By the time everything was ready, it was time for evening chores. When they had passed out the last of the hay to the hungry horses, Ychass dusted her hands off on her shirt and looked at Brice. "It's a great deal of work, to look after so many horses. Whatever would you have done without us?"

Brice grinned. "The same thing—but slower."

All afternoon, Kelly had watched their industry with a mixture of amazement and approval. Now, as she approached the group she smiled warmly. "You certainly know how to work! Brigid tells me you'd like to come along tomorrow, and I just wanted to say I think that's a great idea. The bad news is that we have to be on the road by six-thirty. I'll look for you around five-thirty. Okay?"

As Kelly moved off, the Five exchanged surprised looks. "We

88

are to go with you tomorrow?" Remarr asked carefully. "To what end? Is there not something we can do to find 'Tsan?"

Brigid shook her head. "I don't think there is a step you can take without at least one of us along to guide you; and all of us are committed for tomorrow. If we didn't go, Kelly would be very suspicious. It really is the best we can do. Besides," she added with a smile, "you might find the show fun."

"*Fun?*" Vihena began, outraged; but Iobeh squeezed her hand.

Brigid is worried about us, she signed. *No doubt there is some danger we do not understand.*

Vihena clamped her teeth on further outburst. Brigid looked around at them anxiously. "Are you hungry?" she asked at last. "Shall we go home to supper?"

Remarr managed to smile. "Indeed yes. The longer we remain, the more appetizing your horse begins to look!"

That evening after Brigid left them, the Five held a council. The others settled in the living room, but Vihena stalked around with feverish energy.

"This is *madness!*" she began. "We wasted an entire *day* helping that useless troupe prepare for—for *games* with their horses! 'Tsan is languishing somewhere while we are mired in foolishness. And they want us to waste *another* day at their silly games. The gods didn't send us here to play servants to a collection of pleasure-seeking fools!"

"You are too harsh," Remarr chided. "You mustn't forget that they rescued you, Vihena. The subterfuge may seem pointless to us, but *they* know the rules—and perils—of this world. We would do well to remember that, and to follow their advice."

"And *waste* another day in idleness?" Vihena challenged.

"We were hardly *idle*," Ychass remarked.

Vihena glared. "Very well: are we to waste another day in stupid, pointless makework?"

"What would you propose?" Karivet asked. "I know you are fretting for action, but what would you have us *do*, Vihena?"

"Ychass should attempt to touch 'Tsan's mind."

"I have tried," Ychass said. "Something blocks me."

"Try again," the swordswoman ordered.

The shapeshifter focused her thoughts and sent her mind questing. She found 'Tsan almost at once, but could not get her to respond; 'Tsan was heavily asleep; the sleep was too thick to disrupt. She struggled with it for several moments, then shook her head. "She sleeps. I do not think it is a natural sleep."

"Where is she?" Vihena demanded.

"It's not that simple, Vihena." Exasperation sharpened her voice. "Though I can touch a mind, that touch doesn't act as a map. If only 'Tsan would wake, she could tell me where she is."

"What about the gods?" Remarr ventured. "They said they would help us."

"You want me to cast my thoughts *across the void?*"

"Is it possible?"

Ychass's pale gaze touched each of them in turn. "And which of you will pull me back, should I fail?"

Vihena scrubbed one foot in the carpet, Remarr examined his harp-calluses, and Karivet picked at the upholstery. Iobeh touched Ychass's wrist and signed, *I will.*

But can you? Ychass asked her silently.

In answer, Iobeh funneled her energy into a call, a longing that the shapeshifter felt as distinctly as the tug of a cord. Ychass nodded, closed her eyes, and cast her mind forth.

The void clutched at her, tried to suck away her sense of herself. She fought it, shaping her mind into a dense core she hoped would pierce through without being snared. *Elgonar! ELGO-*

NAR! she called. There was no response. Ychass began to tire. She knew she should draw back into herself while she still had the strength. And then she felt a flicker, a will-o'-the-wisp glimmer that drew her onward. She pursued it, sure she was on the brink of contact, until it dissolved into mocking laughter, leaving Ychass alone in the dark: lost.

Panic clawed at her sense of herself. The tight core of her thoughts began to fray. Then, she felt Iobeh's call—the tug of her longing. She followed it. Ychass's thoughts thundered along the cord Iobeh stretched between them until the world snapped back into place around the shapeshifter. Her deep, relieved breath turned into a violent spasm of coughing. In spite of the strain that showed on Iobeh's face, the girl held the shapeshifter's hands until her breathing eased and she could again speak. Ychass squeezed Iobeh's hands to convey her thanks before she met Remarr's eyes and said, "No."

Karivet shivered. "*Gods!* Are you all right?"

"Thanks to Iobeh. I am not a god that I can cast my mind beyond the void. Simply wanting a thing to be true is not enough. Vihena, I share your impatience, but we must not let our desire for action drive us to rashness. I *believe* I met the Trickster in the void; she lured me beyond my strength to return unaided. If the Trickster is in this, do you see the implications? We must be doubly on our guard for we must not only overcome the dangers of this place, but we must also contend with whatever obstacles the Trickster invents."

"You cannot be sure it was she," Vihena countered.

"It sounded like her laughter."

Remarr stepped in. "It is only sense to listen to Ychass in these matters. But what shall we do about our allies? Shall we fall in with their plans, though it means losing another day?"

"What choice have we?" Vihena asked bitterly. An idea struck her. "Unless we Ask you where she is, Karivet."

Karivet's jaw tightened, but he said, "Ask, then, if you are sure of your question."

Vihena took his hand and met his eyes. "Where is 'Tsan?"

"In this world, 'Tsan exists only in memory," Karivet answered tonelessly.

"What?" Vihena gasped. "Is she dead?"

"It is as though she had never been."

Vihena covered her face. "No! Oh, no!" she cried, her words blurred with sobs. "*Now* what will we do?"

13

For the first time in what seemed like years, Alexandra slept peacefully. When she woke in the infirmary, she realized what a tremendous relief it was to have someone with whom to talk, someone with whom she did not need to keep up pretenses.

Dr. Marchbanks had listened to the whole wretched story: the cult and the missing piece of her memory; the delusions of an alternate world peopled with gods and shapeshifters; her "memories" of herself as chosen savior; the tormenting dreams; even the minor hallucination. As it had spilled out of her, he had listened without judgment. In the end, he had asked her whether she would like to stay in the infirmary, and when she had said yes, he had made the arrangements.

Alexandra got dressed. It was morning; she had slept almost twenty hours. Before long, one of the nurses brought a tray. "Did you sleep well? After you've had your breakfast, Dr. Marchbanks wants to see you."

Alexandra ate hungrily, even though the food was not terribly appealing. Dr. Marchbanks was waiting for her in his office. He was a wiry, small man with curly brown hair and an intense, animated face. He seemed to listen with every pore. He smiled when she came in, waving her to a chair.

"Did you sleep?"

"Very well; and no dreams. But where do we go from here? I can't live in the infirmary."

"No," he agreed. "But I wouldn't say you needed to, either. How does the thought of going back to the dorm make you feel?"

She shrugged. "It doesn't scare me; but I still can't remember what happened to me in the cult. I mean, I feel a lot better having gotten some sleep, but things aren't right yet."

"It will take time, Alexandra. I'll want to see you—well, at least once a week, perhaps more often. If you find you aren't able to cope, you can come back here. What's important is that you understand you don't have to do everything yourself; it's all right to have help. You've been through a lot, and you've managed remarkably well. You're not crazy, Alexandra; but you *have* been under tremendous stress. Just having told someone about it will help; but there are more aggressive therapies to explore if we must. You have options, Alexandra. Try to remember that. Now"—he picked up his appointment book— "we'll set up a regular weekly time. If something urgent comes up, call anytime and of course I'll work you in, but I could give you a regular time—either Tuesdays at one, or Wednesdays at three."

Mentally she reviewed her schedule. "Tuesday would work."

"Very good. If anything comes up in the meantime, call me. Unless I hear from you, I'll look for you Tuesday. Okay?"

She nodded. "Thanks."

After she had gone, Dr. Marchbanks made some notes in her file. "Unusual case," he wrote. "She refers to 'delusions,' but does not believe in her constructs. Indicative of heavy rationalization?" As he laid his pen aside, he shook his head. The world Alexandra Scarsdale had invented was a richly imaginative one—far richer, alas, than the world of the university community. He sighed. The human mind was endlessly fascinating, even if academia sometimes palled.

When the Weaver groaned and opened his eyes, Eikoheh breathed again. The Namegiver and the Dreamer helped him to sit up, and Ohmiden brought him water. After he had drunk, the Dreamer laid his hands gently on Elgonar's bruised throat, and willed power through his fingers.

"El, where's the Trickster?" the Namegiver asked.

The Weaver covered his eyes with one hand. "I wove her across the void," he whispered.

A flicker of amusement crossed the Dreamer's face. "Did you take the language from her?"

"No. It was nearly more than I could do to send her at all. This is serious, 'Ren. I sent her after the Five. I did not have the strength to find another world for her; and I doubt she is trapped. She is stronger than even my worst nightmares."

"Hold!" Eikoheh cut in. "You have sent the Trickster to the same world *as the Five and 'Tsan?"*

"I had little choice, Eikoheh. The pattern is set to span the void to that place. Had I tried to change that, I would never have succeeded."

"I would like to know," the Namegiver remarked, "who threw that pitcher?"

"I did," Ohmiden confessed. "She made me angry."

"Your aim was true, my friend," the Dreamer said. "Your action may well have saved us all."

"I am glad my best stoneware pitcher was sacrificed in a good cause," the Dreamweaver commented. "But how can we aid the Five, now that the Trickster is loosed upon them?"

"If we pool our strengths, we might warn them," the Dreamer said, but the Namegiver and the Weaver shook their heads.

"The Trickster would anticipate that and it would put Ychass in grave danger," Elgonar said. "But the Five must know. Perhaps we could send one of them a dream."

"Send the dream to one of their allies!" said Ohmiden. "Surely the Trickster is unaware of them."

"That is wise," the Namegiver said with approval. "Show us their colors in the pattern, Dreamweaver, so that we may decide which of them will best suit our purpose."

Angel woke with a jolt. The urgency of the dream left her heart thudding. The digital clock blinked reproachfully: 2:47. She recalled the look on the face of the man in her dream. The Weaver wanted her to warn someone, warn the Five; warn them that the Trickster was loose in the world.

The meaning clicked into place. The Five: Ychass, Vihena, Iobeh, Karivet, and Remarr; they had talked about the gods, had even mentioned the Weaver. It didn't sound as though the Trickster was a good guy.

Angel tried to think. Ychass could hear thoughts; maybe she could hear Angel's. But how did one think loudly?

Sleep lured her: tell them in the morning. Then she recognized that she might forget to pass the message on in the morning. So she wrote the whole dream down in as much detail as she could recall, then tucked the paper into the pocket of the riding coat she would wear tomorrow. That done, she went back to bed and fell almost instantly asleep.

When the Five rose at daybreak to meet Brigid, there was not much enthusiasm. Karivet's pronouncement had sapped their hope, in spite of the knowledge that even though Ychass had gotten no direct response, she *had* touched 'Tsan's mind. Anxiety lay heavily on them as they made breakfast and got ready for the events of the day. Vihena's impatience had subsided into lethargy; if 'Tsan existed only in memory, what was the point? Remarr wanted to strangle her, but the others liked her better when she was quiet.

When they arrived at the stable, the place was swathed in a chill morning mist; the excitement of the others was so tangible it made Iobeh twitch. Horses were blanketed, their legs wrapped. Last-minute equipment checks were run before they loaded the trailer and piled people into vehicles. They headed out of the yard at 6:23 exactly.

It was a long day. The Five led horses, ran errands, and acted as extra pairs of hands for their allies. It might have been enjoyable, except for their growing frustration. Ychass and Iobeh both suffered from the unspoken tension; Ychass had shielded her thoughts so much that she nearly missed Angel's mental summons.

As Angel had brushed off her riding coat, the crinkle of paper had puzzled her momentarily. She had fished out a folded sheet from the pocket—and the memory of her weird dream washed over her. She looked around for the others, but realized there was no tactful way to get out of earshot of the adults. *Ychass!* she thought, hard. *Come over here and don't talk.*

Shaken from her mental shell, Ychass complied. *What is it?*

In answer, Angel gave her the paper. Ychass glanced at it, then raised frowning eyes to Angel's face. *What is this?*

Read it! As the thought left Angel's brain, she remembered that none of the aliens could read. She twitched the paper out of the shapeshifter's hand and silently read it, calling the dream to mind. Ychass looked alarmed.

I must tell the others, she thought to Angel. *The Trickster is no friend to us—or to 'Tsan! We must take precautions if she is here. Thank you, Angel.*

Ychass made time among the day's press of tasks and errands to report Angel's dream warning to the others. When she told

97

Remarr and Vihena, the swordswoman's simmering dissatisfaction boiled over.

"With the Trickster herself stalking 'Tsan we are *wasting time* with these pleasure-seeking children and their animals!" she raged. "What insanity possesses us?"

"If we hadn't come along today," Remarr pointed out, "Angel would have been unable to deliver the Weaver's warning."

"*You!*" Vihena snarled with deep disgust. "By all the gods, Remarr, you could mouth comforting words at the end of the world! What good does it do to cling to such *baseless hope?*"

"Hope," the minstrel responded evenly, "is more powerful than despair; and not all courage requires rage to fuel it."

Vihena flushed and raised a hand to strike him.

"*Peace!*" Ychass's voice, underscored by her mind, drew them up short. "When we fight amongst ourselves, surely we do the Trickster's will. Vihena, we have traveled this path before: *we must depend upon our allies;* without their guidance we are at sea indeed. And the Weaver spoke to Angel. Should we not take encouragement from that? If the gods are using these children—despite the weaknesses we see—then they are surely woven into the pattern." She turned away without waiting for a response. With a nod, Remarr led the horse in his charge to another grazing spot, leaving Vihena to her thoughts.

For the rest of the day, Remarr managed, without making his efforts pointed, to stay out of Vihena's way. There was certainly enough work to keep them all occupied. At long last, the games ended. The troupe returned to the stable, did the evening chores, and when the last horse was fed, Brigid took the Five back to her parents' farm and left them.

The Trickster was angry. It was not so easy to ride the winds in this world as it had been in the world of the Loom, and it was very hard for her simply to call up the things she needed. She didn't know whether this was due to some quirk of the world she was in, or whether it was caused by the power she had lost. There were people everywhere. They cluttered the landscape and acted, by sheer force of numbers, as camouflage for 'Tsan. The Trickster had used a shred of her power to confuse watching eyes, to prevent people from noticing that her gray robes and cloak bore little resemblance to local garb. She leaned against the wall of a building and let the herds of people stream past her; she hoped to catch some spark of useful information from their surface thoughts. Though no one knew anything of 'Tsan, the Trickster learned the importance of the paper slips people termed "money." She wasted no time in acquiring some. She was easily the most efficient panhandler downtown Boston had ever seen; if she caught her marks' eyes, they fished in their wallets for the largest bills they had.

She watched people; there was such variation in their dress and appearance. The Trickster wanted to blend in, but she could not spare the power to keep up her eye-confusing shield indefinitely. So she used some of her take to purchase native clothing. She then went to a market that sold mechanical steeds. She 'persuaded' a vendor to sell her a two-wheeled horse at a price she could afford. When he began to talk about "permits," "licenses," and "insurance," she made him forget, and then took the knowledge of how to control the thing from his mind. It took her several moments to work out the balance of the thing, but when she'd stopped wobbling, she roared down the street on her two-wheeled horse.

The Trickster *knew* the Five were here: she had felt the shapeshifter's mind, briefly, when Ychass had tried to bridge the void. If the Five were here, the Trickster was sure that 'Tsan was too. She must find the Wanderer before the others did.

14

"Now what?" Vihena demanded in a tone of almost belligerent despair. The Five were seated at the table in the Chandlers' dining room. "The Trickster is *here*—somewhere; 'Tsan exists only in memory. Our allies are easily distracted by their own petty concerns. What else could possibly go awry?"

"The Trickster could *find* us!" Remarr snapped. "Or she could find 'Tsan before we do. Your Clan would be ashamed of you, Vihena; you are wringing your hands like a silly Vematheh."

"How *dare* you!" Vihena began, but Karivet slammed his fist down on the table.

"*Will you stop bickering?*" he demanded. "I swear by the wise gods I have never seen such lunacy! Vihena, I know you dislike problems that will not yield to a sword, but you are no *fool*. 'Tsan exists only in memory—it was a blow to hear that; but it is the answer to the wrong question. The 'Tsan we know could have no place in a world as bizarre as this. Ychass has felt her mind, but it is not *our* 'Tsan; it is the woman she has become in this place."

"If she is not *our* 'Tsan, will she wish—or be able—to help us?" Vihena demanded.

"We have no other hope," Ychass said quietly. "The fate of

the world rests on our recovering 'Tsan, to heal the Loom with her presence. If she is lost to us, then hope is gone."

"Then we should Ask Karivet."

"*No!*" Karivet, Remarr, and Ychass said together.

"What would you Ask me?" Karivet went on gently. "The wrong question might sap our hope or make us overconfident. And once the word is spoken I cannot unsay it."

"But I want to *know,*" Vihena pleaded.

You want, Iobeh signed, *to be spared the effort of hoping. But we need your hope, and your effort.*

With a lopsided smile, Vihena asked, "So now what? Is there any way to guard against the Trickster?"

Ychass shrugged. "I dare not try to touch 'Tsan's mind again, as I have no way of knowing whether the Trickster can intercept such communication. I will shield my mind, but beyond that, I can see no way to protect us."

Iobeh gave a sudden gasp and gestured toward a large, convex mirror. There was the Trickster's avid face—curiously distorted by the mirror's curve—watching them.

"Cover it! Cover the mirror!" Remarr cried.

Vihena raced to the sideboard for a tablecloth. Together, she and Remarr veiled the mirror.

"Can she hear us?" Vihena whispered.

"How would I know?" Remarr whispered back. "But if she can capture our gaze, or touch us, she can compel our obedience."

"There are other mirrors," Ychass said. "We must shroud them all."

They scouted through the house, towels, sheets, and table-cloths in hand. When they gathered again in the dining room, Remarr shook his head at the others.

"I do not like it that she has found us so quickly."

101

Vihena shrugged. "She is one of the gods."

Do you think she will attack us? Iobeh signed.

"No," Remarr said. "She will toy with us, as a leopard with its prey, until she tires of the sport; *then* she will strike."

"And remember," Ychass cautioned. "She too is looking for 'Tsan. Our search will draw us ever closer to the Trickster."

This is true, Iobeh signed. *But we have allies—which the Trickster will not expect.*

The Trickster punched a fist into her palm. As long as she could *see* the Five, she might snare one of them, but with the scrying surfaces covered, she was barred. A mirror could not give her information—like *where,* in this miserable, crowded, gods-forsaken, filthy excuse for a world, *they were!*

Her fist smacked into her palm again, but with less force. There was no doubt: the Minstrel was quick; and the others had hidden depths as well. It could be interesting, pitting her wits against the Five.

With satisfaction in her smile, she began concentrating on the Wanderer. If she were near a mirror, why then, the Trickster would see what she could see!

Angel stood before the bathroom mirror, fiddling with her hair. The bathroom made a haven—one place where she could be sure she wouldn't be interrupted. She squeezed a little styling mousse into her hand, then began working the front of her hair into spikes. Suddenly, her reflection rippled, then vanished. Looking out at her was a thin, red-haired woman whose eyes were the nearly colorless gray of Ychass's.

Angel. The voice sounded in her mind, not her ears. *I am the Namegiver. 'Tsan is in desperate danger. The Trickster is in your world, and 'Tsan has met someone who can strip away*

102

the things that make her "'Tsan." You must act. There is little time.

"What should we *do?*" Angel demanded. "How can we *find* her?"

Ohmiden dreamed of a place of learning, a vast school, the Namegiver responded, *and the name: 'Boston.' Does that mean aught to you?*

"Boston is a city—south of here. There are lots of schools in that area," Angel replied. "What else?"

The Namegiver's reflection wavered. As the mirror returned to normal, Angel swore softly. She rinsed the mousse out of her hair, while she tumbled the god's information about in her mind.

For a blissful day, things returned to normal for Alexandra. She slept the night through without dreams. But the next morning, on her way through the Square, she caught a glimpse of an odd reflection in a storefront—not hers. She battled panic—so intent that she was nearly mowed down by a taxi.

As Alexandra rushed to her German class, she ran headlong into her German teacher. He caught her shoulders, steadying her.

"Why the hurry?" he asked her.

"I—I didn't want to be late," she stammered.

"It's Saturday, Alexandra," he told her in a doubtful voice that made her feel especially fragile. "There's no class today."

"Oh God, how *embarrassing!*" she said, trying for a light tone. "I guess I've lost a day."

"Or gained one. Listen, let's get a cup of coffee—since you have all this free time." He gave her an engaging grin. "I don't bite—I promise!"

She could see no way to escape. It wasn't an unreasonable

103

suggestion, after all. So she allowed Herr Bergemann to tow her toward his favorite coffee shop. As they crossed the street, Alexandra caught sight of a Harvard Square Character: a tall woman with impossibly orange, punked-out, spiky hair, a black leather jumpsuit, and mirrored sunglasses, who leaned against a massive Harley-Davidson motorcycle. "A Character," she whispered, with a slight gesture toward the biker.

"She'd be hard to miss," Herr Bergemann agreed. "She must be seven feet tall, what with the hair and those boots." The boots were high black ones with four-inch spike heels. "I wouldn't want to meet her in a dark alley," he added.

Alexandra had the uneasy feeling that the biker's gaze followed them until they disappeared into the coffee shop.

Alexandra and her German instructor had a perfectly normal visit and then went their separate ways. She felt cheered until she noticed the spike-haired biker on a different street corner. Alexandra changed her route so she wouldn't have to pass the woman, though she railed inwardly at her own silliness. By the time she reached her room, she was so annoyed at herself that she immediately uncovered all the mirrors and raised the blinds.

I'm getting better! she insisted. *I don't need to obey such ridiculous whims.* She even went so far as to leave a message for the Super asking him to repair her bathroom mirror.

She spent what was left of the morning on her English Lit course, and managed to lose herself in the poetry of William Butler Yeats. But as she got up to go to lunch, her eye caught the mirror over her dresser. It was not reflecting the room; instead, she saw the face of the orange-haired biker—glasses and all. She stared at her own reflection in the woman's glasses. As the biker started to remove her sunglasses, Alexandra spun away from the mirror with such violence that she fell against her easy chair. The skidding chair collided with the table upon which she had precariously stacked her texts and notebooks.

The whole toppled with a tremendous crash. Alexandra lay on top of the wreckage, gasping. Though she heard her neighbor's anxious questions, she couldn't answer. Suddenly, the alarm shrilled as Alexandra's neighbor came through the fire door.

With a feeling akin to relief, Alexandra covered her face with both hands, and howled. None of her neighbors—nor, when she was fetched, the tutor—could calm her; so at last, the tutor sent someone after a car and they trundled Alexandra off to Health Services. The tutor was far too distracted to notice the biker—however flamboyantly dressed—who watched the commotion from across the street.

By the time Isaac Marchbanks arrived at the infirmary, uprooted from his Saturday gardening like one of the weeds he had been after, one of his colleagues had sedated Alexandra.

"Did she say anything?" he asked the man. "Any hint about what set her off? She seemed so much better on Friday."

The other doctor shook his head. "She was completely hysterical, weeping and moaning. I knew you'd want to talk to her, but honestly, Isaac, she was totally incoherent."

Stifling his irritation, Isaac retreated to his office. If he'd only known they were going to sedate Alexandra, he could have finished his weeding. Oh, well; perhaps he could use the time to catch up on some articles. He had barely started reading when one of the nurses tapped on his door.

"Dr. Marchbanks, there's someone out here who wants to visit the new admission."

"She's sedated. No visitors."

"That's what I *said*," the nurse replied, "but I'm not making any headway. It's a real tough customer—dressed like a punked-out Hell's Angel."

"Send him in and I'll talk to him."

"It's a *her*."

105

Isaac Marchbanks' eyebrows shot up. "Send *her* in then."

A moment later, Marchbanks found himself looking up at an extremely tall, outrageously striking woman. Her wild hair, an improbable orange, sprang in spikes from her scalp. She wore clunky metal chains, her black leather jumpsuit was steel studded, and a pair of sunglasses hung around her neck. Her eyes were a blue so deep it was nearly purple.

"I'd like to see my friend," she told him.

"Sorry. She's sedated."

"That's what the woman told me," she said contemptuously.

"Come back tomorrow; then you can see your friend."

"I want to see her *now!*" The crackle of anger made Marchbanks look up in surprise. Suddenly, he was drowning in purple eyes.

"No." The word lacked the intended authority; he sounded dazed. But the suffocating sensation eased a bit.

"*What?*" the woman demanded.

"I said, no." His voice gained strength. "She can't have visitors now. Leave your name; I'll tell her you were here."

The woman put her fists on her hips and glared at him. "I want to see her. *NOW!!*" On the last word, her hand snaked out and prisoned Marchbanks's wrist. Her touch made it hard to breathe.

"I . . . don't . . . care . . . what . . . you . . . want," he said, each word a nearly impossible effort. "You . . . may . . . not . . . see . . . her!"

She touched his brow with her other hand. "Sleep," she commanded.

"*Sleep!*" The outrageousness of her command would have brought startled laughter if he weren't already so angry and unnerved. Instead, a rush of rage burned away the feelings that hampered his mind and his breathing. Isaac Marchbanks leaped to his feet, shaking off her hand. "Who the hell do you think you are? I said no visitors, and that is exactly what I meant! Now, will you leave, or must I call Security?"

She stared at him. Then her lips twitched in a one-sided smile. "I'll go, Isaac Marchbanks; but don't think you've won. Clearly, the Wanderer has powerful allies, but I have not yet plumbed the depths of my strength." Raising one hand in a mocking salute, she went out.

Marchbanks watched to see that she got on the elevator and that the elevator did not stop at any other floors on its descent. He summoned it back to check that it was indeed empty before he returned to his desk. His hands shook as he picked up the article he had been reading. Concentration was beyond him. According to Alexandra, the people in her delusional world had referred to her as 'Tsan, the Stranger—*and the Wanderer*.

15

When Angel arrived at the stable, nearly bursting with her news, chores were in full swing. Each time she thought she had the Five, Brice, and Mark to herself, someone would wander in to interrupt. It wasn't until lunch, when they were seated around the big table in Kelly's kitchen, that she could report her exchange with the Namegiver.

The others listened breathlessly. The Five were excited to have such a definite clue, but their allies counseled caution.

"Boston is a big place," Mark said. "And there are a lot of schools there. It won't be a simple matter to find your friend."

"But there *is* Directory Assistance," Brice put in. "We may be able to get her phone number."

"It won't be that easy," Mark muttered direly.

Angel leaped up and went to the phone. "Let's try it. What's Boston's area code? Six–one–seven?" She punched a string of numbers. "Boston," she said after a moment, "or greater Boston, anyway. Do you have a listing for an Alexandra Scarsdale?" There was a long pause. "Okay. Thanks." She replaced the receiver. "No good. She's not listed."

"If she's at some college," Brice put in, "the school would have her phone number."

Angel gestured to the phone. "Do you want to make a lot of unexplained long-distance calls on Kelly's phone?"

Both boys made faces. The Five had been watching, mystified. Remarr voiced their puzzlement. "'Phone?'"

Angel tried to explain. "Telephone. Phone. It lets us talk over distance. Calls to faraway places cost money. If there were a lot of extra calls on Kelly's bill, she'd get mad."

The Five exchanged glances. Brice grinned suddenly. "You don't need to say it," he laughed. "'This is a strange place.'"

"Why are we bothering with 'phones'?" Vihena demanded. "We know where 'Tsan is. Let us go look for her."

"The Boston area is a *big place,*" Mark repeated. "We couldn't find her by just wandering around. We need to know where to look."

"Very well," Vihena said, reining in her impatience. "But what *can* we do?"

"We can wait until Brigid gets out of work and then go use *her* telephone," Brice said. "We call all the schools and colleges we can think of, and see whether any of them has Alexandra Scarsdale as a student. *Then,* if we find her, we can call her, or at least we'll know where to begin looking for her."

Vihena sighed. With pure mischief in his expression, Remarr said softly, "More waiting."

She eyed him, but instead of exploding, she smiled. "You took my very words, Remarr."

Late that afternoon, Brigid arrived. She looked worried. At the first opportunity she took Angel aside. "My parents will be home on Tuesday. We've *got* to get the Five out before then. How are you guys doing on getting them invited to your houses?"

Angel bit her lip. "My folks are hovering on the brink. Mark thinks his mother will let Iobeh and Karivet stay. I don't know about Brice. I'll really put the push on my folks, but you know how they are."

"I'll check with Brice," Brigid said. "Anything happening?"

109

"Yeah—but here comes Kelly. Can we come over to your apartment this evening? Say yes!" Then, before Brigid had a chance to say anything, Angel sprinted off.

Brigid's apartment was very small, and rather too warm as well. She poured tall glasses of iced tea while she listened to Angel's report and to the plan for locating Alexandra. Then she produced a pencil and a pad. The allies spent some time brainstorming; Mark proved invaluable, as he had already begun to research colleges he might want to attend. The Five listened, baffled. Finally, Brigid tore the page off the pad and gestured to the phone. "Go to it," she said, "whoever wants to be first."

The calling developed into a ritual. The caller would pick a school, call Directory Assistance, ask for the number, call the school, ask for Alexandra Scarsdale, and then cross off the school's name. Then the list would pass to another caller. It was Brigid who called Harvard. With wide eyes, she wrote down a phone number, read it back, and hung up, excitement warring with disbelief on her face.

"I've got it. I can't believe it. *I've got it!*" She looked around at them all. "So who wants to call her?"

"Action at last," Remarr murmured. "Vihena should call."

Vihena took phone. "Show me what to do." Brigid dialed, while everyone crowded around.

"Is it ringing?" Angel asked.

"Yes," Vihena answered. Then she shook her head. "Nothing else is happening."

"She's not *home,*" Angel moaned. "I can't *stand* it!"

Vihena handed the phone back to Brigid, who hung it up. Fixing Remarr with a glimmer of malice, she said, "So *now* what?"

Remarr met her gaze. Suddenly, they were both laughing. "Why, Vihena," he gasped, "*we wait!*"

110

When they had laughed themselves out, Brigid took the Five back out to the farm while Mark ran Brice and Angel home. Each of them planned to sneak in one more try before bedtime, and they all swore to let the others know immediately, if anyone made contact. But bedtime came and went with no success.

For the first time since he had grown into his spirit-gift, Ohmiden fought the dream he was given. It swept him into a swirling world of impossibilities and terrors; he was mired in darkness, imprisoned in a void that held him away from light, away from meaning. There were no beacons to guide him, just whorls of purple and scraps of conversation. The voices were unfamiliar: two or three men, speaking meaningless words.

". . . sedation . . . dose . . . see some reaction . . ."

". . . catatonic?"

". . . stimulate her . . . Adrenalin?"

"A peculiar case."

". . . electroshock therapy . . ."

Ohmiden struggled against the dream. He had the sudden conviction that he was being used, *that this dream wasn't something given, but was instead being* taken *from him. As he struggled, a mesh of violet strands tightened around him. He was being strangled; mired, drowning—in his sleep, he cried out, but his own voice would not waken him.*

Somewhere, eons distant, his shell was shaken. Someone shouted. He could make no response. His inner self was barred from his body; his spirit was trapped, lost in featureless murk. The strength went out of his fighting.

Then he was surrounded by light—wonderful, glorious golden light. His spirit surged with joy. The light came nearer. At its center was a woman, a figure robed in sunlight, with hair like a torch. In her hands she held a pair of silver shears.

Ohmiden understood, and the welcoming fire of his joy

111

damped a bit. This was the Harvester, who cuts the thread from the Loom at life's end. He framed a question: Is it my time?

Her only reply was to hold the shears out to him.

He tested his bonds; they were tight, strong. He sought for other guidance, but aside from the glory of the Harvester's presence, there was no other beacon.

May I not say farewell?

The Harvester held out the shears.

Time stretched endlessly. The Harvester waited. At last, Ohmiden took the shears. With his spirit-sight, he could see his thread trapped and tangled in the binding purple mesh. If he cut his thread, the entangling bonds could no longer hold him; and yet, he hesitated. The cords that bound him pulsed with power—and in their violet light, the glimmer of a plan came to life. Ohmiden shifted his grip on the Harvester's shears. He cut—not his own thread, but the cords that bound him. Searing brightness surrounded him; the old man heard the Harvester exclaim. Then the pain took him. It was worse than the binding; it was like breathing flames. It consumed him; he could not bear it. He could not bear it! *Almost of their own volition, the Harvester's shears found his thread.* Forgive me, Eikoheh, *his spirit pleaded.* I am not strong enough. *Then he cut himself free. As the pain released him, he soared into the joyous welcoming light.*

The Trickster threw her head back and screamed. It had cost her power to use the old man's dreaming gift; as the Harvester's shears sliced through her bindings, the strength flowed out of her. While it did not render her helpless, it was a deep blow.

She ignored her wounding. She was still ahead of the Five: she knew where 'Tsan was; and Marchbanks had said that she could see her on the morrow.

Triumph flickered in her eyes. It would take a mere instant to wipe away all 'Tsan's memories of her time in the world of the Loom; and then the Weaver's hopes would turn to ash.

The morn would see her triumph; the night would feel her hand. The Trickster mounted her mechanical steed and roared into the night, ripe for mischief.

The Dreamweaver raised her head to find the Harvester on her threshold. Eikoheh felt nothing—neither joy nor fear—at her coming.

"Have you come for me, too?" she asked, wary and bitter.

"It is not your time. Dreamweaver, I bring you a gift." She held out her hand. Resting in her palm was a skein of silken thread. The silk captured light and cast it back in a rainbow of colors. The Dreamweaver caught her breath.

"What is this?" the old woman asked.

"A gift from Ohmiden: power he stole from the Trickster. Take it; use it. Nothing will curb her as potently as her own strength."

"How did he get this? Why did he take such a risk?"

"He did not choose this, Dreamweaver. The Trickster tried to bind and use him. He could not triumph, but neither could the Trickster break him. In such a case, death is a mercy it is mine to offer. I gave him my shears, old woman, so that he could cut his thread free." Wonder crept into the Harvester's voice. "He cut the Trickster's bindings instead and loosed the full force of her rage against him. He could not withstand her— Ohmiden was a mortal, and old. But he dealt the Trickster a bitter blow indeed. Use the silk, Dreamweaver, to strengthen the Loom."

Eikoheh studied the Harvester's face, then she took the skein of silk. As Eikoheh's hand closed on the silk, the Harvester vanished. The silk thrummed with power. Eikoheh knelt by the bier where she had laid Ohmiden's body out for burial.

113

"So this is your legacy," she said. "No doubt I should be grateful. After all, you gave everything to gain us this weapon." She looked from his tranquil face to the skein of glowing silk and back. "It seems a poor trade to me, old man." Tears *blurred her vision. "Ohmiden," she murmured, then her voice rose to a wail, "Oh, gods, Ohmiden,* I will miss you!*" For the first time since the old dreamer had ceased breathing, Eikoheh wept.*

16

In the morning, Angel arrived at Horizon Stable radiant with confidence. Things were finally going right. They knew where the Five's elusive friend was (even though no one had gotten her on the phone); and further, Angel's parents had agreed to let her invite Vihena to stay with them. Brice and Mark also arrived with invitations for Remarr and the twins. This left Ychass, but Angel knew the shapeshifter could stay in Brigid's apartment. She went through the morning chores whistling.

Her breezy confidence didn't survive chores. As soon as Mark managed to catch a few moments alone with her, he said, "Angel, I've been thinking. It's summer. What if this Alexandra Scarsdale is away?"

"Wouldn't the school have *said*?" Angel demanded.

"How would I know? But if we don't get her today or tomorrow, we're never going to be able to keep the Five from going down there to look for her."

"A trip to Boston might be fun," Angel suggested with a belligerent optimism that Mark knew well.

"Get real. They'd get eaten alive in the city."

"Okay," she snapped. "Keep your shirt on. We'll think of something."

Angel set her mind to scheming. She needed a plan before she confronted the others with this collection of worries.

In the tack room, she found the Five deep in a heated discussion. They started guiltily at her entrance, but resumed once they realized who she was.

"Won't you at least try, Ychass?" Vihena asked. "How fitting for us to turn her own weapon against her."

"No, I won't!" the shapeshifter flared. "I haven't any training; I'm no match for a god!"

"What's this about?" Angel murmured to Remarr.

"Scrying," he reported, then seeing her baffled look, he added, "using a mirror to see over distance."

"I didn't know Ychass could do that."

"She can't," Remarr whispered back.

"Then why are they arguing?"

Remarr's lips twitched. "It passes the time."

Just then, Brice poked his head in. "Hop to it, guys," he called. "There's a hay wagon coming. Kelly says she needs it unloaded and out of the arena as soon as possible. She has two lessons to teach this morning."

Angel was glad of the mindless work of heaving and stacking the fresh hay bales; it gave her time to think—and she desperately needed to come up with a workable plan.

The Infirmary had a hushed feeling. The Trickster paced the waiting room. What was taking so long? The small woman in white had disappeared several minutes ago. The Trickster wished she had dared expend the power to control the lackey, but she needed to conserve her strength.

The click of heels announced the woman's return. "This way, please." She gestured. "Dr. Marchbanks will see you."

The Trickster stopped short, glaring at her. "I don't want to see Dr. Marchbanks," she said. "I want to see my friend."

The woman wilted, but just then Dr. Marchbanks himself

116

appeared in the doorway, his arms crossed and his expression stern.

"I'm afraid you can't see your friend."

The Trickster rounded on him. "You *promised.*"

Isaac Marchbanks propelled her into his office. "The good of my patient has to take precedence. I'm sure you agree that I must do what is best for Alexandra." He steered her to a chair, indicating that she should sit down.

The Trickster fixed her gaze on his face. "I will see my friend." Her voice pushed inexorably against his reasoning.

"No."

Though the Trickster's temper began to fray, she maintained her persuasive tone. "But I must see my friend; it will make her better to see me. I only need a moment, and she will be much, much better. Indeed, do what is best for her: let me see her."

Isaac Marchbanks felt her arguments like a physical force, but he resisted. "I must decide what is best for her. I do not think it would be helpful for you to see her."

The Trickster's temper broke free. "Then suffer the consequences of your pig-headedness!" she growled. Lashing out with her hoarded power, she took 'Tsan's location from his mind and strode down the corridor. She had not gone far before she realized what she had taken from him was worthless. The place was a maze; the hallways looked alike. She had taken the *image* of the place where 'Tsan was, but not the key to the maze.

In his office, Isaac Marchbanks came to himself. As his surroundings steadied, he reached for the phone. "Security? This is Dr. Marchbanks. There's a deranged person roaming the halls. Could you send someone up here? She's over six feet tall, wearing black leather and orange hair, and she's stronger than you'd expect." He put the phone down and stared at it. His mind felt thick. He was still battling lethargy when the Trickster burst into his office.

"Call them off," she ordered.

He didn't need to ask what she meant. "No. You need help."

"Not their help and not yours. Call them off—or I may be forced to do you harm."

"Forced by whom? If you are threatening me you will have to decide whether or not to hurt me. That choice comes from you, not from some outside impulse. You make your choice, and then you have to live with the consequences of your actions."

She stared at him. "You are standing a hair's breadth from death, yet you are quibbling over words. Do you think I cannot harm you? Call them off."

"I have no doubt that you could hurt me—"

"I could *kill* you. You are extremely annoying."

"Are you in the habit of killing things that annoy you?" he asked mildly.

"If a fly bites"—she ground her hands together—"I crush it."

"People aren't flies."

Before she could respond, there was a knock. A look passed between them, then he gestured with his chin. "Stand behind the door. And don't try to be clever. Yes?" he called.

The door opened about ten inches and a security guard stuck his face in. "We looked all over, Doctor. Your visitor seems to have found her way out."

"Well, thanks for trying."

"All in a day's work." He laughed, then withdrew.

The Trickster studied the doctor for several moments before she spoke. "I don't understand you. You whistled up those hounds; why didn't you tell him I was here?"

"I didn't think I needed to. Was I wrong?"

118

The hint of a smile softened the Trickster's cool gaze. "I don't think so. Will you let me see 'Tsan—my friend—now?"

"No," he said, with a sudden surge in his heart rate. The people in Alexandra's delusional world called her 'Tsan.

"You must enjoy living on the edge of danger," the Trickster purred.

"Not particularly. But I have to stand by what I believe is best for my patients."

"When may I see her?"

Isaac Marchbanks fixed the woman with a serious gaze. "When Alexandra is rational, I will ask her whether she wants to see you; then, if she does, we can arrange a short visit."

"When?"

He spread his hands, still holding her gaze. "I don't know. Tell me your name."

"Antekkereh," she responded. Her eyes widened, as though she had said more than she'd intended. She jerked away from his probing gaze. "Why did you want my name?" she asked.

"So I can tell Alexandra who wants to see her."

The Trickster went to the door. "She doesn't know my name," she said. Before Isaac Marchbanks could react, she was gone.

Eikoheh studied the Fate as she fingered the skein the Harvester had given her. The silk was like nothing else. How could she cast this shifting color into her subtle pattern and expect anything but chaos? And yet she must. The Harvester had told her to; besides, it was Ohmiden's last gift. She sighed.

As her thoughts circled, her fingers began to worry at the silk. It was then that she made her discovery: the silk could be drawn out to a filament so fine it retained only the faintest shimmer of color. It could be stretched until it was delicate as cobwebs, but not broken. Suddenly, the Dreamweaver understood how to

119

use the stolen power. There—yes!—there was a color that would be enhanced and strengthened by a little of Ohmiden's silk. She spun a length of iridescent filament and added the power to the thread she had selected, rewinding the bobbin with care. Then, with a grim smile, she sent the shuttle singing through the warp. Maybe this would give the Trickster pause!

The Trickster left the Infirmary in a state of deep frustration. She couldn't understand how Marchbanks had compelled her name from her! She had lost power, she knew, when the old seer had defied her—but surely not enough to undermine her ability to control mortals. Perhaps Marchbanks had some inborn talent. He was a healer; maybe that made him resistant to her. She frowned. And now he had her *name*. Names were power, and Marchbanks was already strong enough.

She sighed explosively as she mounted her two-wheeled horse. She might not be able ride the winds in this ridiculous world, but she could at least create the illusion with her powerful machine. She roared down the street.

The Trickster shot through traffic with little regard for the rules others followed. When she reached a stretch of clear road, she sped over the pavement like a black-and-orange lightning bolt. Behind her, the air erupted into wails; blue lights flashed in her mirrors. The Trickster laughed; the speed was exhilarating. The wind of her passage raked her spiky hair.

After a time, she was forced to brake. One of the slow, foolish crate-vehicles had wedged itself across the road. It signaled its distress in sharp, bright blue flashes. The Trickster was looking for a way around it when an unnaturally loud voice boomed out: *"ALL RIGHT, HOLD IT RIGHT THERE!!"*

She looked for the source; by the sound, the speaker would be formidable indeed.

120

"FREEZE!!"

The Trickster halted, awaiting further developments. A young man in blue livery approached. "Where's the fire?" he asked.

The Trickster was puzzled. "Which one?"

"Cute. Speed limit's forty. Radar clocked you at ninety-seven. You'd better have a pretty good excuse."

The Trickster was silent.

"I need your license, registration, and proof of insurance."

The Trickster felt a squirm of unease; the man from whom she had bought this thing had mentioned a license before she made him forget it. "Is it terribly, terribly important?" she asked, her voice silken. "For if it is, you will have to wait here while I go fetch them."

"Yes, it's terribly important," he said, mimicking her tone. "But I'm not going to wait here because *I wasn't born yesterday.*" On the last four words, he vented blistering sarcasm. The Trickster stiffened. "Now, do you or do you not have your license with you?"

The Trickster reached for her hoarded power. "Why don't you forget you ever saw me," she suggested. For an instant she thought she had him; then fury blazed in his eyes.

"Forget I ever saw you? I've been chasing you for the past fifteen minutes and radioed headquarters about you. I damn well won't forget I saw you! I don't know what you think you're offering me, but whatever it is, I don't want it!!"

Another liveried man approached them. "Trouble, Simmonds?"

"*Trouble?* Fifty-seven miles per hour over posted limit, no helmet, no license, no registration, no proof of insurance—*and* an attempt at bribery! It's all in a day's work, sir."

"Is the bike stolen?"

121

"Computer's checking."

The older man turned to the Trickster. "All right. Get off the bike; put your hands on the side of the squad car."

She fell in with his wishes, but when he started to frisk her, she bridled. "What do you think you're doing?"

"Looking for concealed weapons," he said coolly. When he had finished, he opened the rear door of the squad car and motioned her inside. "Get in. *Now.*"

The Trickster started to protest, but thought better of it. These men weren't responding at all to her attempts at control. At least Marchbanks had had to struggle to defy her.

"All right, Simmonds," she heard him say. "I'll take her in and book her. Check in with me before you go off duty."

The words made no sense to the Trickster. What did it mean to 'book her'? She suspected the phrase 'take her in' did not mean they were offering her shelter. The two men finished and the older one joined his companion in the front of the vehicle. No one spoke to the Trickster as they started away. Her uneasiness grew and strengthened. For the first time she felt—not irritation, not anger, but—fear.

17

With a satisfied sigh, the Dreamweaver laid her shuttle down and stretched her aching shoulders. It was working: the way she was winding Ohmiden's gift into the pattern. She could feel the stolen power restraining the Trickster.

A faint noise spun the old woman around. The Weaver was there, watching her.

"Don't you knock anymore?" she demanded.

He smiled an apology. "I felt the changes in the Loom; I came to see how you were doing it. That's the power Ohmiden stole, is it not?" At her nod he went on. "Your use of it is brilliant. You've clipped her pinions—yet you still have quite a bit of the silk left."

The old woman nodded. "If the Trickster went after me directly, I'm sure she could break through what I've woven; but for some reason, she seems to be avoiding direct assaults."

"She is devious."

"I don't think so," the Dreamweaver responded. "She faces constraints that are no part of my weaving; the Five face the same. 'Tsan's world is not reconciled to mystery."

The Weaver was silent. "So what next?" he asked at last.

"Should we tell the Five, or their Allies, that we have lessened the Trickster's power?"

Elgonar considered. "Even thus weakened, the Trickster is

dangerous. I would not give the Five cause for false optimism."

Eikoheh raised her eyebrows. "Or cause for real hope? They went feeling very overmatched. This might encourage them."

"I will ask the others." The god laid a hand on the old woman's shoulder. "In the meantime, rest."

His words summoned a prickle of unshed tears as Eikoheh was reminded of Ohmiden. She managed a weak smile, but words were beyond her.

"Brigid!" Angel whispered. "Come here!"

Brigid followed Angel out to the manure pile. "What's up?"

"Maybe nothing—maybe a problem. You haven't reached Alexandra, have you?" At her negative gesture, Angel continued. "Well, Mark reminded me that it's *summer,* and lots of students leave campus. What if she's away? We've got to find out."

"Have you got a plan?"

"Well, the skeleton of one. See, someone needs to call the school and try to weasel out whether she's enrolled for the summer term. I'd do it, but I don't see how I can without causing some problems when Kelly gets her phone bill. Besides, I don't want to worry the others until we know the worst."

Brigid nodded. "Okay. I think I can manage the phone. Cut through the pasture to Kelly's and I'll meet you there."

"You're going to *ask* her?" Angel demanded, almost forgetting to keep her voice down.

"Sure. This is the Brigid Chandler Direct Approach. I ask permission, give her a couple of bucks to pay for the call, and—presto!—long-distance call with no questions asked. Go on, Angel. I'll see you in a few minutes."

A short time later, having extracted the university's phone number from Information, Angel dialed the number.

"Hello?" she said loftily. "I say, I hope you can help me out. I'm trying to get in touch with a friend of mine who's an undergraduate. Her name's Alexandra Scarsdale. I have her telephone number, but she hasn't been home, and I can't remember whether she said she'd be taking classes this summer or not. I thought perhaps you could tell me whether she's enrolled for the summer session?" There was a pause. "Alexandra Scarsdale." Angel looked over at Brigid and held her crossed fingers up. "Yes? She *is*. Oh good. Well, I guess I'll just have to keep ringing her, unless—I don't suppose you could tell me her address, so I could drop by with a note? It would be such a pity to *miss* her." Angel snatched a pencil. "E-fifty-two Dunster House. Thanks *ever* so much. Goodbye." Angel hung up. "Success!" she crowed. "She's there *and* we have her address. How do you feel about a trip to Boston?"

"Something tells me I'd better answer in the affirmative. But I can't get us all into my car, and I'm not doing the negotiating—if you know what I mean. We could go tomorrow; I'm not working on Fridays this month."

"Tomorrow! All *right!*" Suddenly, Angel's face fell. "But tomorrow's the Competitive Trail Ride! We have to work on it!"

"Friday's the only day off I have," Brigid said. "Ask Kelly whether she can manage without you."

Angel thumped her fist into her palm. "She's already complained that she's understaffed. She'll *kill* us if we rat out!"

"*I* didn't volunteer. Tell the Five that I'll take two of them with me to Boston tomorrow." Brigid took pity on her. "Cheer up, Angel. We may get her on the phone before we leave."

Angel managed to smile. "Yeah. Besides, the important thing is finding her, not who's there when we run her to earth. Let's go back. It's got to be time for chores."

The Trickster paced her cage. The men had *told* her she didn't have to answer any questions. She recalled their droning

125

singsong: "You have the right to remain silent . . ." Why were they so angry with her when she chose not to speak? Many of the questions she heard lurking in their minds *had* no answers—or no answers they would accept. If she told them she was a god from another world it would be disastrous. So instead, they kept her caged—waiting for the judge to set bail, whatever that meant. She had no allies, no hope of aid. Perhaps she could pull herself back across the void, but what if she failed? What if the attempt depleted her power still further? Besides, to retreat would be to concede to the Weaver, and she couldn't bear that!

Time crawled past, while she maintained her dogged silence. She paced—and worried.

Miles away from the Trickster, Alexandra struggled with a different sort of prison: she could not find her way out of her own disordered mind. People spoke to her, but their words evoked no response, their faces evoked no sign of recognition. She ate what was set before her—or some of it—and slept when she felt the need. She was passive, withdrawn; nothing shook her.

Isaac Marchbanks stifled a sigh. Talking with Alexandra was worse than talking to a wall. He let his gaze wander around the little cubicle, as he sought another topic of conversation. He noticed that someone had covered the mirror with a pillowcase. "Did you cover the mirror, Alexandra?" he asked. No response. He removed the shrouding pillowcase, watching her reaction. She made a brief, agitated gesture, then turned her back to him.

"It's a mirror, Alexandra," Isaac said as he unhooked it from the wall. "It won't hurt you. It just reflects the room—see?" He held it out to her. She turned away. "What is it that frightens you, Alexandra? Is it something you see in the mirror?" He held it in front of her face again.

126

She shut her eyes. He waited several minutes, but she did not relent. He suppressed a sigh. "I going now, Alexandra, and I will take the mirror away. I'll talk with you again tomorrow."

In the hallway, he ran into a colleague. "How's the Scarsdale girl?" the man asked.

Isaac sighed. "I got a reaction out of her—but not a hopeful sign. She had covered her mirror; when I uncovered it, she reacted with distress. When I pushed her, she closed down completely. Damned if I know what to do."

"Remember what I said about electroshock therapy."

"I do," Isaac admitted. "But I'd rather exhaust other options first."

The other man shrugged. "Well, good luck."

When he reached his office, Isaac propped the mirror up on his desk and collapsed into his chair. Alexandra had told him about the episode with the mirror in her bathroom; no wonder mirrors bothered her. But he had really hoped she would break her silence; instead, she had withdrawn further. Nothing he tried worked. Maybe electroshock was the answer—but not yet. He'd give it a little longer—through the weekend, anyway. Then, if there wasn't significant improvement, he would move her to the psychiatric hospital and see what wisdom his colleagues there could offer.

"Look, isn't there *someone* you want to contact?" one of the Trickster's jailors asked her again. "You can make a call. Surely there's someone who's worried about you."

The Trickster shook her head. She was used to being alone. The worst thing was the boredom. One of the guards had offered her something to read, but she was loath to spend the power now to acquire the written language. In the world of the Loom, only the Vemathi used writing much—and mostly to

127

keep accounts. If only she had a mirror. Scrying did not use much power, and it would amuse her. But there was no mirror in her cell—

She broke off the thought with a muffled oath. Had her wits gone begging? She pulled the cord of her sunglasses over her head and began gazing into their mirrored surface. An image formed slowly. She didn't guide her scrying, just opened her mind to anyone involved in the search for 'Tsan. As the image steadied, her eyes widened. She had expected one of the Weaver's allies, or perhaps 'Tsan herself. What she saw brought laughter to her lips. Of course! It was simple! Why hadn't she thought of it? As she smiled to herself, the image in her glass raised his head and looked straight at her. The shock on his face pulled her into action; she dismissed the scrying swiftly. There was no sense in frightening poor Isaac Marchbanks to death. *He* was going to get her out of this place!

18

It was finally decided that Ychass and Vihena would go to Boston with Brigid. Vihena was so eager for action that she didn't argue when asked to leave her sword behind. Angel, Mark, and Brice turned their energies to organizing Remarr, Iobeh, and Karivet to help out with the Competitive Trail Ride.

The next morning, Brigid and Ychass stopped at the stable around seven to pick up Vihena.

"How are you getting along with the Newcombs?" Brigid greeted her.

Vihena smiled a little ruefully. "In the interests of making myself welcome, I baked a batch of honey cakes. Mr. Newcomb said he wasn't going to let me go back to Greece."

"I wouldn't have thought that, even for intrigue's sake, you would consent to do such a *womanly* task," Ychass drawled.

Vihena didn't rise to the bait; instead, she said to Brigid, "How are you managing with our shapeshifter?"

Brigid laughed. "I was worried about how uncomfortable Ychass would be on my couch. It's not really long enough, and it is *very* lumpy. Imagine my surprise when I found a large gray tabby cat asleep on the cushions!"

Ychass's expression held a hint of feline smugness. "Cats can make themselves comfortable in nearly any situation."

129

The drive to the outskirts of Boston took them a little over three hours. As they drew nearer the city, Ychass and Vihena were astounded at the crowded neighborhoods. "There are so many *people,*" Ychass said more than once. "How can they *bear* being pressed together like grains of sand in a dune?" The city was vast and terribly untidy; there were people and buildings everywhere. They had never imagined the world could contain so many souls.

Finally, Brigid guided the car into a space that seemed several sizes too small. "Well, we're here," she told them. "This is Harvard Square. Come on. Let's look around."

Both Ychass and Vihena watched as Brigid pushed coins into the slot on the meter. When it made a strange, churring noise, Vihena asked why it ate metal. Brigid explained as well as she could. When they reached Harvard Yard, a student gave them complicated directions, then pointed them toward the river and suggested that if they didn't find Dunster House, they ask again when they were nearer.

As it turned out, they found it fairly easily. Dunster House was a huge, sprawling brick structure that looked large enough to house a castleful of students. They went through the main entry hall into a courtyard; there were many doors and over each one was a neatly stenciled legend. Brigid steered them to E ENTRY, and up to the fifth floor. Vihena strode to the door and knocked. The knocking echoed in the stairwell like the pounding of the hand of fate. There was no answer.

"Oh, merciless gods," Vihena groaned. "Where *can* she be?"

"We could leave her a note," Brigid suggested.

"You'll have to write it," Ychass reminded her. "We are not familiar with the written language."

After a moment's scribbling, Brigid read her note for their approval.

130

11:20 A.M., July 26th.
Dear Alexandra: Vihena and Ychass are in Boston for the day. We hope to connect with you before we go back to Vermont. We'll come back around 1:00 P.M., and again right before we head out of town. Leave a note if you can't be here. Our departure time is flexible, and we would REALLY like to see you! If we miss you, Ychass is staying with me, Brigid Chandler, at 115 Harrington St. Apt. 3, Barre, VT 05641. Phone: (802) 470-5758. Please get in touch with us; we want desperately to see you. Brigid, Ychass, & Vihena.

"Can you sign it or make some mark she would recognize?"

Vihena took the pen and scrawled the emblem of the House of Moirre at the bottom of the note. They sealed the note and wedged it between the door and the frame, where Alexandra couldn't miss seeing it. Then, they went in search of lunch.

The Trickster left the police station with Isaac Marchbanks. As he unlocked his car, he gave her a harried look and said, "You owe me, Antekkereh."

"Owe you what?" the Trickster responded warily.

"Well, at *least* an explanation. Let's go back to the Square, get something to eat—then you can explain."

She studied his profile as he pulled into traffic, then said, "I have the right to remain silent." Her words were almost a question. She didn't *want* to explain—but he had used her name.

"I'm not putting you on trial," he protested. "I just want to know what the hell is going on."

The Trickster was silent. When they reached the Square, they walked through the busy streets to a small, quiet café, in the basement of a house. A bored waiter handed them menus. The Trickster watched Isaac, copying him as he scanned the menu. After a moment, he laid it aside.

131

"Do you know what you want?" he asked; then, his gaze sharpened on the menu in her hands. It was upside down.

"I *want* not to have to give you an explanation."

"I meant to *eat,*" he clarified.

"What are you having?"

"A cup of cappuccino and a croissant."

She nodded. "That sounds fine. I'll have that, too." As he ordered for them, she wondered idly what sort of food the waiter might bring. It couldn't be as awful as what she had been eating for the last several days.

"How about that explanation?"

"Where should I begin?"

"At the beginning?" Isaac offered.

"That makes for a long tale," she replied with a shrug. "Before the beginning of history, I came to be, born of the mischief in the Mother's laughter. When she saw what she had done, she told me that I should be the one to keep her other children from growing complacent. Through the ages of my youth—"

"Let's narrow the focus a little," Isaac Marchbanks cut in, a hint of sardonic amusement in his tone. "Or we may be here all week. How did you get the bike, Antekkereh? Did you steal it?"

"I am not a thief!" she blazed. "I understand the game and I don't cheat. I bought it," she added, as an afterthought.

"Where did you get the money?"

"People gave it to me."

"Wait a minute! You have people who would give you enough money to buy an expensive motorcycle, but you stay in jail four days because you can't think of anyone who'd bail you out?"

"There is more to caring than simply giving money."

Isaac Marchbanks sighed. "True enough. So let's leave the bike for now. How do you know Alexandra?"

132

The Trickster shrugged. This was bad. She considered expending the power to nudge the waiter into interrupting, but before she could do this, he arrived with their food. After he left, Isaac tried to pick up the conversation.

"You told me Alexandra doesn't know your name. You can't be much of a friend. Why do you want to see her so badly?"

"She is bedeviled by fear and memory. I want to give her peace."

Isaac said, with a hint of grimness, "Is that true?"

"Would I lie to you?" she parried.

"You certainly might not tell me the whole truth."

This counterthrust startled the Trickster into laughter. "I certainly might not," she agreed, with reluctant respect.

"*How* would you give her peace?"

The Trickster picked words carefully as she blended truth and misrepresentation. "Her memories cause her pain: she cannot believe what she remembers and does not remember that which she believes. I could resolve her conflict—make her belief and memories run parallel again. I am something of a catalyst."

The doctor silently pondered her words. Looking up, he captured her gaze. "Antekkereh. I want you to tell me why you want to give Alexandra peace. Is it for her sake—*or for your own?*"

The Trickster wrenched free of his pinioning eyes, but she could not evade his question. "I want to be free," she whispered. "This is one way to accomplish that. But it would also free Alexandra from her torment." She met his eyes. "I would give her peace, Isaac. I swear it. I swear it by my name."

The doctor's expression clouded. "But is it a peace she would choose, Antekkereh?"

The Trickster looked away. "Isaac, I don't know. But I do believe that it is the only peace she will find, here."

Isaac was silent. Part of him longed to believe her, longed to turn over some of the responsibility for this perplexing case to Antekkereh. But peace meant different things to different people. "Tell me," he said, when the silence began to feel confining. "Of what do you want to be free?"

"I want to be free of restraints."

"But we all have restraints; it is the price of being civilized."

"*Civilized!*" she snarled. "I have no use for order." An avid—almost feral—expression lit her face. "I was meant to be a sower of chaos! I want to ride the winds, laugh with the storm, and dance with fire! And I want to fulfill my destiny to keep the rest of the Mother's children from complacency!"

"It sounds lonely to me."

"*Lonely?*" The word was a scornful laugh. "What use have I for others?"

"That's exactly what I mean." He reached across the table and caught her wrist. "I need your promise that you will give up trying to see Alexandra. She needs peace, but she must find it in her own way."

"Very well," the Trickster replied. "I promise—on my honor." The Trickster's honor, she knew, was double-edged.

His grip tightened on her wrist. "Antekkereh, swear on your name."

She could not break free. Between the binding of her name and the keen edges of her honor there was not space enough to maneuver. Rebellion smoldered in her eyes, and bitterness colored her words. "I, Antekkereh, swear that I will not come next or nigh 'Tsan—whom you know as Alexandra. I swear I will neither impose my will nor use my influence upon her. This I swear on my name, and may the Namegiver hear me and hold me to my oath. Are you satisfied, Isaac Marchbanks?"

"Yes." He released her wrist. "Look, Antekkereh, have you got a place to stay?"

134

His change of subject caught her off guard. "No. But I'll find someplace."

"Come back to the office," he suggested. "I'll give you a spare key and directions to my house. You can stay with me."

"Don't you fear I'll murder you in your bed?"

"I am far more afraid *for* you than *of* you, Antekkereh," he said pensively.

She set her cup back on the saucer with a sharp click. "More fool you."

Isaac Marchbanks smiled. "I don't think so. Not this time. Come on: let's go."

Brigid picked the restaurant: a Middle-Eastern deli called The Hungry Persian. After they'd eaten, they wandered around, watching street-jugglers, and observing the masses of people.

"I've never been to a market this large," Ychass said.

"Nor one with such diversity of dress and behavior," Vihena said. "Look at *her,*" she added, nodding toward a tall woman in black leather, with neon-orange hair and mirrored sunglasses.

Brigid grinned. "It certainly takes all kinds. You know, I think it's time we headed back to Alexandra's."

As they walked back to Dunster House, each was careful not to voice doubts or fears and none of them—not even Vihena—noticed the extraordinarily flamboyant woman following them.

Their note was still in the door, undisturbed.

"Curse the perversity of the gods!" Vihena said. "We are so close to 'Tsan I can almost *smell* her, and"—she spread her hands in exasperation—"she is *not home.* What must we do? Camp on her doorstep?"

"It *is* frustrating," Brigid agreed. "Let's knock again; maybe she was asleep before."

135

Vihena pounded loudly enough to wake the dead. As the echoes died, the door across the landing opened.

A young man looked out. "Are you looking for Alexandra?"

"Yes!" Brigid responded. "We're just here for the day, but we really wanted to catch up with her."

A look of trouble crossed his face. "She's in Stillman—that's the Infirmary. She had kind of a—breakdown, I guess. I don't know whether she can have visitors."

"She's *ill*?" Vihena demanded, before Brigid's hand closed on her wrist.

"She kind of lost it—freaked out, or something. It might have been drugs."

Or a spell? Ychass's thought-voice queried. *Remember, the Trickster is here.*

The young man gave them directions to the Infirmary, and they set out, leaving their note in the door—just in case.

None of them noticed the figure that slipped inside the doorway from which they had come. As they headed to the Infirmary, the Trickster climbed the stairs to Alexandra's aerie. She pounced upon the note like a lioness on her prey and tucked it into her pocket. She couldn't read it, but she knew she could find someone to read it for her. And though she had given her word that she would leave 'Tsan alone, she had made no promises at all regarding the Wanderer's friends and allies!

19

The Infirmary was located in a glass-and-concrete tower over-looking the Square. Brigid led them to the elevator and guided her friends inside. The doors hissed shut and they ascended.

"We'd like to see Alexandra Scarsdale," Brigid told the receptionist. "We're friends from out of town. Alexandra's neighbor told us she was here."

The white-clad woman looked doubtful. "Dr. Marchbanks said no visitors, but if you like, I'll check with him."

Brigid nodded thanks and the receptionist disappeared. She returned a moment later.

"Doctor Marchbanks is with a patient. If you'd like to wait, he should be finished in ten or fifteen minutes."

"Thank you. We'll wait," Brigid said.

Ychass raised an eyebrow. "Actually," she said aloud, "I think I'll run that errand I mentioned. It shouldn't take very long." Under the words, her thought-voice gave a different message. *The guardian doesn't think Dr. Marchbanks will let us see his patient. I'll shift and sneak in to see her.*

Wait, Brigid thought back. *Let me see if I can help you.* "Maybe you could find a nice card for her," she suggested aloud, then turned to the nurse. "What room is she in, so we can send her flowers or something?"

"She's in room six-twelve."

Brigid sent Ychass an image of the numeral 612, and a hint that it would probably be near or on the door. Then, Ychass left the waiting area; she shifted to fly-shape, and made her way past the guardian into the maze of corridors beyond.

It took longer than Ychass had expected to find the room with the proper rune. Luck was with her; the door was open. The shapeshifter flitted inside, to find 'Tsan, pale and terribly vulnerable, asleep. Ychass took her own form, then, very gently, shook the young woman awake. For an instant, there was welcome and joy on Alexandra's face. "Ychass," she said, both aloud and inwardly. Then fear clouded her gaze, and on its heels, rage. She sat up, pointing a shaking finger at the shapeshifter.

"Get away!" she cried. "*You can't be here! You're not real!*"

"But I am here," Ychass said, gripping 'Tsan's hand. "And I *am* real; you know it! 'Tsan, you *named* me!"

"Go *away!*" Alexandra screamed, her voice spiraling upward. "I don't know you! *I never named you! You're not real!! I'M NOT 'TSAN!!!*"

The sound of running feet recalled Ychass to her situation. Instinctively, she shifted—but not to a fly. When Dr. Marchbanks arrived with two orderlies, his patient, her face contorted with terror and rage, was flinging all the movable objects within reach at a cowering gray cat. As the orderlies moved to restrain her, the doctor shut the door. Ychass was trapped in the room.

"Alexandra. Alexandra," he soothed. "It's all right. It's just a cat; nothing to be afraid of. We'll take it out."

At his words, Alexandra's terror eased. The doctor indicated that the orderlies release her. Alexandra buried her head beneath the pillow. Isaac stared down at her in silence.

"I'm taking the cat away, Alexandra. If you want to talk, ring for a nurse and I'll come." There was no response.

Ychass crouched, her ears flat to her skull and her eyes shut tight, the picture of feline distress. She allowed Marchbanks to gather her up but as soon as they were in the corridor, she became a writhing, spitting, scratching beast. They struggled together, the doctor trying hard not to hurt what he thought was a terrified cat. Ychass, outrage blazing in her silver eyes, bit the man. He dropped her. She streaked away, seeking the solitude to shift her shape again and escape.

The orderlies charged after her. Isaac stared at his bleeding, throbbing hand, but saw in his mind's eye the cat's intelligent, silvery eyes. According to Alexandra, shapeshifters could not change the color of their eyes. No wonder, he tried to tell himself, she had been unhinged by the stray cat. He shivered with a mixture of awe and dread.

The orderlies returned. "I can't imagine how it got away," one of them said. "It's as though it vanished into thin air."

The other young man nodded. "We were hoping to spare you the rabies shots."

Isaac shrugged. "You did your best, I'm sure. How do you suppose it got in here in the first place?"

The first orderly smiled crookedly. "The same way it got out."

Vihena and Brigid knew something was amiss. Ychass had sent them a one-word warning, *Trouble,* before she eluded her pursuers. Thus, the two who waited were prepared for the sight of a doctor, flanked by orderlies, his blood shockingly red on the white of his coat.

"Oh, Doctor," the receptionist began before she took in the blood. "Good *heavens!*"

"It looks worse than it is—I hope," he told her with a strained smile. "I'm off to Emergency."

"These young women want to know whether Alexandra Scarsdale can have visitors?"

139

"*No!*" He surprised even himself with the sharpness of his denial. "If you tell me your names," he added more gently, "I'll let her know you were inquiring after her."

"I am Vihena Khesst and my friend is Brigid Chandler," Vihena replied. "Please tell her we are very concerned."

"Vihena?" the doctor repeated, his face going blank with surprise. "*Vihena Khesst.*" Not a question: recognition.

"And Brigid Chandler," Brigid added brightly, hoping to divert him. "Doctor, you're *bleeding*—we don't want to detain you."

"No." His expression grew distant. "No." The orderlies began herding him along. "Wait!" he called, turning back. "I want to talk to you later—when I've gotten cleaned up."

"Fine," Brigid said. "We've got some errands to run; should we think about stopping back around"—she consulted her watch—"three?"

Dr. Marchbanks looked as though he had guessed the falseness of Brigid's suggestion, but the orderlies prevented his arguing. The three disappeared into the elevator; shortly after that, Ychass returned and they made good their escape.

Once back on the street, Brigid towed them to an outdoor café. "Now," she said when they were settled, "what happened, Ychass?"

The shapeshifter reported in a cool, uninflected voice. "It is my guess," she added, "that the Trickster has put 'Tsan under a spell. At the start, she knew me—then, fear and anger overrode her mind. To me, it smells of the Trickster."

Vihena nodded, her eyes troubled.

"So how do we go about breaking her free?" Brigid asked, hiding her own doubts in a matter-of-fact approach. "If we kidnapped her, would that help?"

"*Kidnapped?*" Vihena demanded. "Just how were you planning to do that? From what Ychass tells us, 'Tsan won't be of a mind to cooperate!"

Ychass frowned. "I don't think we three can solve this by ourselves," she said heavily. "We need Iobeh."

"*Yes!*" Vihena agreed. "She could soothe 'Tsan with her spirit-gift."

Ychass nodded. "And without the rage and terror of the Trickster's spell tearing at her, 'Tsan would know us and listen to the message of the Weaver and the others."

"But how to get Iobeh here?" Vihena mused.

"That is harder than you know," Brigid put in. "That doctor—Marchbanks, wasn't it?—recognized Vihena's name. That means your friend has told him about you." She paused to let the import sink in.

Vihena's brow knit. "Is that a difficulty? Surely it means 'Tsan trusts him enough to make an ally of him."

"Unless I'm much mistaken," Brigid said, "that Dr. Marchbanks is a psychiatrist; someone who tries to heal madness. If Alexandra has told him about you, it's my guess he thinks you are all figments of her imagination."

" 'You're not real,' " Ychass quoted, understanding flaring. " 'I don't believe in you.' Oh, Brigid! She has let him convince her that we are the dreams of her disordered mind!"

Brigid nodded.

"But we are *real*. Surely he will have recognized that by now," Vihena said. "And if we are real, then it follows that 'Tsan is not mad."

"I doubt a psychiatrist would be swayed by the coincidence of a name," Brigid replied. "He's much more apt to think Alexandra somehow incorporated real people into her madness—or worse, that *we* are exploiting some weakness of hers for our own ends."

141

The others were silent while they pondered Brigid's words. After some time, Vihena raised an eyebrow and murmured, "This is a strange world." Then she fixed Ychass with a keen look. "Would Iobeh have to be in 'Tsan's presence to work her healing magic? You can cast your mind over distance. Can she?"

Ychass considered. "I'm not sure. I know she can affect people if she can see them, but whether she can touch a mind over distance is a question I cannot answer."

"Could you *ask* her from here?" Brigid queried.

"Yes," Ychass sighed. "But such an undertaking might alert the Trickster to our presence, and thus warned, she might attack. If you think it worth the gamble, I am willing to try."

Vihena spoke first. "Try. If Iobeh can help 'Tsan, we may be able to resolve the whole matter."

Ychass closed her eyes and sent her thought-voice, like a distant trumpet, to Iobeh. Several minutes passed before the shapeshifter opened her eyes. "Iobeh says she cannot touch 'Tsan's heart from such a distance. She would need to be quite close, though not in sight. She has touched 'Tsan from the next room; I showed her the place where we were made to wait, and she *thinks* she might be able to reach from there."

Vihena suppressed a groan. "So how do we get her here?"

"Let me think about that," Brigid put in. "I could always take another 'field trip' next Friday—or actually, *two* weeks from today. Next week everybody will be at that big dressage show in Wellesley."

Ychass heard Vihena's inner fight with recriminations, none of which showed in her expression. "Where is Wellesley?"

"It isn't too far from Boston. Maybe we can get Iobeh here from there, but"—she forestalled further questions with an upraised hand—"but I want Angel's help with that planning. She's really good at that kind of intrigue, and I'm not. Look, do you think we should head back to Vermont now?"

"But you told the doctor we would come back," Vihena protested.

"Nope. I *asked* him whether we ought to think about coming back. So we're thinking—and to me, anyway, it doesn't seem like a good thought."

Ychass's thought-voice, rich with amusement, brushed Brigid's mind. *It is well you had the foresight to consider Vihena's troublesome honor.*

Brigid's lips quirked. *I'm a quick learner.*

Vihena shrugged. "You are too devious for me, Brigid, but in this case, I think we'd best take your advice." She rose. "Shall we?"

Alexandra waited until she was certain she was alone; then she waited even longer. She was trapped in her fear. She knew the cult was after her again; *they* were trying to drive her into madness. She realized it when *they* sent the false vision of the shapeshifter. And she knew that Isaac Marchbanks would be unable to protect her: *he had seen a cat*. If he were truly free of *their* influence, he would have seen *nothing*—for nothing was there. *Ychass was not real*. But Isaac had seen it—not the woman, but the cat. He had *seen* it; he was touched by *them*.

Another thought chilled her. Perhaps he was *one of them!* He was the only person she had told about her delusions. How else would *they* know how to torment her? It made sense. It made all too much sense.

Betrayal burned through her. She had *liked* him. She had *trusted* him! And all the time, he was one of *them*. Cautiously, she sorted through the things the tutor had brought from her room. There was not much of use: several changes of clothing; a hairbrush; a toothbrush and paste; a stick of deodorant; her wallet with thirty dollars and her all-important bank machine card. No weapons; no talisman that would protect her; several

143

useless books. She carefully packed her battered bookbag, adding an apple and two cookies saved from lunch. Then, she waited. During evening visiting hours there were lots of extra people in the halls. She could probably get to the stairway and then it was just a matter of running down a few flights and getting on the elevator from the third or fourth floor. Then, she'd be free—free to disappear to where no one could find her.

Alexandra ate her supper, stowed the roll and orange in her bookbag, and when the time was right, put her plan into effect. It was easier than she had imagined. Long before any of the infirmary staff realized she had gone, Alexandra had melted into the twilight and the crowds of homeward bound commuters.

20

Eikoheh cursed, quietly and passionately, over what she saw in her pattern. They had been so close! *The shapeshifter had actually touched 'Tsan—and for nothing!* She finished all the curses she knew and began inventing new ones. A chuckle stopped her; she spun around.

"You are very inventive, Dreamweaver," the Namegiver said.

"Don't you ever knock?" she demanded testily.

The Namegiver shrugged. "Rarely. It lessens the dramatic effect of my entrance. Tell me what is wrong with your pattern."

"It is plain for you to read."

"Plain to you, or to Elgonar; to me, it is so much cloth."

Eikoheh pointed. "This is the shapeshifter; and that, 'Tsan. They came close—touched, even—but the pattern refused to take the path I had envisioned. You see? These other colors are now coming to the surface, not the ones I chose. 'Tsan's thread is buried within the fabric. I cannot find the Trickster's influence, but it *must* be there. Surely, events would not be so contrary without the guiding of her hand."

"If the difficulty has to do with 'Tsan, the Trickster is not to blame. She has bound herself not to use her influence upon 'Tsan." The Namegiver looked thoughtful. "She called upon me as witness. I cannot imagine who could have forced her to such a promise; but I am grateful."

145

"She won't use her influence upon 'Tsan." The old woman repeated slowly, "Not upon 'Tsan. Not upon 'Tsan! Then she will move against the Five!" She turned back to the loom, pounced on the shuttle wound with the power stolen from the Trickster. A spark of wicked amusement kindled in her eyes. "I know how to be a nuisance. Do you think, Namegiver, that the Trickster would like being thrown in contact with 'Tsan after she has bound herself with her own promise?"

The Namegiver raised her eyebrows. "Can you do that?"

"I can try," the Dreamweaver replied. "I am nearly certain I can tangle the Trickster's thread with 'Tsan's, but it will take some time to arrange. My pattern grows more slowly than events across the void move. I doubt I will be able to prevent the Trickster from striking some blow against the Five—if she knows where they are. I can only hope to deflect the worst of it—and then distract her."

"Do your best, Dreamweaver. I, for one, would enjoy watching the Trickster squirm in the grip of her own rash vow."

When Isaac Marchbanks got home, the Trickster was already there. Her eyes widened at the sight of his bandaged hand.

"What happened?" she asked him.

"It's a long story. Would you toss a couple of Lean Cuisines in the microwave? I'm not up to anything more ambitious."

The Trickster stared at him.

"In the *freezer*," he prompted—to no effect.

She hunched her shoulders. "I don't understand."

"Oh, for the love of heaven." He rolled his eyes. "Lean Cuisines: prepackaged frozen dinners; they live in the freezer in boxes." He gestured to the upper door of an oblong metal box. "Pick out something you can stand to eat—I'm not fussy. Then toss them in the microwave."

146

"What's the 'microwave'?"

"What *planet* are you from?"

She smiled sheepishly. "One that hasn't 'microwaves.'"

Isaac actually laughed. "Look, if you just get those damned dinners out and unwrap them, I'll do the rest." He held up his bandaged right hand. "I'm not up to wrestling with packaging."

The Trickster did her best; the packaging was stubborn. When they were both seated at the kitchen table, and Isaac was awkwardly eating left-handed, the Trickster made another attempt to get him to tell her the tale of his injury.

"You said it was a long story; do we have time for it now?"

"I got bitten by a stray cat," he said.

The Trickster eyed him with mocking severity. "That is a short story. You must have left a great deal out."

Isaac was torn between irritation and amusement. "People generally say something is a long story when they don't want to tell it at all," he said.

"Oh," she replied. "I didn't understand that. I apologize; I didn't mean to pry."

Isaac's lips quirked in a cynical smile. The answering gleam in her eyes showed him he had been right to doubt her.

"Point to you," she conceded. "I should have known I couldn't fox you with that! But I am dying of curiosity."

He studied her for another moment. "You're very good; I wasn't entirely sure I was right. You won't really die of your curiosity, Antekkereh."

"No," she agreed, menace tingeing her voice, "but *you* may."

"Ah-ha! Intimidation!" He grinned at her. "Now I can refuse to tell you and not even feel guilty about it."

The Trickster's anger bled away. "I suppose I ought to have guessed it would have that effect on you," she said dryly.

147

"I've given you ample clues," he agreed.

Slowly, her expression clouded to seriousness. "I don't understand: why *aren't* you afraid of me? Everyone else is."

"Everyone?" he asked her.

She looked up, troubled, and nodded.

"Why are they afraid?"

"Because I'm wild and unpredictable; because they never know what I will do next, and they have no way to curb me."

"Do you want everyone to be afraid of you?"

"I never thought about it," she admitted. "It never mattered before."

"Before what?" he probed.

"Before I met someone I couldn't bully." Her eyes swam with unshed tears.

With his good hand he touched her cheek. "It's not too late to change, Antekkereh."

They were connected by the touch of fingers on a cheek until she pulled away. "Will you teach me to read?" she asked.

"*What?*"

"I thought—you knew I couldn't—"

His common sense kicked in. "Of course I'll teach you—or I should say, I'll try. But you might do better with someone who is trained to teach adults to read."

"I'd rather learn from you," she said. Something in his reaction made her relax. "After all," she added with wide-eyed malice, "how hard can reading be if you can do it?"

It took a moment, but then, they were both laughing.

Alexandra was afraid to sleep. She knew *they* could get into her dreams. She found a diner, and sat, drinking coffee and pretending to read, until she was kicked out at closing time. She didn't know where she could go to get away from *them*. The silent, deserted streets made her edgy. It was easy to imagine

148

that *they* had somehow spirited the other people away, leaving her as exposed as a shell on the beach. Perhaps there were no other people; perhaps they were merely images invented by *them*.

Alexandra fought this train of thought. She knew other people weren't merely one of *their* inventions; some people had to be real. Ahead, she saw a Dunkin' Donuts shop. To her anxious mind, it seemed an oasis of light and safety. There was a bored waiter inside. The smell of doughnuts choked her, but she could always drink more coffee. Morning would be a better time to make decisions, when sunlight could chase away night fears and despair.

The Trickster learned to read with frightening speed. As Isaac thought about reading, and the sound each letter represented, the Trickster lifted the background from his mind, as well as his verbal explanation. Before the evening was over, she had mastered printed matter. Sensing Isaac's uneasiness, she stopped showing him how well she understood and spent the rest of the evening forming the letters of the alphabet with her own awkward hand. After Isaac had gone to sleep, she got out the note she had found in Alexandra's door. She puzzled out most of it and listed a few things that stumped her: "1:00 P.M."; "115 Harrington St. Apt. 3, Barre, VT 05641"; and "Phone: (802) 470-5758." Just as she had finished writing and had hidden away the note, there came a sharp, shrilling sound.

"Isaac?" she called, made nervous by the strange sound. He came into the kitchen, his hair rumpled and his eyes heavy with sleep. He made a grab for a small, oddly shaped thing on the wall and held it to his ear.

"Hello? . . . What? What do you mean, *gone?* . . . When? . . . She's in no shape to be on her own. Have you called the police? . . . Well tell them to list her as missing. She may be a danger to herself . . . I didn't think she was suicidal, but what do I know? All right. Call me if there's any word—and tell the police they can call if they have questions. I'll be in early tomorrow . . . okay . . . goodbye." He replaced the object in its rack. "Why are you still up?" he asked the Trickster.

"I'm not tired. Is something wrong?"

"Alexandra's disappeared."

"Disappeared?"

He nodded grimly. "She packed up some of her stuff and left the infirmary. Antekkereh, she shouldn't be on her own. It isn't safe for her."

"But how will you find her?"

Isaac dropped into a kitchen chair and leaned his head against his good hand. "I don't know. The infirmary called the police—but I don't really expect much from them." He sighed. "I wish those young women had come back. They might be able to offer some insight."

"What young women?"

"Vihena Khesst and Brigid Chandler," he said.

"*Brigid Chandler?*" the Trickster repeated.

"Do you know her?"

The Trickster handed him the stolen note. Isaac gave her a measuring look.

"How did you get this?"

"I stole it; I thought it might be important. Could they have taken Alexandra hostage?"

"Hostage? I hadn't thought of that. Ychass," he whispered. His hand throbbed; he remembered the cool, silver eyes in the face of the stray cat. He shuddered, then forced his mind back to the present. "You're right; this is important. I think tomorrow I'll give this Brigid a phone call."

Phone call: the word clicked in her memory—the magic these people had for talking across distance. "You mustn't!" she

150

blurted. "That will warn her. She must not have wanted to talk to you since she didn't come back. Why would a phone call be any different? She'd think you had stolen her note."

Isaac frowned. "What do you recommend?"

"Can't we go to where she lives?"

"It's in Vermont."

"Does that make it impossible?" the Trickster demanded. "She came here; surely we can go there."

"We?"

The Trickster caught Isaac's wrist, made him look at her. "Won't you let me help you, Isaac? You've done so much for me."

"Let's sleep on it. We'll talk more in the morning." He got up, but stood looking at her for a long moment. "Please go to bed," he said finally. "It makes me tired to watch you."

"I will; I promise. Good night, Isaac."

"Good night, Antekkereh."

There was still no word of Alexandra in the morning. After rehashing her case with his colleagues, Isaac decided he'd better go look for this Brigid Chandler in Vermont. He scooped up his keys, locked his desk, and rose. Then he stopped short. Antekkereh stood in his doorway, watching him silently.

"You were going without me," she said. Her voice was colorless, untouched by accusation.

"I still may," he replied. "Give me one good reason why I should take you."

She hunched one shoulder. "There's no reason I *should* go— except that I'd *like* to go with you. Please, Isaac?"

Her manner was dignified without being haughty or scornful. But he could tell his answer mattered—maybe too much. "Why does it matter?"

"What can I say?" she responded. "If I tell you I just want to

151

be with you, you won't believe me; if I tell you I need to talk to this Brigid Chandler, it will make you nervous; if I tell you I'm afraid the temptation to seek out Alexandra and work my will upon her will overcome me, despite my promise, you will think less of me; if I tell you that I'm curious to see Vermont, you will think me silly and frivolous."

"Why don't you tell me the truth?"

"Isaac, all of that is true."

"But is it the whole truth?"

Her calm shattered. "Of course not! If I were to tell you the whole truth, we'd be here until the sun faded to an ember! Never mind. I'm sorry I asked." She whirled and strode out.

"Wait!" he called. She didn't even hesitate. Isaac hurried after her; he barely made the elevator. They were the elevator's only passengers. Antekkereh pointedly avoided looking at him.

"Do you still want to come with me?" he asked finally.

It seemed a long time before she spoke. "If you were one of my brothers, you would ask that question, and then, if I were fool enough to admit that I did, you would laugh and say, 'What a pity I won't take you, then.'"

"I'm not your brother," he said quietly. "If you'd still like to come, I'll take you with me."

The Trickster smiled sadly. "If I were made of as stern stuff as I like to think, I would now refrain from coming, since I can hear the uneasiness in your voice. But pride is a cold place to live. I'll be glad to come with you."

When they reached Barre, Isaac got directions and they made their way to Brigid's apartment building. She was not there.

"Now what?" Isaac asked. "Shall we sit and wait for her?"

"Lunch?" the Trickster countered. "Aren't you hungry?"

They found a diner and ate, then went back. This time, when they rang the bell, they heard a faint but cheerful voice. "Hang on! I'll be right there." Brigid Chandler answered the door, dressed for riding. Her eyes widened at the sight of them. "What can I do for you?"

"I'm Dr. Marchbanks," Isaac said. "I'd like to talk with you about Alexandra. This is—"

"I'm the Trickster," she cut in clearly, covering her own name in Isaac's mouth.

Oh shit, Brigid thought, then, panic fueling her thought-voice, *YCHASS!!*

The Trickster heard Ychass's prompt response, but didn't pay attention to the exchange. Instead, she focused on the shapeshifter's mind, to locate it like a star in a constellation.

Somehow, Brigid managed to move them inside. Isaac asked her questions about Alexandra, which she tried to answer with as much truth as she could. Finally, she took the offensive.

"Look, I'd *really* like to know how you found me—and why you bothered to come here."

It was Isaac's turn to be uncomfortable. "Alexandra disappeared last evening. She left the hospital without telling anyone where she was going. I thought she might have come here, and that she might have sworn you to secrecy, or something. Miss Chandler, I am concerned about Alexandra; she is delusional and perhaps paranoid. I'm afraid of what she might do."

Just then, they heard footsteps on the stairs. Ychass came in without knocking. "Goodness," she said. "I didn't realize you had company, Brigid."

"This is Dr. Marchbanks," Brigid explained, "and his friend—I'm sorry, I've forgotten your name."

If the Trickster hadn't been trying to follow Ychass and Brigid's inward conversation, she might have forestalled Isaac. When she didn't respond, the doctor said, "It's Antekkereh."

"Right," Brigid said. "Antekkereh."

The Trickster's head snapped up, her eyes blazing. "You

153

have no right to my name," she said, her fierce gaze boring into Brigid's. "Forget. *Forget!* Lest I strip away your memory!"

Brigid fought the pounding surf of the Trickster's power; but she could feel it sucking her under. *Forget! Forget!!* It pulled her toward a place where her spirit would be overwhelmed. *FORGET!* Brigid nodded—surrendered—and the Trickster released her. While the Trickster focused on Brigid, Ychass inched to the door. When the Trickster spun toward the shapeshifter, Ychass was out of reach, already racing down the stairs. With a cry, the Trickster followed.

Isaac stared after her, then turned back to Brigid. "What the hell is this all about?"

"What?" Brigid's eyes were glazed.

He grabbed her by the shoulder and shook. "This Trickster stuff. Who the hell is she—and why are you so afraid? You look like you've seen the dead walk."

"No. Just a god." Color was coming back into her face. "I hope Ychass got away."

"A *god?*" Isaac's voice cracked. "Antekkereh is no more a god than I am!"

Brigid shrugged. "Goddess, then."

"She's a mixed-up, overbearing, and rather disagreeable young woman; I certainly don't see signs of divinity in her!"

"You aren't looking for the right qualities," Brigid told him. A sudden sound from the street drew them to the top of the stairs. Brigid plunged downstairs and Isaac followed.

Traffic had been stopped by a huge, panic-stricken gray mare. The horse trumpeted as she reared and struck out. Brigid dove toward her, shrieking with her mind: *Ychass! Ychass!* The mare pivoted, teeth bared and ears pinned back tightly. As the horse's head snaked toward her, Brigid froze: instead of the silvery eyes she had expected, the horse's bulging orbs were a bright and impossible purple. A flailing hoof caught Brigid in the shoulder, sending her sprawling. The horse charged, while Brigid curled into the tightest ball she could.

"*Antekkereh, NO!!*" Isaac shouted. "Don't hurt her!"

The gray mare reared over Brigid's huddled form; then its heavy hooves crashed down on the asphalt, straddling but not touching Brigid. The horse stopped its frenzied attack, and stretched its nose carefully toward the still form of the young woman. Now, its eyes were gray, and its ears were poked forward anxiously. Beside Isaac, the Trickster tugged his coat. "I wasn't going to hurt her," she murmured. "It's not my fault if that crazy woman flings herself at maddened horses."

Isaac studied the tall woman beside him for a long, stern moment. "We're going home," he told her at last.

The Trickster suffered his examination, then regarded him in turn. "Are you very angry?" she asked him.

"I'm scared to death."

"Of me?" The Trickster sounded sad.

"Of the whole damned business. Let's go."

155

21

Fickle and merciless GODS! Brigid, did I hurt you? Ychass's thought-voice pushed at the edges of Brigid's mind, trying to drive back the panic, as her soft horse-nose nudged the still form, seeking to reassure and comfort. *Brigid, I'm sorry!*

Brigid sat up. She could hear the voices of the crowd the wild horse had attracted and the distant wail of sirens. "*Just* what we need," she muttered. "The police."

Ychass's thought-voice was brittle with sudden unease. *Do not speak aloud!* she demanded. *I can't understand your spoken words. Oh, gods! When she was in my mind, controlling me, she took the language; the Trickster stole the language!*

What do you mean? Of course you can understand English—you're thinking in it!

No, I'm not!! Thoughts are beyond language. Brigid, what are we going to do? The Trickster has stolen my ability to understand your people! WHAT ARE WE GOING TO DO?

Calm down. We'll deal with it—but later. Brigid pulled herself together in the face of the shapeshifter's anxiousness. *Right now, we've got a mess to get out of. I wish Angel were here; she's better at this sort of improvisation.*

By the time Brigid made it clear that she was unhurt, the police officers had arrived. One began taking witnesses' statements while the other approached Brigid.

Act up just a bit, Brigid suggested. *I don't want him coming too close.*

Ychass complied, and the officer stopped at a respectful distance. "Now, miss, perhaps you'd tell me what's going on?"

"I wish I knew," Brigid admitted.

"Well, start with the horse. Is this your animal?"

"Um," Brigid stalled. "Not really. My mother boards her at the farm for a friend of ours. And before you ask, I haven't any idea how she got here; I heard the commotion and came outside to investigate. When I saw Mari Llwyd having a fit, I just acted—I really didn't think."

The second officer joined them. "How are you going to get that horse out of here? I mean, you're holding up traffic."

Brigid thought fast. "There's a halter and lead rope in my car. I'll get it. Come on, Mari," she added to the horse, underscoring the words with the thought, *Follow.* With one hand on the horse's withers, Brigid moved over to her car. The halter was on the front seat. With the horse under control, the excitement was clearly over. Traffic and passers-by began to move again. Brigid turned to the officer. "Here: if you'll hold her for a minute, I'll call my mother; she can bring the trailer down."

"You want *me* to hold her?" the police officer demanded. "I don't know anything about horses."

"Well, she's perfectly calm, now, and I won't be a minute."

A moment later, Brigid returned. "Mother's out," she fibbed; of course she hadn't called her. "She must be looking for the horses. I'll just ride ol' Mari back. I'm real sorry about all the excitement."

"Wait a minute. The witnesses said that horse was wild and dangerous. You can't ride her without a bridle or saddle!"

Brigid exuded breezy confidence. "I can't imagine what got into her. She's usually totally placid. I ride her bareback all the time."

"She *kicked* you!" he protested.

"She didn't mean to—and she was sorry right after. Not to worry: we'll be fine." Then, using the porch steps as a mounting block, Brigid clambered onto Ychass's broad back. *Let's go before they think to ask my name! Or worse, Mother's!*

Brigid chose a route that avoided the more heavily traveled streets and then took a woods road where they could be certain they weren't observed. It was then, when Ychass tried to change herself out of horse-shape, that they discovered the real damage the Trickster had done.

Brigid!! There was an edge of hysteria in the shapeshifter's thought-voice. *I can't change. The Trickster has bound me in this shape!*

But—but how could she DO that? Brigid tried to keep her anxiety under wraps; but it wasn't easy to prevaricate, mind-to-mind.

I don't know, but I'm TRAPPED!! Brigid, I CAN'T CHANGE!!

STOP IT!! We'll handle it! Don't panic! Worries tore through Brigid's mind like hounds on a scent, while the shapeshifter's fear distracted her. *Wait! WAIT!! Listen! Calm down! We've got her name. Surely she can't hold you if you've got her name?*

She took it; I can't remember it.

Well, I can. Dr. Marchbanks said it again, even after she took it back. It's— Brigid stopped. She *could not* make her memory supply the name.

Ychass's thought-voice sounded much more controlled. *You must have agreed to forget; I did. It gives her power.*

I feel so stupid!!!

Horses aren't built to shrug, but Ychass's thought-voice was resigned. *She's one of the gods.*

Brigid watched her friend anxiously. *Are you all right?*

158

I'm calm, if that's what you mean. I panicked because I was afraid that she would strip my mind as well as my shape; it is the only way I know of to do that to one of us: take the shapeshifter's name, memory, and freedom.

Is that why your eyes were purple? Brigid asked, recalling vividly the frenzied mare's attack.

She overpowered my mind, Ychass replied. *SHE was controlling my actions. She must have left restraints behind, to hold me in this shape. Brigid, I'm sorry I frightened you, but what are we going to do now?*

Let me think. I want to talk to Angel. Ychass, you have to stay hidden. I'll show you some good hiding places, but you must stay out of sight until we can explain you to Kelly. Horses just don't appear out of thin air. Don't worry, we'll dream up something. But Ychass, there's more. Alexandra has disappeared. She's left the hospital and no one knows where she is!!!

On the long car-ride home, the Trickster pretended to sleep. It was easier for her to concentrate on the bright mind of the shapeshifter—and to maintain her binding—without other distractions and she didn't know what to say to Isaac Marchbanks. She could hear his recurrent fear that—somehow—he had been sucked into the maelstrom of his patient's madness, and the bitter, unanswerable questions he had about the woman beside him in the car. The Trickster was out of her depth, and she knew it; so she sat with her eyes closed, and tried to savor the predicament she had caused for her enemies. Her triumph was sadly flat.

Then, she felt the shapeshifter try the bonds that held her. She was *strong!* Ychass knew her own name, knew that it was *her* name. Sweat beaded on the Trickster's forehead as she poured power into her binding. It held. Abruptly, the shapeshifter's struggling ceased. The Trickster let out her pent breath in a slow, silent sigh. It was fortunate she had gotten her name away from them; if they hadn't both agreed to forget—she could never have held Ychass in any shape.

It would be hard to maintain this binding, the Trickster knew; but she wasn't trying to do anything but hamper the Five's progress. This was a large world, full of people. 'Tsan would be hard to find; and Isaac clearly felt she was in danger. All the Trickster needed to do, all she was able to do, was to delay them until 'Tsan had fallen prey to whatever harm Isaac feared. Ychass in horse-shape would make for awkwardness— and the added twist of blocking her ability to understand the language might compound it. As she leaned back, feigning sleep, a satisfied smile spread over her face. It was not a pleasant expression. By pure ill luck Isaac Marchbanks chose that instant to glance over at his passenger; the malice on her face didn't reassure him.

"I cannot read the pattern, El," the Dreamer confessed as he studied the work on the Loom in the Weaver's bower. "Are they winning or losing?"

The Weaver spread his hands. "I doubt this quest will make of them either winners or losers. The pattern the Dreamweaver chooses changes the very fabric of Fate; the Loom is different, stronger, for her work on it—but how much of its strengthening can be traced to Ohmiden's death? And was that a victory—or a defeat?"

"Do not be too quick to name events," the Namegiver warned. "Even the Mother and the Arbiter do not see all ends; and not even you can unravel Fate."

"This is your way of saying we won't know how it turns out until it's over?" the Dreamer jibed gently. "Yschadeh, how profound you are."

"I have a question," the Weaver put in. "We know the Trickster has bound herself not to interfere with 'Tsan; but the Wanderer does not respond to our attempts to reach her. Scrying doesn't work; 'Ren touches her dreams, but can awaken no response. How can even the Trickster flout her own vow so?"

"She cannot," the Namegiver said softly, her eyes troubled.

"She must be! What other power could possibly restrain the three of us?"

"I do not know."

"But you've guessed something?" the Dreamer demanded.

"Yes. But it is only a guess."

"Well?" Elgonar prompted, when she fell silent.

"I think it must be 'Tsan herself who holds us at bay," the Namegiver admitted.

"But *why?*" Irenden asked. "Why would she?"

"She doesn't want to come back." There was aching sadness in the Weaver's voice.

"It may be something else," the Namegiver said. "We do not see all ends."

"Surely there is some help we can give them, the Five, or their allies? So much rides on this!" The Weaver's face was anguished. "There have been murders in the City; the Tame Khedathi are turning feral, and the Vemathi are rediscovering ruthlessness. For the first time in nine generations the Priestess of the shapeshifters has called for a blood sacrifice. The Orathi—the gentle Orathi!—are building *walls* around their enclaves." The Weaver swept a hand toward the Loom. "The Dreamweaver guides the pattern, and I must not interfere, but the Loom is weak, and Fate yearns toward chaos! *I cannot sit idly by and watch!*" He buried his face in both hands for a moment; then he looked up at his siblings. "Send me across the void. If we pool our power, we can do it. Send me! I can divert

161

the Trickster—keep her away from the Five. I will lead her a merry dance, the sort of punishment she deserves. *Please.* I cannot sit idle."

"Elgonar. You'd leave the Loom?" the Dreamer was shocked.

"My hands are bound! I can do nothing while the Dreamweaver chooses the pattern. The Loom needs no other guide. Eikoheh is capable, gifted, and brave beyond measure."

"She is also mortal," the Namegiver said sharply, "and old. Were she to die while you were across the void, there would be no guiding hand, no subtle mind behind the Loom's agency."

"That might be no ill thing," Elgonar said bitterly. "The world I weave is very ordered; perhaps that makes it an irresistible target for entropy."

The bower was silent. After several moments the Namegiver turned one hand palm upward. "You have never given me reason to doubt your judgment, Elgonar. If you are determined to go, I will lend you my aid."

"Thank you."

The Dreamer spoke then. His voice was harsh, as though the words fought to remain unspoken. "I will not. You must not go." The Weaver's brilliant eyes filled with tears. "I see it: we will need you here."

Elgonar gripped his brother's wrists. *"What do you see?"*

The brimming tears spilled down the Dreamer's cheeks as he wrenched his face away from his brother's demanding eyes. *"Don't ask!!!* Do not ask me."

The Weaver made himself release the Dreamer's arms. "Very well," he conceded. "I will stay and somewhere I will find the strength to watch."

22

That evening, Brigid summoned Angel, Mark, Brice, and the Five (minus Ychass) and explained the predicament: Alexandra lost, the Trickster found, Ychass trapped in horse-shape and bereft of the magic that allowed her to understand the language. Even Angel couldn't find any encouraging words when Brigid was done.

"So now what?" Brigid cast the question into the silence.

Angel rallied. "First off, we've got to come up with a way to explain Ychass as a horse—before she gets noticed, or caught."

Vihena frowned. "Brigid said Ychass was in hiding on her family's land. Why not simply remain there?"

"No way," Angel responded. "It's hard to hide something that size—and she'll get hungry, too, I'd imagine. Grass is all well and good, but it's not *grain*. Horses are not wild animals around here; people will demand to know who owns her, and if no owner is found"—Angel made a gesture of helpless horror—"some do-gooder animal lover is apt to want to 'adopt' her and take her far, far away. We have to come up with some way to make Kelly—or Mrs. Chandler, even—believe Ychass belongs to someone, and belongs *here*. Now, I have an idea. Brigid, don't you have some dressage-rider friends who want their horse worked while they are away in Europe?"

Brigid began to smile; just watching Angel's imagination at work made her feel easier. "I might have."

"Then listen up," Angel went on. "You tell your mother: this friend wants you to look after the horse; wouldn't Mother like to be supportive and board the animal so you can ride her?"

"Can we possibly come up with a plan that *doesn't* involve my mother? I'm sure she'll feel she should at least have heard of a buddy good enough to entrust a horse-baby to me."

"Okay. Run the same story past Kelly."

"Right," Brigid agreed. "And who's going to pay the board?"

"Your friend, of course."

"*Angel.*" Brigid laughed, exasperated. "Said friend is a figment of your febrile brain!"

"Oh yeah."

"We could all chip in," Mark suggested. "I could probably spare fifty dollars without Mom getting alarmed."

Brice nodded. "So could I."

"I haven't got a cent," Angel confessed, "but I'll do Ychass's stall to keep the board cost down."

Brigid relented. "Let me call Kelly and see if there's room. Maybe I can take Ychass to Wellesley instead of Rex." She shot a look at Vihena. "Wellesley isn't too far from Boston. If Ychass is there, she can help keep us in touch with those of you who go into Boston to look for your friend." She went into the kitchen to make the call. While she was gone, the others continued the discussion.

"You said Ychass was the first situation to confront," Remarr said. "What is next?"

Angel sighed. "Boy, I don't know. Is there anything we can do to protect ourselves from this Trickster character?"

"We probably shouldn't be meeting here," Mark offered, "since she knows where Brigid lives."

"A little late for that advice, surely?" Vihena put in.

164

"I don't think it will matter. If she applied herself, I'm sure she could find the rest of us." Remarr sounded tired.

"What about finding 'Tsan?" Brice asked. "Should we organize another field trip to Boston?"

"Not unless you take Iobeh," Karivet said. "Remember what Ychass told us, that 'Tsan was afraid of her, probably under some spell of the Trickster's. It won't do us any good to find her unless Iobeh is there to soothe her."

I am willing to go to this big City, Iobeh signed. *Perhaps that is what we should do next?*

Brigid came back. "Kelly's got room. I told a whopper to Mother: I said I wanted to practice driving the trailer and could I take it tomorrow. *So* it's all arranged. I'm off to fetch Mari Llywd from Shelley tomorrow."

"Mari *who*?" Angel demanded.

Brigid adopted a superior air. "Don't parade your ignorance, child. Mari Llywd is the Gray Mare in Celtic mythology—a creature of nightmares. I thought it suited our shapeshifter rather well—especially if you saw the performance she put on in the street outside this very window! Shelley, by the way, isn't in Europe after all; she's pregnant and not riding. I thought that would give us more flexibility—you know: people tend to plan when they are coming home from a European trip."

"You're brilliant," Brice said with a laugh, but Brigid denied it.

"*Angel's* brilliant. In case anyone asks, Ychass is visiting friends in Montreal. Now, what else can we do for excitement?"

Remarr looked up at her. "How do you feel about another 'field trip' to Boston?"

Brigid grimaced. "I was afraid someone would suggest that. I really can't take any more time off from work. The earliest I could possibly take anyone to Boston would be next Friday. But if you all go to Wellesley as grooms, a few of you ought to be

165

able to—I don't know, scout the territory?—while the rest of us are riding."

"That's nearly a week away," Vihena said, then clamped her teeth together.

"It is," Mark agreed, "but if we work on it, we may be able to get there sooner. It's possible my mother would let me take the car—and she'd probably be more agreeable if she thought Remarr or Vihena were going, too. I'll ask her tonight; she'll need some time to think it over, but I ought to get a definite answer out of her by tomorrow. Then we could go on Tuesday."

"Good," said Brice. "I think Remarr and the twins ought to go—that will look the most natural, since they haven't been."

"*Rema*—" Vihena cut off the scornful name midsyllable and modulated her tone. "I would like to go," she said reasonably.

"You've been," Angel pointed out. "The others haven't."

"It's such a fascinating place; I'd love to go again."

Remarr matched her colorless, polite tone. "If we don't find 'Tsan on Tuesday, you'll have another chance."

A muscle jumped in Vihena's jaw. Though she made no further protest, she resolved to be included in the next expedition, no matter who tried to keep her out of it.

It was hard, Alexandra found, to use the bank card when her hands were shaking. The little buttons kept slithering out from under her fingers. That last cup of coffee must have been a mistake. Finally, she wadded up the crisp bills and shoved them into her pocket; then she headed for the train station. She had more than enough money to buy a ticket to New York. Rolly Castleman, her late father's literary agent, had helped her before; no doubt he would again.

The Dreamweaver groaned. There was more loose in the pattern than she could control. Ychass—what was wrong with

166

her? Try as she might, she could not use the shapeshifter's thread in the way her pattern demanded. And now 'Tsan's color was moving away from the others, slinking along the underside of the fabric instead of the front where her vivid red could be easily identified and manipulated. She was dreadfully tired; but there was no time to rest, and no refreshing cup of ifenn pushed into her hands by a gruff old man.

Eikoheh blinked back tears, and bent her will to the pattern beneath her hands. It seemed the only thread that would obey her will was that of the Trickster—a fact which frightened Eikoheh more than she could admit.

Early the next morning, Brigid hitched the horse-trailer to the truck, and clattered off. She sent a mental call to the shapeshifter, with the image of a place to meet; when she arrived there, the big gray mare was waiting for her. Brigid snapped a lead to the halter and guided Ychass on board.

Loading sure is easy when you can explain what you want, she thought.

You never know, Ychass responded, her thought-voice quivering with mirth. *I might decide to panic, just like a real horse.*

Despite Ychass's teasing, the trip went smoothly. Ychass's mental complaint told Brigid if she took a curve too quickly, or stopped or started too abruptly. When the trailer reached the stable, swarms of children came to see the new horse.

"Gracious," Brigid said aloud. "It's camp week. I'd forgotten." When Ychass nudged her, hard, she repeated herself mentally; while she readied Ychass to unload, she explained about the horse-mad, beginner campers.

"Easy there, big girl," Brigid murmured. Under the automatic words, she thought, *Back up slowly, and watch your head.*

The big gray horse eased off the trailer, to the oohs and ahs of the kids. Ychass looked around at them all. *Gods. You weren't exaggerating.*

Indeed, no, Brigid agreed fervently, as she and Ychass started down the hill toward the barn. Kelly watched the big horse move.

"That's quite an animal, Brigid; what's her name?"

"Mari Llywd," Brigid replied. "It means Gray Mare in Welsh. Shelley calls her Mari—Nightmare when she's naughty." She walked Ychass around in the arena, then put her in her stall.

Aren't you going to ride me? Ychass thought at her, a little forlornly.

Brigid lingered, one hand on the velvet nose. *Later. You need to settle in—or if you were a horse you would. I'm going to ride Rex first.*

Ychass moved her nose out of range, with a slight toss of her mane. As Brigid moved off toward Rex's stall, Angel sidled up to her. "She's impressive," she whispered. "And I'm not sure I envy you having to ride her."

Brigid only smiled.

An hour and a half later, when Brigid led her new acquisition into the arena, she discovered that almost everyone had invented a reason to loiter in the vicinity. Torn between irritation and amusement, she mounted, admonishing Ychass to hold still. The two of them went over the basic gaits and aids in a workmanlike manner. Gradually, the campers drifted off to find something more interesting. The working students, the Five, and Kelly all remained.

Now, Ychass suggested. *Now can I try something spectacular?*

No rearing.

Of course not. An image accompanied the thought: the springy half-tempo trot-in-place called piaffer.

Where did you learn about that? Brigid demanded.

168

Ychass's thought-voice was smug. *A couple of weeks ago, I asked Kelly to explain the point of dressage, and she made me watch a video tape. The horses performed many impressive feats.*

Go ahead, Brigid suggested as she asked for a slower, more collected trot, and then, Ychass was airborne. It was an indescribable feeling, as though the horse were suspended in the air too long. Ychass kept it up for perhaps half a minute, then moved forward in a perfect collected canter. Brigid's approving enthusiasm rang in her thoughts.

"My God, Brigid," Kelly said, awed. "She's spectacular."

They like me, Ychass thought, pleased.

I'll say, Brigid agreed.

After a time, Brigid dismounted, ran the stirrups up, and loosened the girth. Kelly came toward her, shaking her head. "I can't imagine why your friend hasn't been able to lease that mare. She's gorgeous."

Brigid felt her friend's anxious eyes on her. "Shelley said she had some quirks. I guess I just haven't hit them yet." She gave Ychass a friendly thump. "I'd better go hose her off; she's pretty sweaty."

As Kelly nodded, Brigid led the shapeshifter outside to the wash rack. She picked up the hose, cranked the faucet, and splashed water onto the gray back.

It's cold! Ychass's thought-voice shrieked, outraged. Heads all over the stable yard turned in her direction; with a sick, sinking feeling, Brigid realized Ychass hadn't bothered to shield her thoughts from others.

Ruthlessly, she turned the spray from the hose on the mare's underside. *Whinny or something!* she thought desperately.

Mari Llywd's voice shook the walls of the barn. She pinned her ears back and bared her teeth at Brigid. *Brigid, it's cold!* she thought more moderately. *Stop.*

169

Hold your breath. I'll be quick.

Ychass stood in incoherent, stiff-legged rage until Brigid shut off the tap, squeegeed the excess water off with an aluminum sweat-scraper, and led the mare back to her stall. "Cheer up," Brigid said aloud. "I'll bring you an apple tomorrow."

Apparently, Ychass was able to follow her thoughts on that one, for she replied, *I'd rather have a cup of coffee.*

Brigid laughed as she pictured herself trying to hold a cup to that large, equine mouth.

You're heartless, Brigid, Ychass accused, but her ears pricked forward, and she whuffled softly. Brigid patted her nose and walked off.

23

Sunday evening, as the Newcomb family and Vihena gathered around the dinner table, Mr. Newcomb announced that on Monday he had to go to Boston.

"Would you and Vihena like to go with me, Angel? I'll be tied up in meetings, but I'm sure you can amuse yourselves."

Angel's face was a model of dismay. "Oh Dad, I'd love to go, but I *promised* Kelly I'd work all day Monday. It's Beginner Camp week. I guess we'll both have to take a rain check."

Mrs. Newcomb smiled. "It's nice to see you taking your responsibilities seriously, Angel, but there's no reason Vihena can't go if she wants to." Mrs. Newcomb turned to her. "Not everyone is as horse-crazy as our Angel. You might enjoy a day away from the horses—and the kids!"

"I'd like to go," Vihena responded, "if you're sure I wouldn't be a nuisance."

"Oh Vihena, you can't *abandon* us!"

"Angel," Mr. Newcomb chided. "Don't be selfish. If your friend wants to walk the Freedom Trail, you shouldn't try to hold her back."

"You're right," Angel capitulated, hoping to hide the misgivings she felt. She knew her aliens wanted to get back to Boston, but as Karivet had said, another trip to Boston only made sense

171

if Iobeh was along—and Angel knew her parents. If her parents had decided Vihena deserved a break from the kids, she doubted she could convince them otherwise. "I'm just jealous." She went on with a little laugh. "You know, Vihena, I bet the twins would enjoy going along."

"Yes," Vihena agreed. "I'm sure they would."

Mrs. Newcomb reacted just as Angel had feared. "I know you're too kind to say so, but I'm *sure* you'd like a break from looking after them."

"They're no trouble," Vihena said. "Really. I don't mind taking them, and they would have such fun."

"Now, Vihena," Mr. Newcomb said with the bluff heartiness that Angel knew and dreaded, "the reason I proposed this trip was so that you could enjoy yourself, not to saddle you with your siblings."

Angel intervened, hoping to salvage something. It would be disastrous, she feared, if Vihena went alone; and it would look very peculiar if she *didn't* go at all, having said she wanted to. "I can't go, Vihena, but you'll have more fun if you've got company. I bet Remarr would like to go, too. He was talking about Boston just yesterday."

"Now that's a good thought," Mr. Newcomb said, approving. "Why don't you give him a call after supper?"

"I will," Angel replied. With a sinking feeling, she saw the swordswoman's face go blank with outrage. What *could* she have in mind that Remarr's presence would hinder?

After supper, Angel got Brice on the phone, explained the situation, and begged him to get Remarr to agree. "I have the *worst* feeling about this whole thing," she confided.

"Not to worry," Brice assured her. "Remarr's practically champing at the bit to get to Boston. Hang on. I'll get him."

Soon, it was all arranged. When things were settled, Angel

172

called Brigid. Though Brigid tried to be reassuring, Angel sensed her uneasiness, and she went to bed troubled.

"I know you and Angel expect me to watch over Vihena," Remarr remarked as he and Brice were getting ready for bed. "But what more do I need to know to keep us both out of difficulties?"

Brice shrugged, then smiled crookedly. "A crash course in American culture."

"Oh?" Remarr prodded, his expression puzzled.

"That's my way of saying I don't know where to start. I could try to explain the Transit system, but if you start messing with trains and buses, you're sure to get lost—you can't even read the names of the stations."

Remarr waited, his eyebrows raised inquiringly.

Brice sighed heavily. "I don't think you have any idea, Remarr, how *big* Boston really is. It would be so easy to get lost, and I'm not sure you know enough about how things work here to manage." He trailed off. For a moment, the only noise was the chorus of crickets and night birds.

"Perhaps you are wise to be concerned," Remarr said. "Vihena and I have tasted some of your people's strange ways—and she does not always consider before she acts. If we were to get lost, Brice, what should we do to get found again?"

Brice thought for a moment. "Angel said her dad's meeting was at the Copley Plaza Hotel. If you got lost, you might take a taxi there."

"What is a taxi?"

Brice stared at his friend. "Yipes! That's what I mean. A taxi is a kind of car. You pay the driver to take you where you want to go. It's a lot more expensive than the bus or the subway—" He broke off in the face of Remarr's bafflement. "Bus,

173

subway—*big* magic carts that carry lots of people all at once; that's the Transit system. They follow set routes, but you can't read the station names, and I really think you'd be better off with a taxi. At least you can ask the taxi driver questions."

"How would I recognize a taxi?"

"They're labeled—" He broke off with an exasperated laugh. "And a fat lot of good that will do, since you can't read. Lots of them are bright yellow. They usually have the company name on the side, and a little lighted box on top. But look, if you stand on the curbside and wave like this"—he demonstrated—"saying, 'Taxi! Taxi!' *eventually* one will stop for you."

Remarr was silent for a moment; then he asked, "Would a taxi driver accept a song as payment?"

"A song?" Brice repeated; then his eyes widened. "No! The driver would want money—you know, that paper and metal stuff we use to buy things."

"I haven't any," Remarr pointed out.

Brice pursed his lips in a soundless whistle, then went to his desk, and found a ten, two fives, and three ratty ones. He gave the bills to Remarr, showed him how to tell them apart, and explained the difference in value. When he could think of nothing more to tell Remarr, he said good night, and they turned out the light. He could only hope that the minstrel understood enough to stave off disaster.

Shortly after nine in the morning Mr. Newcomb left Remarr and Vihena on the pavement outside the hotel. He had given them what he called a T Map; but as neither one could make sense of the colored lines and strange black markings, Remarr stowed it in his harp case.

"So," he said blandly. "Have you a plan?"

"Surely you're not at a loss?" Vihena said mockingly.

174

"You've been here before; I haven't. I bow to your greater experience."

"I haven't been to this *part*," she protested.

Remarr struggled with his temper. "For the love of the wise gods, Vihena," he said with hard-won evenness, "what would you have done if I hadn't come with you?"

"Looked for 'Tsan!" she snapped.

"Indeed?" His eyebrows arched. "Without Iobeh? And what would you do with her if you found her? Judging from Ychass's experience, she would be unable to listen to you."

"If you think this a hopeless task, why did you come?"

"Because Brice and Angel asked me to. They were uneasy about your being alone in this place."

"So they think I need a cowardly minstrel for a guardian?" Vihena asked bitterly.

"You have many good qualities, Vihena," Remarr said evenly, "but you are not given to caution."

"*Caution?*" she demanded. "Why you arrogant—"

"Surely we have better things to do than trade insults on the street like a pair of bickering children?"

Remarr's tone brought her up short; her fury cooled to sarcasm. "So controlled, Remarr. So sensible. Don't you ever get tired of being so reasonable?"

"Yes. Often." A glint of emotion lit his eyes, as he continued. "But I live in a world, Vihena, where one word could be my death. I cannot afford to have a temper. I may look like a Khedath, but I have no sword with which to avenge my honor, no Weapons Discipline with which to defend my life. So I am sensible, and I am also still alive."

"You are a coward," she stated, her own voice as colorless as if she had said he was blond.

The minstrel was silent while a range of emotions passed over

175

his face. "How can you say that?" he whispered. "Is it cowardice to refuse to fight over something that is not worth dying for?"

"But Remarr," she said, exasperated, "you don't think anything is worth that price! That's exactly what I mean."

The minstrel's face went blank and ashen; when he spoke, his voice was thick with bitterness. "I spat in the Trickster's face. Have you, with all your posturing, done as much?"

Vihena looked away in the face of his challenging gaze. They made a tableau in the midst of the incurious pedestrians. She couldn't bring herself to apologize—nor to revise her perception of Remarr as weak and cowardly; but she could be spurred to action. Mention of the Trickster had awakened her anger; there *had* to be a blow Vihena could strike against the meddling god! As she thought, a plan began to take shape. She and the minstrel were a gauntlet flung in the Trickster's face—if only she could be made to notice them. And when she came, Vihena would be ready.

"I have a plan," she began slowly. It wasn't a good idea to tell Remarr the whole of it; but she would not sink to falsehood. "We must do something to attract attention—something to proclaim our origin without alarming the people of this world. If you play your harp and I dance, perhaps we shall attract her." (Let him think she meant 'Tsan—she had not said it.)

"Even if she comes, Vihena, what makes you think we can get through the spell?"

"Music is supposed to be soothing," she retorted. "Come, Remarr: it is something to do, and perhaps a hope."

He considered her. "I didn't think you knew how to dance."

Vihena smiled sourly. "I don't—but I know the Forms of the Discipline. If you play music that matches their rhythms, these barbarians will think it dance."

Remarr well remembered the ancient teaching Forms. Vihena was right: it would look like dance to the people of this place. "Where shall we do this?"

Vihena shrugged. "This city is vast. How should we judge? Let us trust in the guiding which led us here." She gestured toward a broad paved square near where they stood. "There?"

Soon, Remarr's harp was tuned and Vihena had finished her limbering exercises. Automatically, Remarr set out his harp case to receive coins, then began to play. He took his tempo from Vihena's controlled, familiar movements, and buried his hurt and anger in the wild power of the harp.

Alexandra's train ground to a halt in Manhattan, spilling sleepy travelers into a gray, muggy dawn. As it was far too early for Rolly Castleman to be in his office, Alexandra went in search of some breakfast. She found a restaurant and was content with tired croissants and indifferent coffee. She had slept on the train, but not deeply, and not long enough.

She lingered over her coffee, reluctant to leave the restaurant's shelter. Here, *they* wouldn't be able to sneak up on her. Her eyes drifted shut for a moment. When she opened them, she saw her father sitting in the chair across from her.

"You're dead," she said, numb. There was no room in her even for fear.

"Yes," Alister Scarsdale agreed.

"Why are you here?"

"I thought you needed looking after."

Alexandra expelled her breath scornfully. "I needed looking after three and a half years ago, but you died; you left me. You didn't care then. Why now?"

"I didn't choose to die—"

"You didn't choose to stay, either! You never thought about me; you never considered my needs. I was never *real* to you!"

Alister Scarsdale's sarcasm bit. "I'd say *you're* the one who's having trouble with reality, Zan."

"What do you mean?" She felt cold.

He turned one hand palm-upward in a characteristic gesture. "I'm dead, remember? I'm not here—but you are talking to me. So what's real, Zan? What's real?"

He disappeared before Alexandra could reply. She looked up with a start to find the waitress hovering with a check. She paid and went out into the street. If she walked to Rolly's office, it would take up the time.

There was a new receptionist, but as soon as she heard Alexandra's name, she saw to it that Rolly was interrupted in his meeting.

Rolly came bustling out and ushered Alexandra into his office. "I'm glad to see you, Alexandra. I've been worried about you, ever since your Dr. Marchbanks called."

"He called you?" she squeaked. She felt as though a hand were closing around her heart.

Rolly nodded. "Saturday. I've been frantic with worry!"

"What did he say?"

"That you weren't well—but I knew that, because the school called me after you were admitted to Stillman." Some of her consternation must have shown on her face, for Rolly laughed apologetically. "Well, good heavens, Alexandra; I'm practically your next of kin. Anyway, he said you'd disappeared and they had no idea where you'd gone."

"Rolly, I don't want to go back," she blurted, desperate. She could see where he was leading.

"But Alexandra, Dr. Marchbanks is trying to make you better."

"He's making me worse. Please, Rolly; you've got to help me." She grasped at a straw. "I think Dr. Marchbanks is connected with the cult," she whispered.

It was a mistake. She knew it as soon as the words were out of her mouth. She could tell what Rolly was thinking as clearly as if the words were written above his head. *Dr. Marchbanks said she was paranoid.* He tried to soothe her. "Now, Alexandra, you're having a bad time, I know; but the cult can't touch you. Dr. Marchbanks is trying to help you. But we can get him to refer your case to someone else. You can get treatment here if you prefer."

Alexandra didn't reply. She recognized Rolly's immovably reasonable mood. She couldn't make him understand that anyone Dr. Marchbanks recommended was bound to be connected with *them*.

"Now," Rolly went on, not noticing her silence. "Here's what we'll do. I'll give you the key to my apartment; you go there and wait. I've got two appointments this morning, but I'll cancel my afternoon ones, and then we can call Dr. Marchbanks and decide what's best to be done. Okay?"

"Okay," Alexandra lied. She knew what she had to do. She took Rolly's key and left the office; she even went to his apartment building, to slip the key into his mailbox, just in case it was his only one. Then she went back to the station. She considered boarding a train bound for somewhere unexpected and distant, but she knew she needed more money if she were to undertake such a jaunt. She would have to return to Boston. Once there, she could close out her savings and checking accounts, and disappear to Toledo, or Phoenix—someplace *they* would never think to look.

Isaac Marchbanks sat in his office, presiding silently over the remains of a roast beef sandwich in its white paper skin. His next appointment wasn't until two. He needed a distraction; his thoughts were too troubling. Briefly, he wondered what Antekkereh was up to—then his thoughts shied away from her.

179

There was too much strangeness, too many inexplicable coincidences. He *would not* think about it.

He shook his head. How human it was to try to override the mind with the will—and how impossible. The intercom peeped. It was the receptionist, wondering whether he would take a call from a Mr. Roland Castleman.

"This is Dr. Marchbanks," he said.

Castleman's voice lacked the urbane quality Isaac remembered. He sounded anxious, almost breathless. "It's about Alexandra Scarsdale. She came to my office this morning. She didn't look very good, but she seemed rational. I never dreamed—I sent her to my apartment; I told her I'd come home early, and we'd talk about what to do. She seemed all right—she really seemed to be comfortable with the arrangement. But she's gone again. She left my key in the mailbox and vanished."

Isaac fought to keep his voice calm. "Think back: did she give you any clue as to what sent her off again?"

"She did say—she told me she didn't want to go back to Boston. I said we could look into getting her treatment here in New York. I was trying not to scare her off, Dr. Marchbanks, but I seem to have done it anyway."

"It's not your fault," Isaac assured him. "Alexandra isn't rational. Things that seem straightforward to you or me seem very different to her."

"That was the thing that made me *know* she was sick: she said you were connected to the cult."

Isaac's voice remained serene. "That's common with cases like hers, to identify the therapist with the perceived enemy. Tell me, Mr. Castleman: what do you think she will do now?"

"I hesitate even to guess," the literary agent responded. "I can't think of any other person she would be likely to seek out. She and her father didn't really establish roots anywhere."

"Do you think she'll come back to your apartment?"

"No, I don't. She wouldn't have made such a point of leaving my key if she had any intention of returning."

"Have you spoken with the police? Refer them to me; I'd be willing to tell them that she may be a danger to herself, if it would spur them to action."

"Doctor, *is* she a danger to herself—or to others?"

Isaac sighed. "I don't know. I dare not rule it out, but I just don't know for sure."

24

The Trickster feigned sleep until she heard Dr. Marchbanks leave for work. She found his bewilderment impossible to face; she felt both guilty and feckless, as though she had damaged something precious, something she had no skill to mend. Remorse was unexplored territory for the Trickster.

Wrapping herself in Isaac's spare bathrobe, she went into the kitchen. She found a note:

I LEFT THE COFFEE POT ON FOR YOU.
PLEASE DON'T FORGET TO TURN IT OFF.
I'LL BE HOME AROUND SIX.

The Trickster poured herself a cup of coffee, turned off the machine as he had shown her, and sat down at the table. Idly, she leafed through one of the strange, glossy, soft-covered books, only looking at the bright pictures. There were many pictures of women—all shorter and more delicate than she was. The Trickster frowned. Then she got up, and taking her coffee with her, went into the bathroom. The smooth, flawless glass of the mirror was not gentle with her reflection. Using a small amount of her power, she ran her hands through unnaturally orange, spiky hair; the fluorescent color drained away to its normal bright copper; the spikes softened and lay flat. Her hair was still shorter than most of the pictures she had looked at, but it would take more power than she dared spend to restore it to flowing waves. Then she considered the black leather jumpsuit. In a blaze of power, she summoned a completely different outfit: a soft blouse of a dusty pale green, ivory-colored tailored trousers with an oversized silk jacket to match, and a pair of flat shoes. She dressed, and without consulting the mirror again went out.

The Trickster didn't have a clear plan of action except to get away from Isaac's place, so she boarded a bus bound for downtown Boston. She watched the other passengers as they got on and off; and she gazed at the passing sights. The city was dirty and crowded, full of summer heat and the unpleasant smell of the traffic. She had been riding for some time when her attention was caught by a lithe young woman moving in a way that looked suspiciously like the Forms of the Discipline. Her gaze sharpened. Yes! It was Vihena—and Remarr was with her. The Trickster did what she had seen other passengers do: pulled the string running above the windows to signal the driver to stop; when the bus came to a panting halt at the curb, she left it.

The Trickster lurked in the back of the smallish crowd as she considered what to do: no open attack; there were too many people, and it would upset Isaac if he had to rescue her from the police again. As she listened to the swirl of harp music and watched the motion of the Forms, she noted that people would step forward to leave an offering in Remarr's harp case before they went on their way. A masterful idea occurred to her. From her pocket, she removed a bus token. She Marked it, embedding an invisible fragment of her power in the metal. Sweat prickled her brow with the effort, but when she was done, the coin called to her inner senses. The Marking enabled her to locate the coin with her mind; if Remarr kept it, she would be able to find him at will. Further, the Marked coin acted as a channel for her influence, rendering the person who carried it susceptible to rash impulses of her devising. This effect was enhanced if the item were carried in a pocket or worn, but even if the token stayed in the harp case, she could subtly color the minstrel's or his companions' thinking. It was not the first time she had used such a device. Her memory supplied the image of Edevvi's engraved silver medallion: it had been Marked. With a smile, she dropped the token into the harp case, then walked quickly away.

During the noon heat, Remarr and Vihena rested. The minstrel deftly sorted the morning's take, separating the bills from the coins and dividing the bills into the groups Brice had taught him. He folded them and tucked them into his pocket. The coins he poured into the doeskin pouch that housed his spare tuning key and his extra strings. He wedged the bulging pouch into the harp case and tucked his instrument tenderly away.

"Shall we find something to eat?" he asked Vihena.

She watched him approach a vendor who dealt in twisted pieces of toasted, salted bread. Remarr bought a pair of them and two cups of cold, vaguely fruit-flavored drink. After they had eaten, they rested until the sun had slipped from its zenith. Then they went back to their task, alternating "dances" with songs. Though they amassed an impressive collection of coins and bills, they saw no sign of 'Tsan—or of the Trickster. A little before four o'clock they went to meet Angel's father.

"Did you have fun?" he asked them.

"It was a very interesting day," Remarr responded. "Thank you for bringing us here."

Mr. Newcomb chuckled. "Don't thank me until we get safely through rush-hour traffic," he warned cheerfully. "Vihena, you look exhausted."

"I think I'll sleep on the homeward journey," she told him, managing a smile. It was one way to avoid both rudeness and falsehood. She was hot, tired, and frustrated; and she suspected Remarr was laughing at her. As she closed her eyes, she heard the minstrel ask about Mr. Newcomb's conference; she fell asleep to the murmur of their talk.

When the Trickster returned to Isaac's house, he stared at her in surprise. After a moment, he managed a smile. "Are you turning over a new leaf?"

"Do you like it?"

He shrugged. "I'm not sure it's you."

"Who else would it be?" she retorted.

"That's not exactly what I meant, but never mind. You look very nice, Antekkereh. Are you hungry? Dinner's almost ready."

As they sat down to eat, there was an awkward silence, one full of scraps of worry and sharp-edged chips of doubt. Isaac broke it, laying his fork down and leaning toward the Trickster.

"Will you explain this Trickster-business for me?"

At first, she could not meet his eyes. When she looked up, there was resolve in the set of her jaw. "If you want me to explain *away* what you call the Trickster-business, I cannot; I respect you too much to lie to you. If you ask me to explain again, I will—but I warn you: I doubt it will ease your fears."

Isaac stared with great concentration at the food on his plate. Then he sighed and raised his eyes to hers. "You'd better explain, Antekkereh; it's worse not knowing."

"Where do you want me to begin?"

"Begin with yourself: who are you, why are you here, how do you know Alexandra Scarsdale, and why does she matter to you?"

The Trickster began. "I am the Trickster, one of the gods in the world from which I come—which is different from this one. The world from which I come is governed by the Weaver and

185

the Loom of Fate; there are people there, as here, and there are shapeshifters—and gods. My coming here was the result of a fight with my brother, the Weaver. I thought I was stronger than I am, and that he was not as clever as he is. I know 'Tsan because, three and a half years ago, the Weaver strung her color in the Loom and summoned her to our world to save the Orathi."

"Wait," Isaac interrupted weakly. "Are you asking me to believe that the things Alexandra calls her delusions are *true?* Are you and the others—if those young women *are* involved—playing some sick game with Alexandra's sanity?"

"It is all true, Isaac. I swear it."

"Can you prove it?"

Though Isaac's words were calm, she knew he was both angry and terrified. She held out her hand. "Give me your hand—the injured one."

"What are you going to do?" he asked as she began unwrapping the dressing.

"I won't hurt you, Isaac," she assured him. She slid one hand under his wrist and laid the other, lightly as a moth's wing, over his injury. She closed her eyes.

Isaac watched as her breathing slowed. The muscles around her eyes tightened with concentration or pain. Sweat sprang out on her brow and cheeks; her breathing grew labored. A tingling sensation began in his hand, spreading slowly up his arm. With a gasp, the Trickster took her upper hand away. Isaac stared. *His hand was healed.* He balled it into a fist, then he turned it over and wrapped his fingers around the wrist of the Trickster's supporting hand. "How the hell did you do that?"

"I *told* you," she said desperately. "I'm a god. It is one of the things we can do."

The mixture of disbelief and fear on his face chilled the Trickster. She hadn't realized, until that instant, how much he mattered to her.

"Oh, Isaac," she whispered; her voice caught on tears. "Please: don't fear me. I would never hurt you—I swear it!"

He said nothing; but slowly, he reached out with the hand she had healed. She did not pull away. He brushed her cheek with one finger, catching a tear. As he drew his hand away from her face, his trembling caused the tear to catch the light and glimmer like a faceted jewel. He looked from the stolen tear to the Trickster's brimming eyes, and his own terror dissolved. "I'm not afraid of you, Antekkereh," he said. And somewhat to his amazement, he found that it was true. "I can't pretend to understand all of this, but I know you would do me no harm."

Relief spilled her brimming tears. "Thank you, Isaac."

He smiled, an impish gleam lighting the depths of his dark eyes. "There go your intimidation tactics!"

"They didn't work anyway," she told him before her smile turned sly. "Besides, how do you know I haven't already come up with something better?"

25

It wasn't until after lunch the following day that the Five (less Ychass) and their allies (minus Brigid, who was at work) were able to slink off to the hayloft to discuss Remarr and Vihena's Boston trip.

Vihena reported in a precise manner that made it apparent she had found the whole excursion unsatisfactory. When she finished, Brice turned to Remarr.

"I hate to seem mercenary, but did you collect much money?"

Remarr dug it out, from his pockets and from the harp case. "You tell me," he suggested. "This includes what is left from what you lent me as well as our earnings."

Angel whistled at the total. "Eighty-three dollars, seventy cents, and one bus token. That's *unbelievable!*"

"A great deal?" Remarr asked.

"Well, yes," said Mark. "You may not have found your friend, but you've made enough money to pay Ychass's board bill for nearly two weeks. I wouldn't call that a wasted day."

"I would," Vihena snapped. "Each day that passes without locating 'Tsan makes the success of our quest less likely. We spent a whole day there, with nothing to show for it."

Remarr took the bus token and pressed it into the swordswoman's palm. "Something to show," he said with a mocking smile. "A token of our appreciation."

188

Vihena's fingers closed around the metal disk. She glared at Remarr for several seconds; then, without warning, she slammed her fist into his face. That would have been bad enough—a hard hit, without warning—but Remarr was perched on a bale near the edge of the loft; her punch knocked him backward, off the bale. He tried to slow his descent, but it was as though he had been shoved down a giant's staircase with no railing. He bounced twice before he reached the edge of the hayloft and plunged into space.

There was an appalled hush before the others erupted into a frantic scramble for the steep loft steps. Remarr lay sprawled on his back in the sand of the arena. They hurried to his side.

"Is he all right?" Angel demanded.

"He's stunned," Karivet replied. "He's breathing, and it does not look as though he has broken bones."

To their immeasurable relief, Remarr groaned and opened his eyes—or rather, one of his eyes. The other was already beginning to swell shut. Mark helped him to sit up while Angel went after an ice pack.

Ychass's voice spoke in his mind. *So what happened? Why did Vihena attack you?*

Ask Vihena.

I did, the shapeshifter protested. *She bit my head off.*

Remarr smiled. *And you are dying of curiosity. Well, I miscalculated. I must have put a bit too much sting in my smile. Yesterday's mission placed great strain on our truce.*

I doubt she meant to knock you out of the loft.

Perhaps not. His thought-voice was a sigh. *It's probably my vanity speaking, but I do wish she didn't despise me.*

"What were you *thinking* of, Vihena?" Angel demanded.

"I *wasn't thinking!*" Vihena returned. "I lost my temper. It was lucky I didn't kill him; if I'd been wearing a sword, I might

189

have sliced him into collops. Have I groveled enough, Angel?"

"You haven't said you're sorry."

"I'm not sorry."

"Well, you sure as hell ought to be," Angel retorted.

"He began it."

"I find that hard to believe. I point out to you, Vihena, that Remarr has never struck you."

"That hardly speaks in the coward's favor. He would never dare raise his hand against me."

"Do you seriously think that Remarr is a coward?" Angel challenged.

"Do you seriously maintain that he is not?"

"He faced a state trooper and a whole hospital full of doctors and nurses for you, Vihena." Angel scowled as she noted the mulish set of Vihena's chin. "You need to think about what courage really is. There's a lot more to it than swaggering around confidently when you already know you have the upper hand."

When Vihena made no reply, Angel snapped, "Don't you think you could apologize to him—in the interests of peace?"

Vihena crossed her arms and glared. "I will not."

Angel stamped her foot. "Vihena, you're being stubborn!"

The swordswoman caught hold of the front of Angel's shirt, and dragged her forward, so they were nose to nose. "*Leave off*," she whispered. "I will brook no meddling." Then, turning on her heel, she stalked away.

Angel drew several deep breaths. It unnerved her to see how shaken the confrontation had left her. She had never seen Vihena like this—frustrated and impatient, yes, but never so dangerously poised for violence. With a deep sigh, she turned her attention to her responsibilities.

The companions allowed the soothing routine of stable work to ease their tensions and uneasiness. Through the rest of the afternoon Remarr and Vihena treated each other with cool indifference. It was clear to all of them that the incident was closed—though neither healed nor forgotten.

Much to her disgust, Alexandra's train did not arrive in Boston until after her bank had closed. She decided to risk a trip back to her room. She needed a shower, and there were things she was reluctant to leave behind if she were truly going to relocate elsewhere.

She reached Dunster House around six and fled up the stairs to her room. Once there, she would not permit herself a light; there must be no sign visible from outside that she was home.

The bathroom was dim but not dark. She luxuriated in the hot water, felt it dissolve both dirt and tension. Afterward, she felt so much better she even considered sleeping. *They* didn't know she was here. This would be the last place *they* would look, after all. She put on her nightgown and went back into the bathroom to brush her teeth.

The Super had replaced the mirror. Alexandra was so relaxed that she stared at her own reflection without even a hint of uneasiness.

It took her a long time to notice that the image in the mirror had changed. It was no longer her face that looked back at her, but the Weaver's serene image. Alexandra felt the way she had when she had faced her dead father across the breakfast table: numb; beyond fear or anger. She finished brushing her teeth and looked back into the mirror. The Weaver was still there.

"I can't even say you're dead. You just never existed," she told the image.

Puzzlement clouded his expression. "But I *do* exist. One might argue that I am redundant, but I *am* real. I gave you my name, 'Tsan; don't you remember?"

"How can I remember something that never happened?"

191

"How can you not remember something that did?"

She thought of the cult, the missing months of her life, which even after three years she could not reconstruct. "I'd like to know."

As he followed her thoughts, her pain was mirrored in his eyes. "This 'cult' is no real thing, 'Tsan. You believe it happened but it was not thus. I wove your color into the Loom. I summoned you into my world, and the Trickster cast you back. Truly, do you remember none of it?"

"None of it is real." Her voice was soft, as though she repeated a mantra.

The Weaver's eyes brimmed with tears. "Oh 'Tsan, forgive me," he pleaded. The tears spilled like quicksilver down his cheeks. "Between us, the Trickster and I have crippled you."

"None of it is real," she repeated. "None of it is real."

In the face of her disbelief, the Weaver's image wavered. For a long moment, the mirror reflected nothing; then it filled again with the reflection of Alexandra, who continued to murmur, "None of it is real."

26

"*Elgonar!*"

The voice jerked the Weaver's head up. He hurriedly dashed tears from his face. He knew that voice; he did not relish the confrontation.

"*Come in, Mother. My door is always open to you.*"

The Mother was an imposing presence robed in green, her fire-bright hair braided and pinned into a coronet. She bent her gaze on the Weaver and he restrained himself from fidgeting like a guilty child. The silence was unshakable, and very awkward.

"*Where is the Trickster?*" *she asked at last, with the air of one who knows but wants to hear the shameful truth from the miscreant's own lips.*

"*I sent her across the void.*" *His voice was neutral, with neither defensiveness nor apology.*

The Mother waited for an excuse then said, scathingly, "How could you?"

The Weaver's voice was unruffled. He answered her words, not her tone. "I used her own power. She lost control and I seized it."

"*Why?*" *There was a warning glitter of outrage in her eyes.*

"*It was the only way I could think of to remove her hands from my throat before she choked the life out of me.*"

193

"The Loom is strong—"

"But the Weaver is not invulnerable; and I was frightened. I have done nothing to prevent her return."

The Mother scrutinized him, as though she could read half-truths and evasions in the lines around his eyes. Then, with a sniff of disdain, she spun away and stalked to the Loom. The Weaver closed his eyes, as though in pain, but his expression was impassive when she whirled back. "What are you doing?" There was more open emotion in her voice than he had ever heard.

"Nothing." His reply was quiet, though he could feel his breath short in his throat. The driving emotion behind the Mother's anger was—fear. *"That pattern is the Dreamweaver's."*

Crossing to him, swift, furious, she gripped his shoulders. *"Are you mad, Elgonar? Do you know what you risk?"*

"Tell me," he whispered.

She shook him, hard. *"The Loom is strong, Elgonar, but it was never meant to hold my world together across the void! My mortal children have no business walking the realms of other gods. You stretch the fabric on the Loom so that at the merest puff, it will tear. Without the Loom to hold it, the world I birthed will burst apart, and then, all will be lost to chaos. Not even the voice of the Star Sower will have power to call back the sundered fragments."* Suddenly, her anger flared. "What possible justification could you have for such folly?"

"The damage was done before ever I sent the Five across the void. I know the Loom. I am the Loom! The wounding you speak of, the weakening, happened when the Trickster cast out the Wanderer. Her thread was torn—torn!—from the Loom; and power streams from the wound like blood. I sent the Five to bring her back, to see whether we could staunch the Loom's wound."

194

"The Wanderer? The one who went to Windsmeet, for the Orathi?" At his nod, she made a dismissive gesture. "But she was a Khedatheh, surely."

"She was not! I met her: neither Khedatheh, Vematheh, Oratheh, nor shapeshifter; something else. Mother, when I strung a Wanderer's color on the Loom, she answered; and now her Fate is woven with ours. 'Tsan belongs to the Loom, and by casting her out, the Trickster has imperiled us all."

The Mother was silent; then she turned back to the Loom. "I have never before had cause to regret putting the Loom in your hands, Elgonar. But even if what you say is true, this has put the worlds out of balance. Even if your mortals are not lost in the worlds beyond the void, there will be a price to rebalance the worlds." She faced him. Her austere expression and the cold fire of her eyes made him swallow. "Summon your allies."

"From across the void?" he temporized.

"Your allies among the gods. Surely you do not expect me to believe that you have undertaken this venture alone?"

"Believe as you choose: I will summon no one. Either I have no allies, or their names are not mine to share."

Their eyes met as their wills clashed. The Mother was the first to look away. "I never imagined, Elgonar, that you would deceive me; some of the others, yes, but not you, my faithful Weaver."

"I couldn't possibly deceive you, Mother—so I must be content with stubborn silence."

"Useless stubborn silence," she snapped. After a moment's study of the Loom, she commanded, in a voice ringing with power, "Yschadeh! Irenden! Attend me in the Weaver's Bower." As she turned back to Elgonar, she surprised the glint of ironic amusement in his eyes.

At her lifted eyebrows, he shrugged. "It is your voice, not mine, which summons them. I find victories in little things."

195

"If it is neither pride nor arrogance, nor lust for power, nor jealousy which drives you to hazard everything on this throw, Elgonar, what is it?"

His answering expression was tender and a little sad. "It is love for this world you have birthed, and my stubborn unwillingness to concede to entropy."

The Mother sighed; when she spoke, her voice was heavy with sorrow. "And what if the cost is more than you can bear?"

"I don't see how it can be," he replied, "unless we fail."

The Mother became aware, then, of the presence of the Dreamer and the Namegiver. Her glance included them all. "You realize that meddling on this scale will require a judgment in the Godsmoot?" At the Weaver's gesture of assent, she went on, more quietly. "And you realize that your punishment could be severe?" Again, he nodded. "And you realize, also, that I cannot impose my will upon the judgment of the Godsmoot? If it had been left to me, the Trickster would never have been bound. So heed me: move quietly and with care. I will not call the Godsmoot against you; but I cannot stop it, if one of the others learns of what you attempt and takes affront." Then, sweeping her gaze across them one last time, she left the Bower.

When the Trickster came down for breakfast, she was surprised to find Isaac, in a bathrobe, lingering over his coffee. "I thought you were long gone," she greeted him.

"Sorry to disappoint. I'm on call this weekend, so I took today off. Besides, I thought you might like a ride to your hearing."

"My what?" she said.

"You don't remember? I thought that was why you changed your hair."

"Isaac, *what's a hearing?*"

Isaac's lips formed a soundless 'O,' as he realized the extent of her ignorance. "This afternoon you have to go talk to a judge about your creative motorcycle driving and your utter disregard for rules and regulations."

"But what do I say?" Panic edged her voice.

He thought about it for a moment. "I think I'd stick to: 'I'm sorry and I won't do it again.'"

"What will happen to me?"

He sighed. "Well, it's a first offense, so they may be lenient. I'd say a fine is practically a certainty."

"A forfeit of money?" she clarified. At his nod, she wailed, "But I haven't any!"

"I have," he said. "Don't worry about that. Now, I don't think this is *likely*, but there is a possibility that you will be given a jail sentence."

"Jail?" The Trickster paled. "Oh, Isaac, I don't want to go back to jail. Should we bribe the judge?"

"*No!* Where did you learn about bribing judges?"

"The Vemathi sell justice. Your people don't?"

Isaac smiled sardonically. "Not officially. Listen, Antekerreh, I had to give the police a name when I came to bail you out. I listed you as Ann T. Carroll. Can you remember that?"

The Trickster smiled crookedly. "Show me how it is spelled, and I'll do my best."

Alexandra didn't wake until after three in the afternoon. She railed at herself for allowing exhaustion to overpower her. Her chances of getting away from Cambridge before nightfall were, she knew, slim. She dressed, then hurried to her bank to get the money she needed for her escape. That task completed, she headed back toward her dormitory room to pack. She was not even halfway home when she started hearing the

197

voices. Like a deer that hears the belling of the hounds, she began to run.

The Trickster and Isaac left the courtroom, very much relieved. The judge had seemed to recognize the real contrition and fear in the Trickster's eyes. The motorcycle had been confiscated, but she was let off with a fine and a suspended sentence.

They decided to stop for a cup of cappuccino on their way home. As Isaac spun his car quickly round a corner, a running figure dashed into the street from between two parked cars.

Time slowed. Isaac slammed on the brakes. Tires screamed on pavement. But the runner was too close, too unexpected. The Trickster's cry rent the air. "*NO!!*" She had seen what Isaac had not: it was 'Tsan!

There was a blast, a silent burst of power that made the car leap into the air. Alexandra was flung like a rag doll, to lie in a crumpled heap nearly twenty feet away. After an impossibly long moment, the car crashed to earth.

"Oh, God," Isaac whispered, shock and horror stealing his breath. "What have I *done?*" As he reached for the release on his seatbelt, he noticed the Trickster. Her face was white as plaster, her eyes vacant. Isaac grabbed her arm, shook it a little. "Antekkereh?" No response. He looked more closely. She looked ghastly; he didn't think she was breathing. "Antekkereh! *Antekkereh!*" He shook her harder. Like a very old woman, she turned her head toward him. Her eyes were still wide, but now they were filled with fear.

"I broke my vow," she whispered. "Oh Isaac, I broke my vow." Then, she slumped forward, apparently unconscious.

"Vow?" he repeated; then he remembered, heard the Trickster's voice: 'I, Antekkereh, swear that I will not come next or nigh 'Tsan. . . . I swear I will neither impose my will nor use my influence upon her. This I swear on my name . . .' He sat perfectly still while the implications exploded in his brain. "Alexandra," he whispered. The screaming of sirens recalled him; passers-by had gathered; police were moving, official and blue, calming fears, taking statements. An ambulance squad arrived and began tending Alexandra. One of the policemen came over to the car.

"You all right, sir?"

Isaac was having a hard time breathing. "I—yes. Is— is she—" He gestured weakly toward the paramedics. "Is she alive?"

The officer nodded. "They'll get her right to the hospital. Is your passenger all right?" he added, as he noticed the Trickster's still form.

Isaac turned to her. "Antekkereh?" He jostled her, to no effect. "She must have fainted," he said. His voice sounded desperate, even in his own ears.

A moment later, one of the paramedics came over. He put his hand to the Trickster's throat, then looked up, alarmed. "Let's get her out of the car. I don't feel a pulse."

She was lying on a stretcher almost before Isaac could get out of the car. One of the paramedics started CPR. Isaac took her hand. "Antekkereh. You can't leave me. *Antekkereh!*"

The woman on the stretcher drew a shaky breath and opened her eyes. "Isaac?" Her hand tightened on his.

"I'm here," he said. "You're going to be all right. Just keep breathing."

"'Tsan?"

"She's alive; I don't know any more."

The Trickster sighed. "Good," she said, her voice a little stronger. "Then it was not for nothing."

The Trickster's cry rocked the Loom. The Weaver heard it; it shook him out of his patient scrying meditation. As he turned toward the Loom, the Trickster's burst of power flared through warp and weft like chain lightning. He flung up one arm to shield his eyes and he heard the Dreamweaver's scream. Wrapping himself in wind, he hurled himself to her cottage.

Eikoheh sat, frozen before her Loom, the shuttle upraised in one hand, while the Trickster's wild power limned her in eerie purple light. Elgonar wrested the shuttle from her hand, channeled the Trickster's power back into the Loom. He wove feverishly, strengthening the pattern, diverting the killing force of the Trickster's oathbreaking blast. Something resisted him, some power—not the Trickster's—prevented him from draining her to a husk; he was stopped short of reclaiming her forsworn name and destroying her. Finally, exhausted, Elgonar set the shuttle down and turned to the Dreamweaver.

With trembling hands, the Weaver gathered the old woman into his arms. She breathed, but he could feel her fragile, birdlike bones; he could see the toll her long weaving had exacted, and he did not know hope. He was too drained himself to attempt any healing magic. He settled her as comfortably as he could, and took his place by her side to wait.

27

Long after the working students and their friends had gone home to their suppers, Kelly came back the stable to give the horses their evening grain. As she turned the lights on, a whicker of anticipation swept the barn.

"That's right, kids," she told her charges. "Suppertime."

Ychass started violently. She had *understood* Kelly, understood the *words!* She tested the strength of the Trickster's binding and shifted to human shape with no resistance at all. It was all she could do to restrain a cry of exultation. Suddenly, she realized that Kelly was approaching. She shifted back. Kelly was standing at the stall door, a perplexed look on her face. Her thoughts were troubled: *Am I seeing things?* Ychass whickered and nudged Kelly gently with her nose. With a shrug, Kelly dumped Ychass's ration of grain and continued down the aisleway.

Ychass waited until Kelly was gone before she tried to contact her friends. She realized she couldn't simply vanish; but she was mortally sick of horse-shape. She needed advice.

In the end, it was Brigid's mind Ychass found. And it was Brigid who came up with a plan. They spent some time consulting over details, then sought their rest with lightened hearts.

The Dreamer and the Namegiver joined the Weaver's silent vigil in Eikoheh's cottage. Together they were able to give the

201

Dreamweaver strength to keep her spirit in her body—but that was all, and it drained the gods. The night waned; dawn, stealthy as a thief, crept closer.

"Should we let her spirit go?" Irenden asked in the quiet.

"'Ren, it's her *pattern*." Desperation tinged the Weaver's voice. "I don't know how she intends to bring it full circle."

"And El may not be permitted to weave it, if the Moot is called," the Namegiver pointed out bleakly. "I have no doubt that the others felt the surge in the Loom even as we did. It is only a matter of time before someone demands an explanation."

"And we will be undone."

"Not you: I *will* be undone," Elgonar insisted. "I will take responsibility. It was I who let my anger rule me when I wove to save the Dreamweaver. I have put the Loom's energies all askew. It is my fault: I will take the blame."

"To what do you refer?" Yschadeh asked him.

His eyebrows rose. "I thought you knew: I tried to kill the Trickster when she broke her vow."

"But El! She broke her vow in 'Tsan's defense."

The Weaver bowed his head. "I know."

"Tried?" Irenden broke in. "Only tried?"

Elgonar did not look up. "Something prevented me, some force I did not recognize."

"So who is most likely to call the Moot?" the Namegiver asked. "The Trickster herself?"

"I doubt I left her power enough to do it; but she is not the only one who has chafed under my control. I would guess the Warriors or perhaps the Arbiter, himself." The Weaver's face was anguished. "If a Moot is called, it will find against me: I am in the wrong. Even I see that."

A moan from Eikoheh cut off their discussion. The Namegiver laid her thin hand on the old woman's brow and

202

murmured, "We are here: the Weaver, the Dreamer, and I. Is there aught you need?"

The Dreamweaver opened her eyes and the three gods stifled gasps. The old woman's eyes were the color of blindness: blank, white, and opaque. Her groping hand found her face; despair etched lines in her face.

"I can't see. I'm blind. Blind!" Her voice climbed to a wail. "How can I finish the pattern if I cannot see?"

There was an aching silence. Then, the Dreamer strode to her loom. "Use my eyes, Eikoheh," he told her, linking his mind gently with hers. As he looked at the pattern, passing what he saw to the old woman, the color drained out of his face. "El?" he whispered, his voice a mere thread of sound. "El, look!!!"

The Weaver sprang to his side. His face mirrored the Dreamer's horror. Only the Namegiver saw understanding dawn in the Dreamweaver's expression, and the tears that left silver trails from the corners of her sightless eyes.

The pattern had changed and the tension of the warp was uneven, giving the work on the loom a curiously rippled effect. But that was not all. In the last several inches of the pattern, the vibrant, gleaming purple of the Trickster's color began to fade to a muted shadow, and in the same space, 'Tsan's red gained intensity, glowing and pulsing with the iridescence of a god's color.

The Trickster did not find the hospital a restful place. White-clad workers flitted in and out of her room, checking this or that, while machines clicked and beeped. Isaac could visit only for short periods; and he looked so frantic that she fretted long after he had left. The Trickster was so drained she couldn't even feel the minds around her without straining.

She lost track of time. The light never changed in her windowless room. Isaac came and went. The Trickster let herself float, hoarding what strength or power was left to her. Finally, Isaac came in with another man, who had the air of one used to respect. He checked all the machines, read the notes on the clipboard at the foot of the bed, and looked as though he was weighing important matters.

"Well, Ms. Carroll, all your readings are normal. I can't see any reason not to let you go home. Is there someone who could stay with you for a day or two, until you're really feeling better?"

Her eyes slid, almost involuntarily, to Isaac. He looked relieved. "Yes."

"Good. Now do you have any questions?"

She hesitated for a moment. "I don't think so."

He waited, as though to make sure she wouldn't change her mind, then turned brisk. "Very well. I'll write up your paperwork, and we'll get you discharged." He left, but Isaac stayed.

"Are you really all right, Antekkereh?"

"I'm very weak. I feel drained—drained of power. I think someone tried to use my forsworn oath to destroy me."

"Will they try again?"

"I don't believe that's possible." She smiled shakily. "What I don't understand is how they failed. A name is a powerful binding; a forsworn name is usually deadly."

"But you broke your oath in order to *protect* Alexandra. That should count for *something.*"

She took his hand. "Clearly it does: I'm still here."

"Thank God," he murmured. "Listen: it will take the hospital a while to process your discharge. In the meantime, I'm going to go see what I can find out about Alexandra. All right?"

She nodded. He kissed her forehead before he went out.

When Isaac reached the wing where Alexandra had been taken, he found the shifts had changed. "Are you family?" the day shift nurse asked him.

204

"No," he replied. "I'm her psychiatrist, Dr. Isaac March-banks."

Her eyes widened; then she smiled. "Dr. Milton will be glad you're here."

Isaac raised his eyebrows. "Oh?"

"The patient seems to be suffering from lapses of memory. I'm sure Dr. Milton will appreciate any history you can give."

"Is Dr. Milton with Alexandra now?"

"No," the nurse replied. "But I'll have her paged."

Alexandra was sitting up in bed. Her eyes followed Isaac as he entered. There was something different about her, he thought, but it took him several seconds to realize what it was: for the first time since he had met her, Alexandra's face was serene.

"Hello, Alexandra."

"I don't know you," she said calmly.

"You don't remember me," he corrected. "I'm Isaac March-banks, Dr. Marchbanks."

"I don't know you," she repeated.

He made a gesture of concession, then held out his hand. "Let me introduce myself. I'm Isaac Marchbanks. And you are . . . ?"

She looked at his hand as though she had no idea what it was for. "Dr. Milton tells me that I am Alexandra Scarsdale, but I couldn't say for sure that she's right."

It was then that Dr. Milton came in. She was a young woman with a friendly smile and a brisk manner. "Dr. Marchbanks? I'm Vivian Milton. Alexandra has made the most remarkable physical recovery—we were quite concerned about her when she was brought in." She smiled at her patient. "Now, if we could just help you to remember some things . . . ! I hope you won't mind if I steal your visitor for a few minutes?" At Alexandra's shrug, Dr. Milton herded Isaac into the hallway.

"It is a most perplexing case. I saw the x-rays of her skull injury that were taken yesterday. I ordered another set this morning because her pupils were reacting normally. The pictures are completely different; there's no visible fracture this morning."

"A lab mix-up?" Isaac suggested.

Dr. Milton spread her hands. "Who knows? But this morning, there is no evidence of head trauma—which leaves me without a physical explanation for her amnesia."

Isaac nodded. "Her amnesia may have a psychological explanation. Alexandra came to me several weeks ago showing symptoms of severe neurosis, or possibly psychosis. Since then, her symptoms have intensified; she has become quite paranoid. It's possible that this amnesia is the mind's attempt to free her from the pain and uncertainty of the last few weeks."

Dr. Milton considered. "That sounds plausible—but what on earth do we *do* with her? She's perfectly well, physically; there are no medical reasons to keep her here, but we can't exactly turn her loose."

"We could request a transfer to a psychiatric hospital. She certainly is in no mental state to be wandering the streets."

"That's probably best. But those x-rays—I just don't understand how it could have happened." She shook her head, then turned toward Alexandra's room. Isaac followed, thinking of Antekkereh's healing powers, and wondering whether she could have unconsciously healed Alexandra. She had certainly been worried enough, and perhaps it would explain her terrible weakness.

Alexandra was watching the door when Dr. Milton and Isaac returned. "If I am well," she said, "why won't you let me go?"

"Where would you go, Alexandra?" Isaac asked.

She smiled faintly. "No doubt something would occur to me."

"It's not quite that simple," Dr. Milton put in. "You need to have a little more of your memory in order to function. Just think what could happen if you didn't remember about traffic."

"But I *do* remember about cars and traffic," she said with a patient air. "I remember many things—surely enough to get by."

"We're not sure of that," Dr. Milton responded. "Trust us: we only want to act in your best interests."

"Don't you think I can judge my own best interests?"

"Frankly, Alexandra, no." Isaac's concern softened his words. "You haven't been doing very well at it, lately. We would be failing our duty to you to discharge you right now."

"Preserve me from senses of duty!" she snapped. "I want to be out of here. It is so *airless* and stifling!"

"If it's too warm—" Dr. Milton began, but Alexandra cut her off with a violent gesture.

"ENOUGH!!"

"Maybe you'd better get a couple of orderlies," Isaac muttered. "I don't like what I'm seeing."

Dr. Milton complied, hurrying out of the room.

"Why don't you run away, too?" Alexandra demanded. "I don't want you here either, and I'm angry. I might hurt you."

"I'm not afraid of you."

"You are lying," she said. "Fear rises from you like mist."

"All right," he conceded, "I *am* afraid. But not enough to keep from doing what I think right."

"You are a fool."

"Probably; but there it is."

"Do you seriously believe you can chain me?" she demanded.

"Who said anything about chains?"

"Imprison, then. Bind. 'Locked ward in McLean's'—I've taken that from your mind. You cannot hold me, Isaac Marchbanks."

He wanted to protest, to erase the hostility that showed in every line of her body. How could he make her trust him when he was so full of doubts and anxieties? If she were taking things from his mind, what else could she do?

"What else?" she echoed. Her laughter was wild, her mood change mercurial. *"Watch!"* She flung out one arm, pointing stiffly at the window. The air seemed charged; the hair prickled on the back of Isaac's neck. A thread of reddish light sprang from Alexandra's finger to the window. The light spread over the glass, growing in intensity. Suddenly, without a sound, the glass was gone. Isaac smelled the tainted breath of the summer city. *"Wind,"* Alexandra commanded, and the room was filled with swirling air. She strode, her ridiculous hospital gown fluttering, to the window edge. She mounted the sill, leaning into the wind, then looked back at Isaac. "I cannot be pent up. You cannot hold me. I am as free as the air."

Suspicion crystallized into certainty in Isaac's mind. "Alexandra, wait!" he cried.

She laughed at him. "I am not Alexandra. That name has no power to bind me."

"Then what are you? Who are you?"

"I don't know. But neither do you." Then Alexandra jumped.

She did not scream. After an impossibly long moment, Isaac went to the window and leaned out to view the courtyard, five stories below. There was no broken body, no knot of horrified bystanders: no sign of Alexandra at all.

The door behind him opened. Dr. Milton and two orderlies swept into the room. "Where—?" she began. "What—? Oh, God." Then she and both orderlies crowded to the window.

Isaac was out the door and down the hall before they realized it; he ducked into a stairway and fled to the Intensive Care Unit

208

where Antekkereh was waiting for him. He called a taxi and when it came, he wheeled Antekkereh to the lobby and helped her into the back seat. As he was climbing in after her, he could hear the hospital P.A. system: "Paging Dr. Marchbanks. Paging Dr. Isaac Marchbanks."

28

That same morning, Mark had an unpleasant surprise. When he led Ychass out of her stall, the big gray mare moved as though she had a broken leg.

"*Kelly!*" he shouted. Ychass's laughter bubbled in his mind. *Don't panic. I'm not hurt—but Kelly must think I am.*

Tell the others, he advised before calling out again. "Kelly! Something's wrong with Mari Llywd."

Kelly checked the horse over and then, baffled, called the vet. "I can't find anything, Janet," Mark and the others heard her say, "but she's absolutely dead lame." She listened for a moment, then thanked the vet and hung up. "Janet's coming out sometime this morning," Kelly told them. "Keep Mari in." Then she sighed. "I'd better call Brigid."

Brigid soon arrived. "I thought Shelley'd better know," she told Kelly. "And you know what? She said something like this happened once before: a mysterious lameness. They never did figure out what was wrong. She hopes Janet will have better luck."

Of course, Janet didn't. Ychass limped dramatically, but the vet couldn't discover anything specific. In the end, Kelly sent Brigid off to call her friend again. Brigid returned to say that the last time, Shelley had laid the horse off for a couple of months.

This time, Brigid reported, Shelley wanted her to take the horse to an equine specialist.

Brigid enlisted Angel and Brice to help her hitch up the trailer. Before very long, she rolled out of the yard towing Ychass behind her. She stopped several miles from the farm, made sure no one was around, and invited Ychass to join her in the cab of the truck. The two of them drove halfway to Colchester, found a restaurant with a big parking lot, and had lunch.

"You can't imagine how sick I am of grain," Ychass told her friend. "And *hay*. If I *never* see another blade of dried grass, it will be too soon."

After lunch, Brigid dropped Ychass off at her apartment. They had decided it would be too much of a coincidence for Ychass to reappear as soon as Mari Llywd was out of sight.

"Prepare the ground for my return," Ychass had agreed. "There's no need for me to join the rest of you until we are ready to leave for that competition."

Much against everyone's better judgment, Eikoheh insisted on taking her place at her loom that afternoon. The Dreamer sat beside her, lending her his eyes. The Weaver stood behind her, his hands on her shoulders, channeling his strength into her frail form. She worked feverishly, as though she knew there wasn't much time. As the Weaver watched, his uneasiness grew. He could see how the luminous red that was 'Tsan's color eluded her control, but it was beyond his powers of vision to tell how the Dreamweaver intended to resolve the tangle.

As though she had read Elgonar's thoughts, the old woman sighed. "I don't know what to do. I have no way to guide 'Tsan's thread. Ohmiden's gift gave me a certain hold on the Trickster, but it does not affect 'Tsan. She is a random force, a mad god. She will pull the pattern apart."

211

"If strength will not move her, might not persuasion?" the Weaver suggested.

The old woman gestured to the thread in her hand: the shapeshifter's color. "It is all I know to try."

In Brigid's apartment, Ychass settled on the sofa and prepared to cast her mind forth—though she doubted she would be able to influence 'Tsan's troubled mind. At least, she could worry at the defenses in 'Tsan's mind, which denied that the shapeshifter and her friends were real; and at best, who knew? Perhaps the shell was ready to break. 'Tsan had always been so sensible. It wasn't like her to stray from reality.

She brushed many minds, each preoccupied with daily concerns, pointless things, useless regrets. Suddenly, she touched a shining mind, bright with vigor, blazing with energy: a god's mind. She tried to pull away, but the other had sensed her.

WHO?

Against her will, her name was drawn out of her. *Ychass.* She framed her own question, *Who are you?*

The only answer the god gave was fierce laughter. With no warning, the god seized her memories, ruthlessly sifting through them. Ychass was defenseless, unable to shutter her inmost thoughts. The god sought, and found and took what was wanted, leaving Ychass weeping with useless fury.

But she did not allow herself the luxury of weeping long. Though unable to resist, she had felt the god's reactions to the uncovered memories; and clear in her mind was the god's triumph at finding Vihena in the shapeshifter's memories. She called to the swordswoman, called with enough force to startle her.

What do you want? Vihena snapped, surprise spurring the anger that slept so close to the surface of her feelings.

212

Ychass related what had happened, and shared her fear that the god might come after Vihena.

Who was it? The Trickster?

I don't think so, Ychass said. *I have touched the Trickster's mind, and this felt different; but I cannot imagine who else would have cause to seek us.*

It's all futile, anyway, the swordswoman's thoughts snarled. *What the hell am I supposed to do against a god?*

Cling to your name. Be warned. Seek Iobeh's advice. Don't be trapped in fatalism!

Fatalism!? The swordswoman's ire burst its restraints. *What are we if not mere toys of the gods? Our every step is woven for us. They sent us here on a hopeless errand, claiming our talents were needed, and what do we find? A world rife with pleasure-seeking idiots who have no honor, who hire mercenaries to keep their laws for them with evil, fire-spitting weapons. When we find 'Tsan, she has been damaged beyond repair by the madness of this place; and still we go on, hoping that some miracle will restore her to us. And now you tell me there is yet another god, one we don't know. And then you dare to caution me against fatalism. The gods know I am no seer, but even I can tell that I am nothing if not a cursed puppet of the meddling gods!*

Ychass could feel Vihena's fury building; she could glimpse, behind the blazing rage, the specter of violence. She was frozen, afraid even to whisper into that dazzling, chaotic wrath. Then she sensed another presence, a balm of cool sense: Iobeh. *Go carefully, Iobeh,* Ychass thought. It was more than half a prayer.

DON'T SOOTHE ME!!! Vihena's mental cry thundered in Ychass's mind. Then the scalding rush of hostility toppled Vihena's fragile balance. Violence broke free. Ychass recognized the intent bare instants before Vihena acted upon it.

213

Vihena, no! NO!! The last cry ripped through the minds of the Five and their allies, as Ychass flung herself into hawk-shape and plunged into the sky. She was already too late, but she fought the knowledge with heartbreaking effort.

She who was no longer Alexandra followed the bright threads of the shapeshifter's memory: 'Tsan; she had been 'Tsan, but she was 'Tsan no longer. Memories of her own, lured by the brilliant treasure plundered from Ychass, surfaced. They were only shadows—a story that had happened to someone else; but she remembered: a singer's voice, lonely in the vast silence of the dry lands; a boy with vision-haunted eyes; a girl-child whistling a sparrow to her hand; an old woman, industrious at a loom; a red-haired stranger with gray eyes that promised peace and calm. Tears stung. What had she lost? Where were the clear, sharp feelings, shared joys and pains, that should go with these misty visions?

She dashed away her tears. Whose memories would jolt her own into focus? Ychass had given her shadows; who would give her substance? *Vihena. Her mind snapped to the inconsistency: in her shadow-memories, the swordswoman's face was different from Ychass's recent memories. There* was a story— *and some answers.*

The one who was neither Alexandra nor 'Tsan wrapped the world's winds around her and bade them carry her to the place in Ychass's memory. The world's winds balked, but she insisted; it was not a smooth ride, but it served. She wove a glamour around herself, so that she might approach unseen, and made her way down the hill to the large, low-slung barn.

In the guest room bed at Isaac's, the Trickster sat up with a start. "Isaac!" she cried.

214

He came so swiftly she almost wondered if he had been waiting by the door. "What? What is it?"

She took his hands in hers and clung to them, her eyes wide, her breath coming in fear-tightened gasps. "There is power stirring," she said at last. "It frightens me."

Isaac sat down beside her, still holding her hands. "What can I do?"

"Stay with me."

Her panic subsided. She managed a smile; it didn't go very far toward reassuring him. Then, her eyes widened, with sudden pain. "Oh no," she breathed.

"*What?*"

"Do you hear it? The singing?"

Isaac shook his head. "No."

Her hands clutched his. "Don't let go. Promise?"

He pulled her close. "I promise."

Vihena's anger left her like a lantern snuffed by wind. Time froze; only her eyes moved, surveying the tableau before her. Iobeh—little, gentle Iobeh—lay where the force of Vihena's blow had thrown her. She was still and her body lay with her head at an odd, unnatural angle. Brigid, Angel, Mark, Brice, Karivet, and Remarr were caught like beetles in amber, their faces fixed in expressions of mingled shock and horror.

"What have you done? Vihena, *what have you done?*"

The voice, so familiar, so unexpected, unfroze time for the swordswoman. She turned, found herself facing—'Tsan! No, not 'Tsan. She faced one who wore 'Tsan's face, used her voice; but there was none of the spirit of Vihena's friend in those stern eyes. She stood too straight for 'Tsan; she radiated power while 'Tsan had only hinted at it. This was a god, wearing 'Tsan's face. This was judgment.

For an instant, their gazes locked. Then, with a wail, Vihena flung herself at Iobeh. "*Iobeh!* Oh, no, no, no." As her cries turned to sobbing, movement returned to the others.

"Call an ambulance!" Angel cried.

"Is she breathing?" Mark demanded in the same instant.

Vihena looked up, snatched Karivet's hand. "How could I have hurt her?"

His seer's voice was cold. "Because you would not bridle your rage." He pulled away from her and felt for a pulse in his twin's throat. "Iobeh, don't leave us."

The one who wore 'Tsan's face laid a hand on Karivet's shoulder. "May I? There may be something I can do."

He moved aside as she knelt beside the girl. She straightened the crooked body and put her thin hands on either side of Iobeh's face. She closed her eyes. They could see the muscles bunch and tense in her shoulders; there was a flash of power, felt more than seen. They heard the thunder of wings as a hawk swooped from the sky, flinging itself earthward to become Ychass. There was a moment of profound silence. Then, the one who was no longer 'Tsan gathered Iobeh into her arms and rose.

"Come," she said softly. "All of you. It is time for the judging." She summoned them with her eyes: Angel, Mark, Brice, Brigid, Karivet, Vihena, Remarr, Ychass. They clasped one another's hands; then, Ychass took the god's outstretched hand. At the touch, a sensation like a charge of electricity ran the length of the line. In its wake, they all heard something they had not before noticed: a high, clear voice, singing, calling, compelling.

"What is it?" Ychass asked.

"The Star Sower," the one who was no longer 'Tsan replied. "She is calling the Moot of the Gods."

The Weaver swayed on his feet. He did not have much left to give the Dreamweaver. He blinked hard at the pattern;

216

something was changing, but he couldn't identify it. His mind was slow, fuddled by the strain of sustaining the old woman. Suddenly, he heard something: a pure, clear voice. His eyes went back to the pattern, and he understood.

"What are you doing?" he asked, his voice a mere shadow of itself. He knew, but he couldn't believe it.

The Dreamweaver hunched one bony shoulder. "I'm sorry, Elgonar. I'm weaving the Moot. There's no other way."

The Weaver buried his face in his hands. He was so tired, so drained. "Now?" It was a moan.

"I'm sorry, Elgonar," Eikoheh repeated. She swayed a little on the bench without his sustaining power.

"I must go," the Weaver said to his siblings, "but you need not. Stay, 'Ren, to guide her weaving; and stay, Yschadeh, to lend her strength."

"I must stay," the Dreamer answered. "But Yschadeh should go with you. You should not be forced to face the Moot alone." He stood behind the Dreamweaver, as Elgonar had, with his hands on her shoulders while she used his eyes to weave her pattern. "Go," he said. "I will stay for you both."

"Go," Eikoheh echoed faintly. "I have places for both your threads in the weaving to come."

Elgonar turned to his sister. "I am too weak to ride the winds," he told her. "Will you carry me?"

In answer, the Namegiver put her arm around his shoulders, wrapped them both in wind, and carried them to Godsmoot.

217

29

The Hall of the Godsmoot was vast, the shadowy vaults of its ceiling supported on columns like forest giants carved of luminous gray stone. The floor was patterned with tiles of every imaginable glimmering color that swept in wide, random swathes across ice-white marble. On three sides of the Hall, tall arched windows stood open to wind and mist; the great dais, dominated by two massive thrones carved of obsidian, was shadowed and mysterious, the only part of the hall where no window shed pearly light. Behind the thrones was a huge silver candle stand, shaped like an apple tree, with thin white tapers fitted into each of its blossoms. None was lit, and in the dimness, the sculpture looked like a winter tree, bejeweled with frost and icicles.

A throb of air wound through the hall, and left in its wake the Star Sower. She wore a robe of blue velvet, stitched with gleaming points of silver. Her dark eyes surveyed the empty hall; then, she threw back her head, swept wide her arms, and began to sing. Her voice filled the Hall of the Godsmoot until the stone glowed; then, as the winds took the sound and carried it, one by one, the gods answered her summons.

First to come were the twin Warriors—so alike that even their siblings could not tell one from the other—arguing as always. On their heels, the Forester, and with her, the Mariner.

Then, in a dizzying group, the Stormbringer, the Dancer, the Talespinner, the Pathfinder, and the Harvester. Talk swirled as the gods greeted one another.

Another gust of wind brought tatters of fog into the Hall of the Godsmoot. The Messenger arrived, then the Lovers and the gentle Rainmaker. The Star Sower's song gained in power and intensity, as though she were reaching for someone nearly beyond the range of her voice. There was a mutter of thunder; sudden, vicious winds slashed at the assembled gods. The Trickster and Isaac appeared, faint and wavering like images seen through water. The Star Sower's voice roughened with effort until their shadowy forms steadied. A murmur of shock ran through the gods.

"A mortal?" It was the Talespinner's beautiful voice. "Has the Trickster lost her mind?"

But the Star Sower sang on, calling: demanding. The Namegiver arrived, supporting the Weaver, and a gasp shook the assembled gods. "If the Weaver is here," the Messenger whispered, "who is weaving the Moot?"

The Star Sower's song did not falter, but grew, pulsing with energy. The candles on the dais burst into flame as the Mother and the Arbiter entered the hall. They ascended the dais steps and took their seats while the Star Sower spun her song into the sudden silence of the assembly. Then, there was a howl of wind that tore the mists surrounding the Hall of the Godsmoot. A shaft of sunlight lanced into the shadowy dimness, and in the center of the dancing color it awoke on the patterned floor, a Stranger god appeared, with a young girl in her arms and a string of eight mortals by the hand.

As the Star Sower's song concluded, the Arbiter rose to his feet. "Who calls the Moot and on whose behalf?"

"I called the Moot," the Star Sower replied, "on behalf of the void between the worlds. Some power has upset the balance, so

219

that even the stars cry out in pain. I summoned the Moot to see whether all of us together might heal the rift ere it rends the worlds asunder. My Lord Arbiter, we are not all here. I have called and called, but the Dreamer will not answer."

"The Dreamer is absent, but the Weaver is not," cried the Messenger. "Who weaves the Moot?"

With great effort, Elgonar raised his head and spoke; his voice was ragged with weariness. "My Dreamweaver, Eikoheh, wields the shuttle, and the Dreamer lends her strength."

"Surely that is your place, Weaver?" snapped one of the Warriors.

"I think not," he replied.

The Mother rose and with a gesture stilled the angry and alarmed mutterings. "Peace. Much must be explained ere we can make a judgment. Let us hear the whole of it in an orderly fashion. Elgonar, begin."

The Weaver met her eyes in a flash of panic. That she had used his true name was not an encouraging beginning. Despair and weariness settled around him like a cloak of lead. He stared at the tiles beneath his feet and tried to assemble his thoughts.

"The tale begins, I suppose, with the Forester. She asked me to string a Wanderer's color on the Loom, to protect the Orathi." His voice was weary, gray, defeated. Suddenly, he felt a touch on his shoulder, felt strength pouring into him. The Namegiver had moved to share her strength with him. As he told the tale of 'Tsan and the quest to Windsmeet, his words gained power. The gods' silence was charged—listening, not condemning. As he told of the Trickster's cruel gifts, and ultimate casting out of 'Tsan, there was a subtle shift of anger toward her; and he knew the others heard his desperation, understood his driving anguish. He told of his alliance with the Dreamer and the Namegiver, told of 'Tsan's five companions, told of the support of Eikoheh and Ohmiden; but when he

220

reached the point in the tale where he and his allies had sent the Five across the void, he faltered to a stop.

"I cannot tell of the Five's trials and adventures, for I could see only Eikoheh's pattern as it grew on the Loom."

The Mother nodded. "Indeed not. We will hear from them, ere we make our judgment. Tell of your own actions and trials, Elgonar, and leave nothing out."

So he did. He told of the three gods' attempts to contact 'Tsan; he told of the Trickster's interference and attack, and his own sending her across the void. When he told of Ohmiden's death, and the power his sacrifice bought them, the Five murmured and Karivet turned to Ychass for comfort. The Weaver told of the Mother's visit, and repeated their conversation. And in a cool, uninflected voice, he related his own attempt to destroy the Trickster with her own forsworn name—despite the fact that he knew she had broken her vow on 'Tsan's behalf.

When he finished, the silence was heavy—and cold. Elgonar felt the other gods' disapproval pushing against him like a physical force.

"But I didn't." It was the Trickster's voice, harsh as a crow's. "I didn't really break my vow on 'Tsan's behalf."

"But you did!" Isaac protested. The gods' attention shifted away from the Weaver.

"No." Tenderness softened the Trickster's expression as she answered Isaac. "I didn't. Myself, I didn't care whether 'Tsan lived or died. But it would have hurt you to have been the cause of her death." She turned to the Weaver. "My name was yours to take, truly forsworn. Weaver, what stayed your hand?"

"No!" Isaac cried. "It's not right! They can't destroy you for acting bravely and unselfishly—no matter what the letter of the law permits, Antekkereh!"

Understanding and wonder blazed on the Weaver's face. "He's right. Yes! Trickster, your name wasn't mine to take; you

221

have given it to your friend, and he *would not give it up!*"

"Very neat, Elgonar," the Arbiter cut in coldly. "Yet you have stolen the Trickster's power—a wrong, surely; and by your own admission, you have upset the balance between the worlds."

"I do not feel *wronged,*" the Trickster said. "And I ask no recompense." Her expression turned sardonic. "The Moot may still pillory the Weaver, but neither at my behest nor on my behalf." She took Elgonar's hand. "I regret I've been such a thorn in your side these ages past. In my heart I knew you were no enemy, but you were near to hand, and your tail was all too easy to twist. Can you forgive me?"

His hand tightened on hers; tears thickened his voice. "We have all wronged you, bound you, sought to destroy you—I no less than any other; and yet you ask me for forgiveness. You amaze me. Of course I forgive you, my sister. I only hope you can find it in your heart to forgive me."

The Star Sower stepped into the circle. "The balance is not as desperately skewed as it was, but my stars still groan in pain." She turned her fathomless eyes on the Stranger god and her companions; then she looked back to the dais. "Perhaps we should hear from the Five."

The Arbiter inclined his head. "Speak, then, mortals."

Ychass, Vihena, and Karivet all looked at Remarr. Iobeh stirred in the Stranger god's arms, but her eyes were closed.

"Me?" Remarr's whisper echoed in the lofty vaults. "But—"

"Who else?" the Talespinner responded, laughter quivering in his voice.

Remarr bowed politely. "I am a minstrel, lord, not a story-teller."

The Talespinner pointed to Remarr's harp case. "So sing the tale. I'll not hold you to speech."

With shaking hands, Remarr got out his harp, swiftly tuned

it, and began. The music stitched threads of joy and sorrow, laughter and pain, under the words that he sang. His music roused Iobeh, and the Stranger god set her on her feet. Remarr's song told of their adventures, the strangeness and frustration of the new world, the surprise and delight of loyal friends, the pain, the tension, the dangers. He spun everything that had happened into the song. He cast his voice like a net into the hall, and when he ended, the gods were awed, expectant.

Into the pregnant silence, the Mother spoke to the Stranger god. "I would hear your tale."

The Stranger god laughed, a sound full of bitterness. "I do not sing, nor can I speak as eloquently as the Weaver. I have no gift of forgiveness to lay like a balm on this company. I have only stolen power, and imperfect memories, lured out of my own damaged mind by an act of violence against the Shapeshifter who was once a friend. I have no name, no place, no purpose. I cannot remember my story and thus cannot share it with you. No doubt I am the aberration that keeps the worlds out of balance. Destroy me and have done."

"No!" It was Iobeh. Her voice was no longer the harsh croak the Trickster had given her. Her eyes widened in surprise and her hand tightened on the Stranger god's. "The balance could be restored by that sacrifice, but too much would be lost."

"What can you know of it, girl?" the Arbiter demanded. "These are weighty matters, not to be swayed by emotion."

"There is no greater weight than emotion!" Iobeh cried. "The heart must sway the mind, lest you have only justice, never mercy. Look at the Trickster! She stands before you whole and healed—"

"She has been stripped of her power—" one of the Warriors began, but Iobeh's voice overrode his.

"Whole and healed! Look at her: she is happy, at peace. Have you ever seen her thus?"

223

"She is so drained of power she is almost a mortal," the Arbiter said.

"No," Iobeh retorted. "She is so full of power that she could restore the Loom and the balance by herself."

"How can you know such things?" the Arbiter asked.

"I hear the speech of the heart. It is my gift! And the voice of the Trickster's heart is so strong, it knocks me breathless." Iobeh could feel the gods' rejection of her words. "How can I make you listen?" she added in a broken whisper.

The Stranger god went to Karivet. "May I Ask you?"

His lips tightened. "Are you sure of your question?"

Her smile was cynical. "No—but has that ever stopped me?"

After a tense moment, Karivet held out his hands to her. "Ask," he said softly, "and I will answer."

She grasped his hands, met his calm, brown eyes. "How may the Trickster restore the Loom and the balance?"

"She must make her heart's choice. Then her power must be named but not bound, and each must return to the proper sphere."

The Stranger god sighed. "The oracle is obscure; perhaps someone may better interpret it than I."

"It's perfectly clear to me," the Trickster said calmly. "My 'heart's choice' is a choice about who I am and who I would become. Do you remember, Isaac, telling me I could change if I chose? Is it still true?"

He nodded. "It's always true. Do you wish to change?"

Her smile was tremulous, her eyes vulnerable. "I would become someone who needn't leave you, if you would have me stay."

His arm encircled her shoulders. "Of course I want you to stay—but will they let you go?"

"Oh, aye." She laughed, with her unique blend of stubborn recklessness. "It is my heart's choice."

224

"But without your power—" one of the Warriors began.

"It is no longer my power," she cut in. To the Weaver she added, "Do with it what you will—as you have."

The Namegiver's eyebrows rose. "'Named but not bound,'" she whispered. Her eyes sought the Weaver's before she turned to the Stranger god. "I name you." Her voice rang in the quiet. "I name you Wanderer, for you are unbound; and I give you freedom, for freedom you must have, freedom to use your gifts as you choose: to heal or blight, to build up or break down, to create or destroy. I name you a wild power, a free power, ungoverned, ungovernable." As she spoke, the Namegiver approached the Stranger god. "I give you every gift it is within my power to bestow: courage, clear-sightedness, compassion. And I give you your secret name, which is yours to keep or to share: even I will not remember it after I have spoken, for so you must be: free to choose without restraint or binding." Then the Namegiver whispered in the Wanderer's ear.

Silence lasted for an aching moment; then the Wanderer demanded, "Where is freedom in this for me? I have no freedom! You have made all the choices for me!"

"No!" the Weaver answered. "Did you not hear the Namegiver? Even the Loom cannot influence you; you must make your own choices—whatever they may be."

"Ha! I'm stuck being a god, in any case. I can hardly go back to a normal life in the world of my birth."

"Indeed you can!" the Weaver contradicted. "It is your choice to hold or release the name and the power you have been given, to accept or deny the gifts you have been given."

"And what happens to you if I reject it all?" she demanded.

Before the Weaver could reply, Karivet spoke. "If you answer that question, you take away the Wanderer's ability to choose in innocence."

225

"I will not choose blind—that's not freedom, it's heedlessness. So tell me," the Wanderer added to the Weaver, "what becomes of you if I reject it all?"

"Fate rides on the Dreamweaver," he replied. "If she cannot rechannel the loosened power, the pattern will unravel utterly."

"If you were at the Loom, could you rechannel the power?"

Elgonar shrugged. "I doubt it. But if it had been left to me, I would never have dared to weave the Five across the void."

The gods held their breath. Power thrummed in the silence; then the Wanderer sighed. "I will stay. There is nothing in my past to call me back to the world of my birth." She turned to the mortals. "One thing remains," she added. "Are you prepared to return to your proper spheres?"

"Can we say our goodbyes first?" Angel asked.

"Of course."

Farewells were said, with hugging and some tears. The Wanderer spoke to Isaac and the Trickster. "The Namegiver gave me a new name. Perhaps I'd better give you my old one—and some memories as well. It will make it easier for you to explain your presence, if you have things like a Social Security number."

"I'm to become Alexandra Scarsdale?" the Trickster asked.

"Alexandra Eleanor Scarsdale," the Wanderer corrected. With a touch, she conveyed a few specific memories—enough, she hoped, to allow the Trickster to fit herself into her new niche. Then, when the farewells had been said, she wrapped her power tenderly around each of the earthlings and sent them home.

The Five remained, looking lost and rather forlorn among the bright company of the gods. The Wanderer went to them. "Should I take back the Trickster's cruel gifts?" she asked them. "I've already changed your voice, Iobeh."

Ychass responded first. "No. I like being able to speak, mind to mind, with my friends."

"It doesn't matter," Karivet shrugged. "I decided, long since, that I would answer when asked; the ability to choose makes no difference to me any longer."

"I never thought a minstrel needed courage," Remarr said dryly, "but I find I've grown used to it."

Vihena was silent. When she met the Wanderer's eyes at last, her own were full of tears. "Even a month ago, I would have leaped at the chance to shed this form; I thought I hated the way I looked. Now I find I rather hate the way I am inside. Could you, do you think, teach me to govern my temper, so that I never again hurt my friends in anger?"

"That is beyond me." The Wanderer's voice was free from either regret or disdain. "You are the only one who can control your rage. It may be a bitter lesson for you, but there are no shortcuts. It will be hard, but you will learn."

"Then leave me as I am," Vihena said finally, "to remind me of my task."

"As you wish. Shall I send you home? Are you ready to go?"

"Where is home?" There was a world of bitterness in the Minstrel's question.

"'Home is a place in the heart,'" the Wanderer quoted softly. "I will send you to the Dreamweaver's cottage; she needs you. There you may make decisions together about where you will settle and how you will live."

When they were gone, only the gods remained, regarding the Wanderer with watchful, guarded eyes. She returned their scrutiny, her own face impassive. When it became clear that she would not speak further, the Arbiter addressed the assembly.

"Is our judgment accomplished? Star Sower, are the worlds in balance?"

"It is an unfamiliar balance, but it causes no distress."

"Surely we must yet punish the Weaver for his outrageous foolhardiness!" one of the Warriors cried. "His actions

227

imperiled the very foundation of the world. He has shown himself unfit to cast the shuttle of Fate."

There was no mutter of agreement. After a moment, the Mother spoke. "It is unfair to lay all the blame at Elgonar's door. He strove to heal the Loom after the Trickster's meddling—and this he has done. Could any of us have done as well? Is the business of the Moot complete? May we disband?" When silence greeted her words, she dismissed them.

The gods departed as they had come, until only the Weaver, the Namegiver, and the Wanderer remained. They regarded one another warily. Finally, the Wanderer spoke. "Do you truly not remember the name you gave me?"

"I truly do not," the Namegiver replied. "Mine is Yschadeh, but yours I do not know."

"It is Antekkereh," she told them with a peculiar smile.

The Weaver gasped. "The Trickster's *name," he whispered, but the Namegiver began to laugh.*

"The workings of power are curious," she said at last. "Do you suppose you are the Trickster as she was meant to be?"

"I suppose I am meant to be myself," the Wanderer said.

"No doubt," Yschadeh agreed. "Now, shall we fetch Irenden?"

"With your aid," Elgonar replied with a weary smile. They linked arms, and the winds carried them away.

EPILOGUE

The summer was long past; a dismal October rain drummed on the corrugated roof of the horse barn. The comfortable odors of hay, horses, and leather were mixed with the smell of wet leaves, and the damp, chill air ate its way into one's very bones. Angel scrubbed at the caked dirt on Gabe's bridle. Mark buffed his show boots, preparatory to storing them for the winter months, and Brice worked on an overdue English assignment. When Angel sighed, Mark glanced up, his brows raised.

"Nothing ever *happens* anymore," she answered his look. "It's so bad Brice is doing *homework!*"

"Hey!" Brice protested. "So go ride in the rain. I'm not stopping you."

Angel clicked her tongue and rolled her eyes. "It's not the rain. Don't you feel it? Life is so quiet without the Five."

Neither of the boys said anything.

"Hey, come on!" Angel said. "Don't mess with my mind. You're not going to pretend it never happened, are you?"

"My mother got a very nice thank-you letter from the twins," Mark said, studying the shine on his boots, "with Greek stamps on it."

Brice nodded without looking up. "Ditto, from Remarr."

"So ask me to explain everything," she snapped. "But it happened! You know it did."

229

When neither of the boys offered any further comment, Angel went back to her task. As she laid the clean brow band out to dry on the old newspaper she was using, something caught her eye. She leaned closer to read it. There was a photograph, one of the awful, posed-couple kind, over a short column of text. "Hey! Listen to this," she crowed, excitement chasing petulance out of her tone. "'Alexandra Eleanor Scarsdale and Isaac Nathaniel Marchbanks were married in a private ceremony yesterday. The bride, who is the daughter of the late Pulitzer Prize winning author, Alister Scarsdale, expects to receive a degree in philosophy from Harvard in June. The bridegroom is a noted psychiatrist and author. The couple, after a wedding trip to'—get this!—'Greece and Italy, plan to make their home in Lexington.' There's a picture; it's not very big, but it's definitely them." She shoved the paper under Mark's nose.

Mark sneezed. "Okay," he bleated. "I believe you. Get that smelly paper out of my face!"

"So, Angel," Brice drawled, looking up from his English assignment, "what will you do for an encore?"

She got her sponge good and gooey before she threw it at him.

J
F
HIL   Hilgartner, Beth

             The feast of the
             trickster